TASTES AND CONSEQUENCES

TASTES AND CONSEQUENCES

Flynn's Crossing Romantic Suspense Series
Book 4

Yvonne Kohano

Nanokas Press

A Division of Kochanowski Enterprises

TASTES AND CONSEQUENCES

FLYNN'S CROSSING ROMANTIC SUSPENSE SERIES BOOK 4

Nanokas Press/KE Press books may be ordered through booksellers or by contacting:

Kochanowski Enterprises/Nanokas Press
PO Box 1274
Clackamas, OR 97015-9594
www.yvonnekohano.com
yvonne@yvonnekohano.com

Tastes and Consequences is a work of fiction. People, places, events, and situations are the product of the author's imagination. Any resemblance to actual persons, living or dead, or historical events, is purely coincidental.

This book contains an excerpt from the forthcoming book *Blooms on the Bones* by Yvonne Kohano. This excerpt may not reflect the final content of the forthcoming edition.

Any people depicted in stock imagery provided by Thinkstock are models, and such images are being used for illustrative purposes only.

Certain stock imagery ©Thinkstock
Cover design: John Kochanowski

ISBN: 978-1-940738-34-5 (sc)
ISBN: 978-0-989330-52-7 (e)

Original Publication: 2/11/2013
Nanokas Press re-release date: 6/18/2015

Also by Yvonne Kohano

FLYNN'S CROSSING ROMANTIC SUSPENSE SERIES

Pictures of Redemption, Book 1
(Serena & Dane)

Flashes of Fire, Book 2
(DK & Vince)

Naked Intolerances, Book 3
(Gabby & Rick)

Tastes and Consequences, Book 4
(Mac & Roxy)

Blooms on the Bones, Book 5
(Tess & Powers)

Wine Into Water, Book 6
(Marguerite & Deke)

Love and the Christmas Tree Nymph, A Flynn's
Crossing Seasonal Novella

Love's Touch of Justice, Book 7
(Jake & Marlee)

This Proposal Between Us, A Flynn's Crossing
Seasonal Novella

Measure Twice, Love Once, Book 8
(Geno and Agnes)

And more to come!
Learn about upcoming releases at
<u>www.YvonneKohano.com</u>.

Subscribe to Yvonne Kohano's enewsletter to be among the first to learn about new releases and special offers. Visit www.yvonnekohano.com for more information.

Follow Yvonne at www.yvonnekohano.com, on Facebook as Yvonne Kohano, and on Twitter @yvonnekohano to learn what tickles her about being a writer, and at www.GooseYourMuse.com for creativity tips.

TASTES AND CONSEQUENCES

Prologue – Fifteen Years Ago

She wanted to savor the lazy feeling for a few minutes longer. The bed still held the warmth of his body, and she hoped that he would return quickly. After all, neither of them had to get up today, no early calls to capture the right lighting or endless steam trays to fill for service. Today, they would begin the rest of their life together.

She waited, wondering what could possibly be taking him so long. His pager had beeped an incoming message. A summoning, an urgent long distance call, he'd said. He hadn't looked at her as he dressed quickly in the clothes laid out for today and headed out the bedroom door.

It had been half an hour now. She knew how he got when he was conducting business, probably some incredible new deal. Rain strumming the windows of their San Francisco hotel room finally lulled her back to sleep.

"Madeleine? Madeleine! You need to get up!" The voice was abrasive and demanding, someone used to having everyone jump to attention. Madeleine sat up quickly and looked around the room in a daze.

"You'll need to be getting your things and going now, young lady." The gray-haired woman looked disapproving. She would undoubtedly purse her thin pale lips even tighter if she realized that Madeleine was bare-assed naked under the sheets, rosy from a night of lovemaking and lax-muscled from the considerations of her lover.

But what was this woman doing in his suite?

"I, ah, I don't understand?" Madeleine heard the timid question in her own voice.

The woman bustled around, impatience in her movements, as she gathered Madeleine's clothes and dumped them without ceremony on the foot of the bed.

"I said, you need to get dressed and go, now!" She stood with hands on hips as if she expected Madeleine to jump right up, naked or not, and comply. The seconds stretched to minutes, and finally, Madeleine felt she had to say something.

"He's going to be right back, but there isn't any place we need to be today. He said so. He's just taking a call."

The older woman smiled with malice in her expression and harrumphed. She pointed towards the door. "Now."

Madeleine still didn't understand. They were going to take a few weeks off, Rome and maybe more of Europe he'd said, and then they'd head to LA and some post-production work. And after that? They'd figure it out.

She had to be assertive and put this forbidding woman, whoever she was, in her place. Madeleine drew herself up and looked the old biddy in the eye, hoping that she adopted the same haughty stare she'd seen some of the movie stars use.

"You're mistaken. He'll be right back. Then we're going to the airport and taking some time off."

There was no show of compassion, no sympathy and no fear. In fact, if anything, the callousness became more prominent on the woman's face.

"No. You're the one who's mistaken. Why do you think he sent me in here? To tell you it was time for you to go! That's part of my job description. I clean up after his... mistakes." She spat out the last word as she glared at Madeleine.

Madeleine literally felt her head spin - she was sure it must be because this made no sense. He'd said – well, he'd said a lot of things. But she knew they were taking off today for a little vacation, because he made sure they both packed their bags after the movie's wrap party last night…

And that's when she noticed it. Her bag was sitting on its wheels, next to the clothes she'd set out for today.

And in the place where his bag had stood beside it, empty air.

Chapter 1

"I told you this was a good idea, didn't I?" Alejandro Degas lazed in the chair across the desk in the small office and smiled at his boss, triumph predominant on his face.

Roxy LaFollette rolled her eyes at her number two and wanted to rant, but she couldn't. The man was right, even when she knew other things were very wrong.

"Yes, Alej, you're correct as always when it comes to personnel matters. The extra interns for the summer are a good idea. I, on the other hand, excel on the financial end of things. But when it comes to the seasoning in that pasta and grilled vegetable salad, you are still wrong."

The man smiled, accustomed to her jibes after all their years together. She would never find a better chef or business partner. He knew her so well. Their styles combined like the perfect menu. But she, at least, was the better chef.

"Look, we have this great contract with the movie people. We have the agreement to back up Cal Fire if anything blazes up close by. There's another movie coming to the county in the fall. We'll have to think about another crop of interns if these end up wanting to move on."

He hadn't stirred, draped across the facing molded chair in a position of ease. Roxy knew differently.

She couldn't have grown her brand without him. When they'd met in the basement of that San Francisco kitchen fifteen years ago, little did she know that the man who helped her perfect her ability to break down a side of beef or filet a whole salmon would still be a solid rudder on her gourmet ship all of these years later. His energy was limitless, as was his devotion to those he cared about.

Everyone made the mistake of assuming they had something going on. Alej let them think that, protection for her he said. He'd been there at the beginning, when she'd needed to rebuild her heart and her confidence just as she was building her cooking skills and chef's craft. They'd tried to make it something more once upon a time, and by mutual and laughing agreement, they'd moved past it to be best friends.

Roxy eyed Alej now, knowing that she hated keeping a secret from him, even if it had nothing to do directly with the continuing success of their business. She was, after all, the majority owner and the nationally known executive chef. Sometimes, secrets were necessary.

"Let's see what they've got before we discuss keeping them on. They looked good on paper, passed their interviews with our staff, and cooked in their trials with reasonable skill. But they all seem to have… issues."

Alej snorted and rose from the chair, stretching like a jungle cat from his native Brazil. "You will always be suspicious, won't you, no matter what? Maybe some people, like these interns, are just who they appear to be, some wannabe cooks who hope to grow into better chefs under your fine tutelage." His broad smile made his teeth flash in the darker skin of his face as he winked at her, then made a quick exit out the door as her pen flew across the room.

Roxy smiled, despite the flying office supplies. Other than the girl tribe, there were few people who could get away with calling her on her vices – high expectations in the kitchen and a soft heart that she tried to hide when it came to helping people.

This time, though, it was time she hid, period.

*****

"I really appreciate you taking this on, Rox, really." Girl tribe member Serena Williamson looked a little frazzled as she flipped through the large three-ring binder on the table, their winemaker friend Marguerite Devereux at her side. "It seems like there's so much left to do, and it's just two weeks away!"

Serena wasn't usually this agitated at the thought of organizing anything. In fact, she was usually the foundation of calm in an otherwise crazy world. But this was Serena's own wedding to her dream man she was stressing about, and she wanted it to be perfect.

"Serena, relax! Roxy and I have talked to the executive chef and the sommelier at the resort at length. Every little detail is taken care of, we promise you. You and Dane will have the wedding of your dreams on the beach, down to the tropical sunset that will light the skies. Of course, you will have to keep that new husband of yours from plucking the camera out of the wedding photographer's hands when that green flash happens as the sun dips into the ocean!"

Roxy envied Marguerite her ability to find just the right thing to say. Serena tensed, then laughed, and finally slumped in the chair in what passed for relaxation. Roxy knew that if she'd been the one delivering a similar sentiment to her best girlfriend, she'd have come off sounding brash with the wrong words spewing out of her mouth. She wasn't very good at relaxed banter these days.

It hadn't always been this way. Her parents recognized her talent for all things cooking early on, and they encouraged her to pursue it even when they didn't fully understand her. In high school, she was content buoying the spirits of the crowd she ran with, no matter what kind of trouble they got into. She was the one who propped up her friends in culinary school when the instructor would hurl their dishes into a trashcan in disgust.

But that was before she was the one whose foundation crumbled. For those first few months afterwards, she moved in a fog and would have run into a few pillars along the way if it hadn't been for Alej. His caring nature gave her time to grow a thick shell around her heart. Now she rarely let it crack open, and the only reason her hard core ever peeked at the light of day was for her girl tribe.

Serena's wedding was going to be the consummate beach event, she would make sure of it. For now, it gave her a good excuse to get out of town and duck for cover at an exclusive Hawaiian resort. It was too bad she couldn't stay in the background for the next couple of months, long enough to allow trouble to blow out of town. And unfortunately, she'd stumbled into its sights through her own business decisions. She had only herself to blame.

Chapter 2

"I know you'll find everything you need right here in town, Mr. Smythe. And what you or your staff can't find, I'll find for you!" The woman gushed, and he stopped the cringe on his face only a second before it appeared.

What was her name? His memory wasn't what it used to be. They'd been talking on the phone for a few months now, but she was unmemorable even in person with his wandering mind. He prided himself on being polite and charming to everyone. He cursed inwardly again. This thing that had taken him over, whatever it was, was making his life harder than it needed to be.

His assistant Martha came up, old-fashioned clipboard in hand, and thanked the woman with her usual efficiency. "Ms. Campstrom, we appreciate everything you've done for the actors and the crew. I'm sure we're going to have a wonderful experience here in Flynn's Crossing." As she led the still-chattering woman away, she shot a hard look at him as he stood without moving.

Campstrom, that's right. How many times had he heard it now? Good thing Martha was on top of this crap, because he couldn't get his own shit together.

MacGillan Smythe rolled his neck and turned again to inspect the neat main drag of Flynn's Crossing. It fit perfectly for the movie, not needing any of the major alterations film people often use to make a real-life set work. Main Street was six blocks long, with shops and eateries tucked away in courtyards that opened off the sidewalks. Some of the buildings dated back a hundred years or more, and the exposed brick, gracefully arched windows and turn of the century stone detailing couldn't have been recreated without considerable cost.

Thankfully, the shops also fit their plot line. The old bank at the center of town converted into a bakery and coffee shop, the peaceful plazas between the old buildings that now sported fountains and intimate seating, and the lack of any major chain or brazen advertising let everyone know this was Small Town America at its best. Cheerful unique displays filled shop windows, and baskets of colorful flowers hung from the old-fashioned streetlights. The residences up the hill at the end of the street dated back to the beginning of the 1900's, he'd been told, and the old Victorian that housed a flower shop anchored the homes to the commercial area.

Martha was still talking to the county employee, the woman who had put on such a campaign to get the movie production company to use Flynn's Crossing as its location. He was grateful that his senior assistant had the patience to run interference. His patience, what was left of it, was worn painfully thin.

Some people said he was worn thin as a reed as well. Gray wove heavily through his dark brown hair, and it shot through his beard when he bothered to try to grow one. A beard could hide the grooves carved next to his mouth, the ones that used to be labeled sexy little dimples. The lines flaring from his brown eyes were now too deep to be called dashing, the deep circles giving away the long empty nights without adequate sleep.

He tried to hide it, the exhaustion that sometimes made lifting his head off his pillow in the morning a colossal chore. The pain eating away at his gut was all in his head – or in his lifestyle – according to his doctor.

"Mac, you need to lay off the fancy booze and the greasy food. You need to work out and get some rest. And yeah," the doctor had raised his hand to stop Mac's protests at that point, "I get that there are expectations of you in your big manly movie star life. But you won't have a life at all if you keep this up."

He wouldn't be getting into any trouble around here, that was certain. The days would be filled with directing, running the rushes, and approving script changes before prepping his shooting plan for the next day in the evenings and falling into a restless sleep.

Yes, not much to do other than work. And maybe he'd run over to a real city, to San Francisco, for the weekends. He could get into a lot of trouble there. Mac smiled at the thought, even though an old ache poked sharply at the edge of his memory of the city by the bay. On second thought, it was probably best to let the past stay in the past. There was nothing left of that man or that time anymore.

*****

"How are we doing on hiring the extras?" Mac knew that as small as this town was, everyone and their long lost relations probably applied to work in the movie. Too bad there were just a hundred or so bit parts and walk-ons.

The industrious young man sitting across from him consulted his notes. Barry made a good details guy as his production assistant, precise and to the point, willing to take care of whatever Mac needed on the film. When Martha got ready to retire – though the woman seemed to have endless energy and would probably outlive him under the present circumstances – Barry might make a good replacement. His earnest nature and willingness to please were earning him major kudos.

That, and his ability to keep his mouth shut when Mac needed it.

"We've filled all the minor speaking parts, and the cameos where we need someone who can capture a particular expression. The crowd scenes are still left, but I hope to have those done by the end of the week."

Mac smiled. Good to know that someone else can carry on with things when he was – what should he call it – indisposed. As in, when he was puking his guts out for no good reason that he could think of. Hell, even when he had been a party animal in his earlier years, it had never been this bad.

"Good job, kid, good job."

Barry beamed behind his glasses and Mac felt a pang of guilt that he was taking advantage of him. After all, he had looped Barry into some activities for the movie that he as the director should have been handling. But he didn't feel like he could do it.

"Anything else we need to cover?" Mac looked at his watch and thought that with luck, he could wrap up some location visits today and retire to the rental house to hide away for an early and hopefully restorative weekend.

"I, um, I talked to the caterer today. 'Roxy's' it's called. The boss wasn't there, on a trip out of town for a wedding, but the guy I talked to, a Mr. Alejandro Degas, is going to be the chef on site. He said he'll make sure everyone's well taken care of." Barry hesitated and frowned. "This is the first large scale continuous catering gig they've done. They have a restaurant and a gourmet grocery store. They cater individual events. But never something this big." Barry paused again.

Great, amateur hour. He'd warned his production staff about this kind of thing, finding good coverage for supplies and essentials in a rural location, even with the quote-unquote big city of Sacramento an hour away. Small potatoes in his mind. In fact, people from LA tended to forget it was even the capitol of the state.

"What about this Roxy? Is it just a name or a person? Why did we pick a company with no experience?" His irritation was rising, and he knew that meant he'd feel the worse for it later, but it was hard not to get mad at his crew for missing important details like this. The stars in this movie were picky when it came to what they ate, and the crew wasn't much better.

"It's a woman, a nationally-acclaimed chef. I ate at her restaurant when I was checking out possible locations and finding accommodations for everyone. It was great. No, scratch that, it was one of the best meals of my life!"

Barry's eyes half-closed as his glasses slid down his nose, and for the first time in the past hour of their meeting, he leaned back in his chair with an indulgent smile on his face. He was clearly in the throes of some incredible foodie memory, Mac realized. Guess he'd better try the restaurant at some point. Anything that could make his uptight assistant look like he was having hot sex with a bevy of well-endowed beauties was worth checking out.

"Okay, if there are any problems, let me know. Otherwise, I'm trusting you to stay on the caterers. Remember that Sheila has very specific food allergies and needs her particular menu and Justin is snotty about his likes and dislikes, so they have to accommodate them. Hell, everyone has a food requirements list these days."

Mac laughed at the thought. Back a decade ago if he'd demanded a certain menu be made available on location as part of his contract, big star or not, he would have been laughed at. But in today's world, everyone had an imagined need for something they could or could not eat. He remembered what the starlet Sheila had said when she'd signed the contract for the part. 'The wrong food could kill me, Mr. Smythe!' And she believed it.

It was a different world now, with stars easily forgetting to honor their contracts and overlooking how their sometimes-tarnished public images reflected back on the movies they performed in. A part of him thought with longing about the old days, when all he had to do was learn his lines and show up, act his heart out, and party in private until the next day. Now he had all of these heavy responsibilities.

No wonder he felt like crap most of the time.

Chapter 3

The quiet whine of jet engines provided a soothing drone, and the rest of their group slept heading east across the Pacific. Roxy found that airplanes, particularly when everyone was absorbed in their own stuff or asleep, were always introspective places. You couldn't help but crawl into your own memories then. And an old one kept bobbing to the surface as the seconds dragged by, no matter how many times she shoved it back down.

A week wasn't long enough.

The wedding had been everything she and Marguerite had assured Serena it would be. The location was incredible, a soft white sand beach overlooking the setting sun at a high-end resort that cocooned them in old Hawaii. The reception was perfection too, and even when the sun dropped into the ocean, Dane only had eyes for his bride, effectively missing the famed green flash.

Roxy smiled as she thought about the devotion of her friends to their newfound mates. Vince Cassidy, a world-traveling lifestyle writer who she still didn't completely forgive for his snarky nature, clearly doted on her girl tribe buddy DK McGiven. And to think they'd met and got off to such a rocky start over a piece of DK's metal art.

Gabby Cooley-Burke and her son Jeremy were the perfect pair for her love Rick Chagres and his son Will. The young boys were remarkably well behaved during the ceremony. It was only when the Kailua lobsters came out for dinner that they couldn't help but start rolling their eyes with declarations of 'gross' and giggling like loons. Gabby and Rick definitely had their hands full with their little family-to-be, but it didn't look like either one of them minded a bit.

Even the single women were hooking up, it seemed. Tess Willowspring, proud owner of Buds and Blooms in Flynn's Crossing and organizer of the many tropical floral decorations for the wedding and reception, was thrown together with Dane's brother Powers. Tess and Powers already hated each other, though why wasn't completely clear, and it was only because they were standing up for Serena and Dane as maid of honor and best man that they called an uneasy truce. But at one point, dancing after the wedding in the balmy air of the tropical evening, the sparks flying between the two of them rivaled the torches the flame dancers were juggling.

And her partner in crime, winemaker Marguerite, was seen with her head bent in deep amused discussion with the resort's sommelier, someone she met setting up the beverages for the event. Marguerite seemed intent on Roxy and the resort's executive chef, Phillip, completing a foursome for a helicopter adventure of volcano watching and then maybe some stargazing from the observatory at the highest peak on the island. Roxy had a brief talk with Phillip, but the unrest she was feeling from what awaited her at home was enough to unnerve her, and she'd be bitching and complaining before long if she decided to go.

Marguerite was disappointed. "You never let yourself have any fun, my dear. What is wrong with this? He is a nice single man, you are a nice single woman. You work in the same field, so you have common interests to discuss. There are no expectations, just a day of relaxation and mutual enjoyment."

When Roxy protested, claiming she had to work on the new summer menu ideas and her schedules to buy from the local farms for the season, Marguerite shook her head and closed the corridor entrance to their shared suite with an unusually hard snap, letting a tinge of her French temper leak out.

It wasn't like she didn't want to have fun, Roxy mused fussily, pleating the thin blue airline blanket repeatedly in her restless fingers. She looked at Gabby's head on Rick's shoulder in the row across the aisle from her, both sound asleep with Gabby's son Jeremy leaning into the pair on one side and Rick's Will on the other. Each parent had small smiles on their faces. Hell, she would so appreciate having something like that in her life, someone to share experiences with and a shoulder to rely on, and maybe even a family some day.

But she'd learned the hard way that she was better off on her own. Ultimately, she was the only one who could protect her heart, and none of her Flynn's Crossing friends knew the full story about why.

*****

"You need to meet with them today, Roxy. They've been working hard for the past week. I know you had Serena's wedding to take care of, but that's past and they're here now. They'll work a lot harder knowing that you too are looking over their shoulders."

Alej was adamant, and she knew he was right. The interns had started their work in the various components of what her girl tribe teasingly called her little empire. Little, hell. If they only knew how much money was tied up in this, they'd shriek on her behalf. But it was all worth it, because the hard work was paying off.

Besides, she's been an intern herself once upon a time. She didn't like to think about that period of her life, the emotional pain too great even in distant memory. But on days like today, there was no turning away from it.

Roxy knew what it was like to have tens of thousands of dollars tied up in an education, knowing that until you hit it big, or even found a comfortable but responsible position, you would be making ten bucks an hour and living in a hellhole and your student loans would be threatening to drown you. You land in a kitchen with a temperamental chef and you get yelled at all the time. You mess up, and you can be out on the street between salad service and the main course.

Luckily, she'd had Alej to guide her back then, particularly since her first chef was a pompous asshole. Fortunately, that pompous asshole was also a culinary genius, and Alej was a people person who could provide the guidance that Chef Bart Paush lacked. She had learned and learned well, despite the personal turmoil of that time.

She sighed and stared at her calendar in the computer, knowing already that she had no excuse today. "Okay, Alej. Let's get the three of them together between two and three pm today. I can give them the inspirational pep talk, and then they can finish up dinner prep for tonight and catering prep for tomorrow."

Alej shifted from one foot to the other in the doorway, appearing unusually worried.

"Is that not going to work?" Roxy ground out the words in exasperation. He had to make up his mind.

"Ah, yeah, that will work. It's just that, ah, there was something that came up while you were gone."

Roxy waited. She stared. Alej shifted again, making a show of examining his nails and then checking the buttons on his chef's coat.

She could outwait him. And it was highly unusual for him to be so uncomfortable about anything. Roxy let the silence stretch.

Alej finally gazed back at her, his expression slightly pained. "It's four."

"Four o'clock? That will be too late. Dinner starts at 5 pm and there is so much to prepare for tomor –"

He cut her off mid-word. "Four interns. I hired four interns for us."

He had the grace to look a little sheepish.

"Why four? I thought we agreed on three. I distinctly remember that we decided on the final three together, though it was a difficult choice among a number of strong contenders. What's this four thing? Who's the fourth intern?"

Her steam was rising. Yes, she and Alej were partners in most of the business, but ultimately, it was her name and mostly her money on the line. To commit to another intern, someone else to keep busy for the season? What was he thinking?

"I know when we discussed them, we kept coming back to only needing three. But with the movie business, and maybe the fire season, and the store continuing to thrive and the restaurant with a lot of major bookings already for the summer…" He trailed off, meeting her stony glare.

Shit, another little mouth to feed. She glared harder at Alej, hoping that somehow, this was a big joke and he'd be laughing and telling her how he'd got her again any second now.

But he wasn't, and he was leaning against the doorjamb now as if he was supporting the weight of the building on his shoulders.

Finally, he shifted and gave way, sputtering a little in the process. "It's special circumstances, okay? Just wait until you meet her. Then I think you'll understand why I decided this without you."

Roxy sighed again, making a point to exaggerate it because she wanted to get Alej's goat. She rolled her eyes at him and put her forehead in her hands, then on her desk, and she groaned, loudly.

She didn't miss the small chuckle from the doorway.

"Okay, I'll meet the four," she emphasized the count, "of them this afternoon."

She picked up her head and stared at Alej again, frowning her disapproval. It didn't work. He was back to his jaunty self, hands resting on his hips and one cocked in a triumphant stance.

"You won't be sorry, Rox, really. They all want to work hard and get ahead. I think you'll be pleased," he paused and winked at her before adding a snotty "BOSS!"

And he spun out the door before she could find anything handy to throw at him this time.

Chapter 4

"And, ACTION!"

Mac watched the actors carefully for the nuances their characters required to sell the believability of the story. The young starlet, Sheila, worked hard at her role. She knew her part forwards and backwards, made good suggestions about minor changes that would target the traits of the woman she played more accurately, and took direction quickly and with good humor. She never needed to be reminded about anything twice. In effect, she was a dream to direct.

The leading man, Justin, was another story altogether. He was an asshole, a-number-one. He had his own ideas about the part and he would play it the way he wanted, whether it worked for the plot or not. Staying true to the story meant nothing to him, and cues about this were now a broken record as far as Mac was concerned. His character was supposed to be sympathetic, someone the audience could relate to and root for.

Hell, at this point the murderer made people feel better.

"CUT!"

Justin had gone off-script once again in a direction that made no sense. Too bad he couldn't fire the guy. He could, however, make his life a living hell on the set and let everyone else in the industry know what a dick-head he was to work with.

"Justin! What the hell do you think you're doing, man? Your wife," Mac emphasized the last word and waved at Sheila, "needs you to be kind and understanding because she's afraid that a murderer may be running around town. Why do you think it's okay to yell at her right now?"

"Hey, man, I'm in my zone, okay? This is what my powers, my inner actor mojo, are telling me the guy does right now, okay? He's not buying her shit, you know what I'm saying?" Justin's hair was now in his eyes with his adamant headshakes and the make-up-and-hair team was having conniptions on the sidelines.

"Uh, Justin?" Sheila put a gentle hand on his arm, and Mac appreciated again what a professional she was being, given the situation. "A woman's not going to feel protected and close to her husband if he's doubting her, you know? And if she doesn't feel that closeness and he's not trying to protect her, there's no point to the movie. We're the good guys, not the bad guys." Her eyes went large and luminous and she smiled sweetly at the leading man, and Mac had to admire her acting talent.

Justin stared at her and blinked hard, instant goofiness written all over his face, and in that second, Mac traveled back in time to a woman who'd made him blink in just the same way when he was only slightly younger than Justin was now.

She'd laid a hand on his, and told him that no matter what anyone said, it was a terrific movie, one that would turn hearts and heads. He was a great actor, she'd said. No one had ever said that to him in quite that way before, no fawning or pretense.

Just honest feelings.

Or so he'd thought.

Chapter 5

"I'm Angel Rivera and I come from LA. I been cooking since I was a kid. My folks own a place in the old neighborhood, ya know?"

He didn't look like he was much older than a kid yet in Roxy's opinion. And the expression on his face and the stance of his body spelled trouble. He thought he was hot shit, probably wouldn't take guidance easily and would do whatever the hell he wanted.

Still, he had cooked well for his interview and he had good recommendations. If he got too cocky, Roxy knew she could take him down a peg or two. Maybe he'd work out.

"And what do you like to cook, Angel?"

His arms crossed on his chest and he puffed up, though with his short stature, the posturing had badass attitude with a capital B written all over it.

"I can cook anything, Chef. I can do any station, ya know what I'm saying? I like living on the edge!"

And he winked at her.

Double shit. She caught Alej's eye as he lounged against a wall behind the interns. He lifted his shoulders as if to say, what can you do?

Without a change in her neutral expression, Roxy turned to the next intern, a tall chunky African-American woman who appeared to be in her late twenties. The woman stared back uncertainly.

"Hi Chef. My name is Leticia Robertson. I come from just outside Atlanta, and I attended Le Cordon Bleu there."

The woman appeared to be shy and her voice was so quiet that Roxy had to strain to hear it. Her references had mentioned that she cooked well and had good food instincts, but she didn't trust her own skills.

"You said on your application that you like to cook soul food and Deep South staples, right Leticia?" Roxy knew she'd unintentionally softened her voice, but she was afraid she'd scare this one off right away.

"Yes ma'am, Chef. But I want to learn from you, how to cook healthy stuff with all of those fresh ingredients." She looked pained. "And you can call me Ticia, that's what everyone calls me." Now she smiled tentatively.

"Well Ticia, we certainly want you to learn about our farm to table efforts here at Roxy's. But you have to stay true to your culinary point of view. Do you have one?"

The woman looked confused, then worried. "No ma'am. Other than the food my family grew up on, I mean. I learned a lot at school, though, different cuisines and such." Hope entered her gaze. "I like making salads and appetizers and such things like that."

Roxy sighed inwardly. She didn't need another *garde manger*, the position in the kitchen that prepared the salads and appetizers for immediate delivery to a table. It was a challenging station since it required a chef who could use a wide variety of techniques and seasonings for both cold and hot foods. And it was an easy place for a restaurant to get in the weeds on a busy night since it was often the first course.

On the outside, she tried to be encouraging. "Chef Alej says that you are doing a good job on preparations for the movie set catering, for their salads and first courses. That's a good start, Ticia. I'm sure you'll do fine." She hoped.

The next young man was tall, broad, and overwhelming. His hair was buzz cut, his chef's coat squeezed him in a few places, and his hands were the size of omelet pans. Scratch that, more like fry pans. Thinking about the sometimes-tight confines of a commercial kitchen, Roxy had to wonder at his choice of profession.

"And you're Ren Guanglie, am I pronouncing that correctly?" Coupled with his size, he was first generation American from Chinese parents, a fact he pointed out proudly in his application letter, making the big man even more unusual.

"It's actually *Guanglie* Chef, but that's my first name. Ren is my last name. Most people, that is, my American friends, they call me Bob." He was eager but nervous, and his voice boomed out in the space of the narrow conference room.

"I'm sorry I massacred your name. Bob it will be. And what are your culinary aspirations?"

The big man got an excited gleam in his eye and he started talking with those big hands. "I love pastry and desserts, Chef! The intricacies, making sugar dance into something spectacular, the delicate nature of a soufflé. That's me, Chef. That's what I'm all about!"

Whoa, was all she could think. He'd made a decent main course for his audition, and while his references said that he could master any technique or dish well and quickly, they hadn't said anything about desserts.

"Is this is a, ah, new interest, Bob?" Roxy kept her eyes on him.

"No ma'am, not at all. But I thought I should learn as much as I could about every station, just in case I ended up in some other position in the kitchen." His expression changed to anxious. He'd do whatever was asked of him, she suspected, but his heart would always be in desserts.

Roxy had to believe he had other skills in the kitchen, something that would translate more appropriately to a wider array of restaurant settings. On the other hand, the most unlikely stars rose from places least expected.

Those were the three human versions of raw ingredients she and Alej had agreed to develop into chefs, the ones who had auditioned for the staff and cooked well enough to prove that they could handle the labors and strains of the real thing. Granted, it wasn't a competition and they had some flexibility in the pace that was set, but they'd prove themselves worthy – or not – soon enough.

And that left lucky number four, the intern that Alej felt strongly enough about to hire without a consultation with Roxy. She was still heated up about that, but it was a low simmer now and she was willing to trust his instincts and see why he'd made such a major decision without talking with his senior business partner.

The woman was average height and build, though it was hard to tell much more than that from her oversized chef's coat and pants. Everything hung in baggy folds around her, not necessarily the safest attire for an active kitchen. She stood silent and watchful, no expression on her face, and just waited. Roxy waited too as she looked at the woman. It would be a game, she guessed, as to who would speak first. The young woman looked vaguely familiar.

Glancing down at the resume in front of her to review her credentials, the name on the page popped out. Jeannine Paush. Roxy's head came up sharply as she stared at the young woman. The age was right, about mid-twenties. This couldn't be a mistake. Paush was not a common name. And the facial features were distinct.

"Thanks to the rest of you for taking time out of your busy afternoon to meet with me. I promise I'll be in the kitchen shortly to see how you're all doing. I'd like to meet with my final intern for a few minutes in private."

One by one, the first three interns filed out with various versions of 'thanks Chef' ringing out in the silence. Alej moved away from the wall as if to follow them and she stopped him. "Chef Alej, would you please join us? We haven't had the opportunity to talk with Ms. Paush before."

Or had they?

Alej looked pained, a longing glance following retreating backs, before taking a recently vacated chair and pulled it closer to the conference table next to the young woman. He turned and smiled reassuringly at her, his good cop to her bad cop Roxy supposed. The intern stared back, drawing in a fast breath. Alej winked at the young woman, and for a moment, it seemed he would take her hand.

Then he looked back at Roxy, intensity in his gaze. For once, she didn't know what to make of his expression.

"So, Ms. Paush, we do know each other, don't we?" Roxy stared across the table at the young woman.

"Yes ma'am."

"And you talked with Chef Alej while I was gone and somehow, you two decided that this was the place where you wanted to work. You had other opportunities I'm sure, didn't you, Jeannine?"

The woman wore a pained expression as oversized as her chef's coat. Roxy stared hard at Alej, willing an explanation from him that made sense, given the circumstances. He turned back to the young woman, smiling and leaning forward.

Some resolve broke in the girl as she looked between the two of them, and she suddenly welled up with tears and hid her face. Alej half-rose from his chair to reach towards her before dropping back into it with a dull thud. Roxy felt her own heart stab with regret as two drops leaked from Jeannine's eyes to fall rapidly on to her puffy chef's coat.

When the silence dragged on for more than a minute, Roxy thought she'd have to restrain Alej, who was vibrating in his chair as he stared in open anguish at Jeannine. But when the woman raised her teary eyes, she stared directly at Roxy with a forlorn expression. On a deep breath, she broke apart again.

"Oh Chef, I needed some place safe to go!"

Chapter 6

"Cut! Justin, goddamnit, can't you follow the script?" Mac didn't know what would kill him first, the pain in his gut or the stupid moves of the leading man in this film. Both right now were in an even heat to bring him to his knees.

Justin had the brains to look embarrassed this time. "I know, I didn't bring this up at the script meeting this morning, but it was like a last minute thing, you know? An inspiration!" He lit up like this was the explanation to everything and looked around him at the crew, anywhere but at Mac, trying to find someone to agree with him.

"Justin, let me explain this to you again. I am the director of the movie. This is because I direct what the actors – that would be you – do on the set. If you would like to recommend a script change, you should do that during the script meeting, okay?"

Struggling to keep his temper in check, Mac almost doubled over as the pain slammed into his gut not far above his groin. It was worse today. He froze and pulled in a big breath, not willing to let on that anything was wrong.

"Lunch!" He yelled it so loud that several people jumped and his assistant Barry boggled his electronic tablet, but the wave of pain made it difficult for him to control his volume. It felt better to yell rather than fall into a heap on the ground and blubber, which was the likely alternative.

The crew put equipment to the side and in pairs and small groups, they moved away, most heading towards the area where the catering truck was set up. Today they were out in the country, away from Main Street and in a setting that represented the remote location where the family destined for death lived. Unfortunately, it wasn't remote enough, and periodically they had to call a halt to filming to allow the noise of a tractor in a field or a small plane from the nearby airport to fade into the distance.

Noises carried far in rural areas, Mac had learned, particularly in these canyons and hills. If he screamed, they'd probably be reporting it on the evening news in Sacramento.

And he wanted to scream, wanted to find an outlet for the pain and attendant frustration. All in his head? Hardly! Something was wrong, something that was more than his diet and lack of exercise. He'd fire that quack doctor and find someone else to treat him, someone who could figure out what this torture was all about.

Just then, he felt eyes on him. He was a star, after all, and people stared at him all the time. He'd learned to ignore the prickle of rapt attention drilling into his back. For the most part, they represented groupies hoping for an autograph or women hoping for a roll in the famed Smythe bed.

He bit off a bitter laugh, thinking how surprised they would be to find out that the famed Smythe bedroom talent was a thing of the past. Hell, he had a hard enough time making it through the night without puking up his guts. Making love through the night was so far off the radar that he almost forgot what it felt like.

The hairs on the back of his neck stood up and a chill ran down his spine. He thought about the saying 'someone stepped on my grave' and wondered if this is what it meant. Icy tentacles spread along every nerve ending. This was more than the appreciative stare of a fan.

This felt ominously personal.

His pain fading in the chill, he got up from the chair quickly enough to tumble it backwards on to Barry's unfortunate toes. Martha, who had been conferring with Barry, gave Mac a frown and opened her mouth to speak, but Mac raised a hand to stop her, turning in slow circles and looking at the crowd, the crew, and their surroundings.

"Mr. Smythe, is something wrong?"

Martha and Barry were both staring at him now, the chair still in the dust and the script that had been suspended from its arm in the dirt as well. Barry's question hung in the midday heat.

He circled again, searching out faces and trying to pinpoint the source of the stare. It brought a premonition of danger and sadness and he wasn't sure what else. The eyes were still on him, he could feel them. They seemed to be coming from the direction of the catering line, but no one there was paying any attention to what was happening on the set. Just one woman in ball cap and sunglasses was even facing this direction, one of the extras he guessed. He continued his circle, his gaze moving over and past her with only a brief pause.

And then just as suddenly, the sensation of being watched was gone.

*****

Her crew worked efficiently on the line, ladling hot food from steamer trays, preparing grill orders, and answering the eager guests' questions about what they were being served. As Roxy had drilled into her staff, they were guests first and foremost. They always were, no matter what the venue.

Ticia kept the cold foods well stocked, and since at least part of this line included Hollywood types who were concerned about appearances, salads were popular. She worked hard to stay out of people's way and avoid conversations, Roxy noticed. The one time a crewmember engaged her in some good-natured ribbing, she'd blushed warmly enough to have it show under her coffee-colored skin before turning away without responding.

The girl would have to grow some backbone. Ticia wouldn't last a second in the kitchen of a chef who bellowed and screamed when a table waited for more than a minute for the delivery of the first course. Sighing and thinking that she should have a heart-to-heart about standing up for herself, Roxy realized that her own days of screaming were far behind her.

Soft, that's what she was getting. Couldn't help it anymore.

She turned to the steam trays, where Angel and the improbable Bob were serving sides and taking grill orders. Bob was quiet for the most part, though when the crew talked to him, he responded in an easy tone. Angel, on the other hand, was dishing it out, both the food and his repartee. Roxy doubted that many of the Los Angeles based crew members had ever spent considerable time on the streets that Angel was from. But the kid was treating them as if they were all neighbors.

Some of the crew looked uncomfortable with the conversation, if you could call it that. It wasn't Angel's Latino heritage that had them squirming, since many of them came from multiple ethnicities themselves. No, it seemed to be the nature of the dialogue. Roxy sighed, realizing that this was another discussion she would have to have, and it probably had less of a chance of success than the one with Ticia.

And that left her intern number four, Jeannine. Roxy had to give the girl credit, she was doing an awesome job on the grill station. She moved with confidence, handling the multiple proteins with ease. Her touch was sure as she flipped a tri-tip for that final char before it rested for slicing. The salmon that was a special order for the leading lady of the movie was moist and juicy without being undercooked.

Yes, she had a ton of potential. But what about the rest of her story? Alej was taking an unusual amount of interest in her, often stopping with an extra word of encouragement. More than once, Roxy noticed them laughing, heads falling close together. Frowning, she realized she'd have to talk to him too. Flirting with an intern was not on the menu.

The early bird guests were often the go-fers for the stars and those well down the totem pole of command on the set. Those in charge were in the middle of the action. The chefs never knew exactly when lunch would be called, but as soon as they were set up and standing at their stations, people flowed over.

"Cut!" Even at this distance, Roxy could hear the director bellow the command. Alej had been hanging around enough already to get the gist of the story line. A thriller, a hapless family, a cunning murderer who wormed his way into the family's good graces but then turns on them, all but the little girl who is herself possessed by demons in some way.

Yeesh, Halloween in Hollywood.

As she stood between the set and her catering line, she heard the intense voice that sent a charge of energy up her spine to lodge in her brain. The voice was pressured, angry but subdued, as if holding everything in. A man's voice, one that forced her to turn.

He stood at the edge of the cameras and equipment, face to face with the leading man. Even making a point to the taller actor, he sat slightly stooped over, hanging on to a camp chair with a grip that looked like it could tear the fabric into shreds. Discussion over, she heard the distinctive word 'lunch' ring out and the crowd around him dispersed, all except for a young bookish-looking guy and an older woman with her back in view, his personal go-fers no doubt.

He had changed, and not necessarily for the better. His hair, once a thick and lush dark sable brown, was now heavily streaked with silver and hung in lank exhaustion, even at this distance. His star quality build was still impressive, but he had lost muscle tone. She had kept an eye on him as time passed, and he was aging faster than the years were flying by.

Suddenly grateful for the disguise of ponytail pulled through her ball cap and her large dark sunglasses, Roxy couldn't help but take three steps forward to improve her vantage point. It was like an irresistible pull, the opposite of oil and water, which was probably an apt description for their two worlds.

He pressed a hand to his belly, a gesture that looked like something he used often and was trying to hide from the two people behind him. Strange, his skin color was pale and he appeared to be sweating, despite the coolness of the late spring morning. She felt a twinge of concern, and just as quickly, she set is aside and called up the anger she'd held so closely over these years instead.

The chair he'd been sitting in crashed backwards to the ground as he stood suddenly, and his minions stepped forward in concern. His head was up now, circling the crowds around him as if searching for something. His gaze didn't pause as it flowed over her, and Roxy felt twin emotions of relief and disappointment. She couldn't take this. This was as close as she could get, as close as they would ever be again.

Chapter 7

"Do you want me to call Dr. Levinson for you? He would be happy to fly up and examine you. Or come into the office over the weekend if you want to fly home." Martha stood next to his desk, or rather the dining room table that served as his desk in the rental house. Martha herself was staying in a hotel about 20 minutes away, saying she preferred the distance so that she could relax in the evening.

Setting herself away from him, Mac thought, after she'd been with him for so many years. Originally, she worked for his agent's company, a go-fer on loan whenever Mac's fledgling movie career required him to be on a location or promoting a film. Martha latched on to him early and refused to be supplanted, and over time, it seemed more appropriate to hire her himself, since she was spending most of her time in his entourage.

She'd run the drab and ordinary everyday parts of his life since then, and things had pretty much gone smoothly. Anything that he needed to have taken care of, Martha fixed. Granted, in the past decade she'd succumbed to Hollywood pressures and dyed her hair an attractive streaked blonde-gray, changing her wardrobe from old lady polyester to more modern form-fitting natural fibers. Rumor had it that she was seeing a gentleman or two. Mac didn't care, as long as Martha did her job.

She'd been the one to remind him of his well-played parts and console him about his failures. When he overdid the partying and needed a ride home, she'd find someone to come get him. Over the years, she'd saved him from starlet-wannabe's and over-enthusiastic stalker fans by her sheer presence alone.

Barry would have to work on that, since he didn't look the least bit forbidding.

In all the years that he'd known Martha, she'd only been off her game and uncertain once, years ago in a time he'd rather not remember either.

"No, let Ari stay home with his family for the weekend, and I'm not flying down either. I feel fine, I told you that already. You can go, Martha." He took a sip of his single malt Scotch whisky and felt the heat's welcoming slide.

The woman looked unconvinced, fidgeting in a way that was unlike her. Mac waited to see what she wanted to say, since she almost always needed to have the last word.

"Mac, I..." He put up a hand to stop her.

"No, Martha, I am fine. It was the stress of having to deal with Justin, believe me. I feel fine. See? I'm eating my dinner right now." He took up a fork and speared some asparagus, dipping it in Hollandaise sauce and shoving it into his mouth. His taste buds were delighted.

He just hoped his stomach would wait to voice its opinion until after the woman left.

Martha sighed deeply, expressing the kind of staged hurt and disappointment that could only come from someone based in the make-believe world of Hollywood. Uncertainty ruled her gaze, though.

"No, I believe you if you tell me you can eat that and keep it down, I really do. It's just that I have something else to tell you, something I discovered only yesterday but was able to confirm today."

Mac chewed, considering. Martha was prone to dramatic flare-ups of her own. Now that she was close to retirement, they seemed to come more often, as if she felt threatened by Barry's impending promotion despite her departure being her own choice.

"Does it have to do with the production?"

"Not directly, no, but – "

"Did one of the actors die, become disfigured, run away?"

She looked decidedly put out now. "Well of course not, but – "

Mac waved a hand in dismissal. "Then it can wait until tomorrow. I'm tired, you're tired, and we have an early call tomorrow so that we can shoot the morning scenes on Main Street before we lose the light. Then we have the entertainment for the town tomorrow evening. It will be a long day. Head out." He raised his glass for another sip and gestured with it to the door.

Turning back to his desk and the pile of notes he'd made about tomorrow's shooting sequence, Mac waited while Martha hesitated before turning abruptly and leaving, quietly clicking the front door shut on her way out. A minute later, he heard the engine of her car start up and pull away.

He finally let himself slump over the desk. The dinner, sent over by the movie caterer, was delicious. Aromas from the plates washed over him. The restaurant, some kind of bizarre name that reminded him of showgirls, offered to send in whatever he wanted if he was working late. He always worked late, and he had quickly decided it was easier for them to select something for him than for him to try to make up his mind about choices.

Earlier this evening, the server, a young woman who looked tongue-tied to be in his presence, could barely mumble out the ingredients as the head chef, a man whose name Mac couldn't recall in his present haze of discomfort, stood by watching. An intern, the chef had said the young woman was. At least the apprentices produced decent quality food.

If only he could keep it down.

His crew was in heaven. They loved the locations, with mid-spring green an almost painfully bright color in the northern California foothills. The temperatures made for pleasant warm days and cooler nights. Most of all, they seemed to love the town itself, which had opened its arms to the production company.

Mac had seen little of it so far, only what was necessary for shooting and scouting out locations that needed to be changed. Minor modifications to a script happened on any set, and theirs was no exception. The crew traveled in a small caravan of semis, actors' trailers, mobile dressing rooms, and SUVs and smaller trucks to carry all of the paraphernalia that movie making required.

And the catering truck. It had a mobile kitchen, huge prep area, and huge grill, big enough that it could probably accommodate hundreds of meals. Barry told them where the crew would be the next day, and they were set up and ready to serve breakfast, snacks, lunch, even the occasional dinner buffet.

He thought back to lunch time today, experiencing again the prickly feeling of eyes on him. He was sure it had come from some place near the food line. It unsettled him still. Was one of their staff videoing the movie-making process? That was strictly forbidden in their contract.

No, that couldn't be it. There were too many of his people up close and personal with the workers on the line for them to have a chance to take pictures of anything.

That left the crowd, and there weren't many around today because the extras weren't needed for these scenes. And they were too far off the beaten path to attract a random gathering.

Mac thought back again to everything he'd see as he turned around, convinced intense eyes were upon him. Maybe he was being foolish. Maybe it was part of whatever this illness was, causing delusions or something. He guffawed at his own thoughts. Now he really was losing it.

His mind's eye suddenly settled on the woman in the ball cap and sunglasses. She'd been watching him, though at the time, he'd dismissed it because he thought she was an extra. Looking back, though, she had been staring in his direction and her disquieting gaze had been intent.

Something about the woman rang a bell, but he wasn't sure why or where it came from. It made him vaguely uneasy. He'd been the target of stalkers before, but this felt different, less threatening but more dangerous nonetheless. The feeling of premonition stayed with him.

It was this thriller movie, he thought, shaking his head. What was he doing, scaring himself? He chewed another spear of asparagus, unable to help himself despite the later consequences, and spun the glass of Scotch, watching the light change its colors along with his mood.

*****

"So what's it like, catering to the stars? Are they uppity, or are they down to earth like us?" At the head of the table, Gabby peppered Roxy with questions as they sat around the small dining room in the house she shared with Rick and their sons. DK and Marguerite sat across from Roxy and Tess. Serena, still on her honeymoon, was the only one missing from the girl tribe meeting.

"And the men, are they as hot up close as they are on film?" Marguerite reached for a dumpling with toppings, then stared directly at Roxy as she shoved it into her mouth in one messy bite and moaned in appreciation.

"All I know is I'm looking forward to being able to see them all for myself tomorrow when they have the town meeting. You're coming, right Roxy? You can get us behind the scenes." DK waved her wine glass in Roxy's direction for confirmation.

Roxy didn't want this, didn't want any of this. "I, ah, I can't. The restaurant – "

"Will be closed," chimed in DK. "Tomorrow is Tuesday."

Roxy squirmed in her seat, wondering how she'd get out of it. They expected introductions and had already said so.

She couldn't risk getting that close. It had been perfect these past couple of weeks, being away for Serena's wedding and letting Alej take the role of head chef on the catering line. The interns filled the staff spaces. She could stay in the background, a dark and remote distance in the background.

And now, her friends expected her to accompany them to the movie crew's public presentation tomorrow night.

"I really can't. The interns need to be overseen."

This time Tess waved a hand in dismissal. "You said already that Alej is handling that. No, we want you, the famous Roxy, caterer to the stars, to give us a behind the scenes tour, and introductions to all of those Hollywood hotties." Girlish giggles punctuated the chewing.

She was trapped. She could come clean and tell them why she didn't want to get any closer to the cast and crew than was necessary. But then she'd have to share the whole disturbing story.

There wasn't enough wine in Gabby's house to make that happen.

"If you need to get passes or something, get enough for the guys too, okay? They all want to come." DK smiled and grabbed an empanada.

Roxy blanched at the thought that this display was going to get even bigger. Not that she didn't love the other halves of her friends, but soon they'd need a private tour operator for the whole gang.

"And the boys," Gabby added. "Jeremy wants to see how the cameras work, and Will wants to meet a stunt man." Her gaze clouded with immediate worry. "There aren't any, are there, on this movie? Because he doesn't need any more crazy ideas in his head..."

Great, party of twelve? Your table's ready.

"This is very exciting, I must say. Who would have thought that the great Mac Smythe would have come to Flynn's Crossing? Why even in Europe, he's a big star." Marguerite punctuated her comment with a stab of the skewer from her chicken kebob before dropping it empty to the plate. "Ah, Roxy, you live a charmed life, my dear. Who would have guessed that the minute you thought about taking up big location catering, a production company would come knocking on your door with a contract."

Roxy smiled weakly as she looked around at their eager faces. No way could she tell them now. No way she might ever be able to tell them.

Charmed life? Hardly!

Chapter 8

"This is the coolest thing ever!" Jeremy's eyes were wide as he examined the cameras used to film the movie. His soon-to-be-official half-brother Will was equally impressed with the lighting and sound gadgets that were set up behind the barricade on Main Street.

Roxy couldn't help but grin at the enthusiasm of the boys. They were completely uninterested in the famous celebrities who were graciously entertaining questions from the audience half a block away. Even the young starlet didn't warrant a second glance. At the age of eleven, they were still at the 'girls – yuck' stage of life. The equipment and the gaffers who ran it, though, inspired their devoted worship.

The big boys were another story. Gabby's fiancé Rick and DK's similarly committed Vince were both on the edge of the makeshift seating area, standing with two of Gabby's friends from her former job at the county, Dave and Steve. While the male stars were being interviewed on stage, the four guys had been having an intense sidebar conversation. But as soon as the female leads were speaking, particularly the young starlet cast as the wife, their rapt attention focused on the podium. Teeth showing and all but panting.

A wolf pack. Of course, half of them had their incisors removed already, but still…

"What are you smiling at with such a huge grin?" Gabby handed a plastic glass of white wine to Roxy and put a companionable arm around her shoulders. DK linked arms with her on the other side, and Marguerite and Tess came to stand behind them.

"Look at the guys. I'm surprised they're not drooling. You'd think they'd never seen a young woman with enhanced boobs before."

The girl tribe laughed and Gabby added, "Barely engaged and already I'm thrown over for a twenty-something in spandex. Yeesh!" But her Cheshire cat smile at the end of the statement indicated that things were, in fact, very, very good at home.

"I've decided they need a name," Roxy continued. "We have the girl tribe, after all. It's fitting that they have a tagline too."

Tess pursed her lips in thought. "Ideas, anyone?"

"This is like a team name, *non*?" asked Marguerite. "Or something more, how shall I put this, earthy?"

Roxy didn't hesitate. "I thought we'd call them the wolf pack. After all, Vince and Rick were lone wolves before they found Flynn's Crossing and their lady loves."

Gabby was already nodding vigorously. "Perfect! Of course, Rick's fangs are gone..."

"Exactly what I thought!" Roxy laughed harder now at the synchronicity of their thinking.

She didn't want to be here tonight, but if she had to show up, she was grateful she had back up. It was warm and right to have friends like this, and landing in Flynn's Crossing a few years ago was the best choice she'd ever made. She'd cooked from San Francisco to Portland and Seattle before she decided that northern California and preferably someplace rural was where she wanted to put down roots. She'd had enough of working in someone else's kitchen. It had been time to strike out on her own.

Back then, when she saw the sale notice in the trade paper, she'd called the real estate agent and made an appointment for the following day. On her rare day off, she'd flown to Sacramento, rented a car to drive up into the foothills, and viewed what was undoubtedly a great candidate for one of those reality TV shows where a celebrity chef has twenty-four hours to remake a restaurant. Or a month. Or maybe six.

As much of a mess as it was, it came fully furnished and outfitted, both dining room and kitchen. The owners also had the small grocery store next door on the corner of the intersection of two major county roads a couple of miles outside of Flynn's Crossing proper. The location was good. The open land had potential.

And eventually, it was all hers.

Best of all, though, she'd found these great friends through her restaurant. Serena and Tess had known each other first. Gabby helped both start their businesses when she worked at the county, and soon she too was part and parcel of the group. They met DK at a cooperative gallery in town where the artist's metalwork was sold. DK was already a regular diner at Roxy's, and the foursome asked at the end of their meal to meet the woman chef who was already making news as the star behind the menu.

Roxy sat down that night, accepted the proffered glass of wine from the group, and the rest, as they say, was history. Before long, they'd added winemaker Marguerite to their girl tribe, her French humor and sensibilities adding an international flare. Six wonderful women who'd each built themselves into what they wanted, with successful careers and rich lives.

And three of them had now found their true loves, Roxy mused, happy for her friends. She had hope for Tess and Marguerite too. They deserved to find men who could fully appreciate their exquisite talents and hard-won successes.

For herself, Roxy had no such hopes. She was wedded to her empire, and she was growing it every year.

"Roxy, what do you think?" Marguerite looked at her expectantly.

She shook herself back to the present. "Ah, sure, of course." She wasn't sure what she'd just agreed to, but she assumed they were still on the whole name-the-guy-gang discussion.

She hadn't been lost in memories for that long, had she?

"Perfect. Alej said he was able to hold the seats for us because of Roxy, so it's only fitting we make our way up there and take our places with the royalty. Besides, I want to be close to the front when that incredible man, MacGillan Smythe, comes on stage. He's always so gorgeous in his movies! What's the best American idiom, a hunk? I wonder what he'd be like in person." Marguerite's eyes were dreamy as she considered the possibilities.

Roxy's feet locked up and she stumbled, but carried along by the force of nature that was the girl tribe, she was swept to an area next to the small stage. There, five seats were being held with 'reserved' signs, and Alej loomed over them, making sure no one took their places.

She couldn't do this. She couldn't be this close. She didn't want to be seen, and this close, there would be no way to avoid it.

Berating herself for agreeing to attend this circus, she started to make excuses to the other women, trying to break off from the unceasing march to the front of the audience, and she cursed herself again for not coming in some sort of disguise.

Of course, if she had, she would have needed to explain to her friends why she was dressed in a disguise and who she was hiding from. And she didn't want to go there.

"But – but he's not on the schedule to speak tonight, is he?" She stuttered her confusion to Marguerite, focusing in on her last statement about wanting to get a good look at Mac.

Marguerite patted her shoulder and urged her forward. "Alej told me that it was a last minute decision. He's going to come out at the end, say a few words of thanks to the town, then take some questions. Exciting, *non*?" Her French accent became more pronounced in her anticipation.

Roxy silently recited every swear word she'd ever heard in any kitchen she'd ever worked in. Then she started over, double-time. Still, she was being pushed forward, and the inevitability of what was about to happen washed over her. There was no escape, not without making a scene that would require even more explanations. She'd fooled herself into thinking that since the director wasn't on tonight's program, he wouldn't be here. And up this close, she couldn't hide in the shadows. She'd been in heavy-duty denial on all counts.

"Rox, you're impressed, right? I saved the seats for you and your friends. I've got an in with the assistant to the director. Cool, huh?" Alej looked very pleased with himself.

She could only give him a wan half-smile and turn away from the stage.

"Oh, and Rox? The director, Smythe, is going to ask you to stand up too."

This is what the condemned must have felt like when they walked to the guillotine. When an anguished groan escaped her lips, Roxy knew that this time, there would be no chance to hide.

*****

Usually he loved this kind of event. It brought the mysteries of movie making to their audience, and the more that people were intrigued by the processes, the more likely they were to buy tickets or videos or downloads of the end result. Or so Mac thought.

Tonight, though, was different. He felt like crap. He'd eaten what he thought was safe food today, a plate of pasta with a little olive oil and parmesan, forgoing the beautiful red sauce that was his favorite and the Alfredo cream that was a close second. The catering buffet continued the Italian theme in salads and olives, and dessert's tiramisu was to die for according to Martha and Barry.

Even with the safe food, though, his gut clenched and he spent a considerable amount of time mopping the sweat from his forehead in the evening breeze. It was only the years of training, and the inevitable run-ins with paparazzi that required a cool head and picture-perfect smile, that allowed him to carry this off.

Sheila and the other women in the film were on stage now, finishing up with the audience's questions. There were the expected proposals of wedded bliss shouted at Sheila, which she laughed off in a gentle way that let the men maintain their egos and said a world about her maturity. She was head and shoulders above that idiot, Justin, and Mac was glad he'd taken a chance on her short resume when he gave her the part.

"Boss, almost time. You need anything?" Barry was standing at his side, his ever-present tablet at the ready to type in any instructions. Mac took the water bottle Barry handed him and drank deeply, hoping the cool liquid would do something about the fire of acid bubbling up his throat.

"It's time." Barry took the bottle and cap and gave Mac a gentle shove out the store entrance that was serving as backstage. Mac paused a second, gathering his wits and pasting on his smile, as he heard Sheila say, "And now, our world-famous director and leading man himself, MacGillan Smythe!"

The wave of enthusiastic applause drew him forward, as it always did. He loved an audience, just about any audience and at any time. The calls of the women and the hoots from the men only made it more fun. When they started using the names of characters he'd play in the past, his big grin got genuine.

There was little in the way of professional lighting, as they'd opted to use the city street's quaint lights for greatest effect. Only a couple of smaller floodlights blanketed the stage and the first few rows of the audience area in detail. The rest was vague and indistinct. But even in that dim light, Mac could see people were on their feet and clapping.

"Thank you, thank you so much. You're being very kind." He hoped that he wouldn't keel over right here on small town Main Street in front of all of these nice folks. "Thank you. Thanks." And in front of the TV cameras that were set up in the back for the evening news feed.

He'd used his words of thanks often enough that they rolled off his lips once he got the crowd settled. He thanked the county film commission and leaders, the city of Flynn's Crossing, the extras, the residents who put up with the closed streets and messed up traffic. He made a few jokes about the nature and wildlife they'd encountered to good-humored laughter.

At some point, he realized that something buzzed inside him, something that layered over the pain to a point where it was no longer the deepest ache he felt. It was that same feeling of being watched he'd had before, but this was stronger and had a desperate edge to it.

And it drowned out everything else.

He scanned the crowd as he continued with his comments. They were quiet as they absorbed his words about making movies and what it meant to him. Many nodded their heads in agreement when he related seeing his first movies as a kid and being dazzled. None of this was new material, but hearing it in person made people happy.

Nothing seemed out of the ordinary. But then why did he have this strange sensation that things were about to change, and change drastically?

"And now, ladies and gentlemen, I'd like to thank some of the businesses that are doing such a great job of supporting us on location." He ran through the list, giving each vendor a chance to stand up and take a bow, making a comment or cracking a joke. He always left them feeling good about their contribution, he made sure of that, and he let them know he respected them. He considered it the honorable thing to do. Honor was one thing he carried forward from the Hollywood of his own wild youth.

"And finally, one of your greatest sources of pride in the culinary realm, we'd like to thank Roxy's Catering for making our meals not only nutritious and delicious but also the starring hours of our day! And I understand that Roxy herself is with us tonight. Chef Roxy?"

He looked stage left where Barry told him the chef would be sitting. He was curious about the woman who had built such a tasty network for foodies in this rural area. He always respected ingenuity and business success. She'd make a killing in LA, based on what he'd tasted.

An average-built blonde, back turned to the light spearing her, was arguing with women around her in the seating area, and if this was Roxy, she didn't look like she wanted to stand up to acknowledge the applause. Mac started clapping harder and got the audience going louder, and soon the crowd was chanting 'Roxy, Roxy'. She had a hand up to her eyes as the second floodlight swung to pinpoint her.

Finally on her feet, the woman waved to the crowd. She looked at the people, back at the assistant Mac knew as Alej, at the women seated around her, everywhere but at him. It was as if she was trying to hide from the stage.

But he already knew. His heart figured it out first, and it leapt into his throat before pounding so hard he was convinced it would choke him. The sweat he'd tried to hide broke out on his forehead in earnest and he swiped it away impatiently. Bile and pain warred to see which would erupt first. He wondered if he would pass out.

Trapped as she was, she was running out of options, and Mac saw her gaze moving in his direction. It was happening in slow motion, so slow that he heard each individual pair of hands clap and pause in the crowd before the next meeting of palms, each catcall drawn out to a long moan, each chant of her name, Roxy, in syllables that seemed to last for minutes.

She met his eyes, hers wide and fixed unblinking in the noise. The hairs on his neck rose and prickled as she kept her face neutral. He'd know those eyes anywhere in the world.

Madeleine?

Chapter 9

"So tell me, what was it with you last night?" Gabby took her seat at the long table in the restaurant kitchen and turned back to Roxy.

"Yeah, I swear, when the two of you locked eyes, I could see lightning flash. And it took you forever to break the look." DK pulled out her own chair but waited, staring back at Roxy as well.

She didn't want to get into it this. It had been disturbing, full of memories and a dense punch of lust despite the years. The ache of remembered pain settled in her heart, just as the pummel of desire sent recollections to that other center between her legs and shocked her with its strength.

Memories. They'd always been so good together. But that was years ago.

In her absence of comments, her friend continued. "Granted, he's losing something of his handsome smooth movie star polish, don't you think? But he still looks, I don't know, rugged and dangerous, something you want to indulge in even if you know it's bad for you!" DK giggled and Gabby joined in.

The thought of their last night together, the passion of undisturbed hours and no need for sleep, just need for each other, blocked her vision. The highs never could climb any higher for her with anyone else, despite the occasional affairs over the years. The pit of darkness that followed made remembering so harsh that she wondered if she would survive it.

"Roxy? Rox!" The women were now openly staring at her, not bothering to hide their curiosity. As she blinked at them in confusion, they began to laugh.

She shook herself free of the memories. "Ah, excuse me? You two are almost married, right? What is this?" Roxy pretended a gruff severity and twirled a lecturing finger at the women, who laughed harder in response.

"We've claimed ours, Rox, but we're not dead! If we didn't look once in a while, how could we know we've picked exactly the right men and appreciate them appropriately?" Gabby's expression was so serious as she laid out their logic that Roxy felt her own bubble of laughter break out in response.

"You two are incorrigible! Do Rick and Vince know about this?"

"Are you kidding? Did you see them, all of them, fawning over that actress last night? Wolf pack is a great nickname for them, no doubt about it!" DK shook her head in mock concern.

"But don't change the subject, Rox. Did you feel a big zing when he looked at you? His eyes fastened on you like a heat-seeking missile. I hear he's not seeing anyone right now. And he'll be in town for at least another six weeks. You've got an in, being his caterer. Why aren't you more interested in Mac Smythe, particularly since there's such electricity between the two of you? We all saw it last night!" Gabby pressed her point again.

Roxy considered what she wanted to say. She wasn't ready to share the past, and if she was lucky, she could avoid it entirely for the next six weeks. But she didn't believe in luck. Hard work was the only guarantee of success.

"It's nothing. In fact, I'm betting he couldn't even see me, what with the lights and all. And me? I was shocked to be the center of attention." She shifted uncomfortably at the tall tale. "Besides you two know I don't have the time or inclination to date." As she turned to the table, she saw Gabby frown and open her mouth to reply.

"Chef? We're ready." Bob's voice echoed from the back of the kitchen. Saved by the bell.

"Okay, you need to listen to their explanations, taste the food, ask any questions, and finally, rate the selections so that we can decide what's going on the catering menu." Roxy slipped into chef mode with relief. Here, at least, she was comfortable and in control.

Roxy had purposely said nothing about the interns' backgrounds, letting them introduce themselves and their dishes much as they would in a competition. Not that any of them were being eliminated, but their food preparations might not make the final cut. Gabby and DK looked up eagerly, two foodies who loved to eat more than they liked to cook. Roxy could swear that DK was already drooling, and she smiled at the thought of how much food she knew her skinny petite friend could pile away.

Ticia walked in first, placing a small colorful plate in front of each of the three women with a shy smile. She'd worked very hard on this dish, puzzling over the selections of local produce that were still somewhat limited so early in the season. At Roxy's urging, she'd even visited the farmers to see what would be ready in the next few weeks so that she could plan for the evolution of her dish.

"Hello, my name is Ticia, and I'm from the south." Her velvety voice gave away her roots, and that only added to the charm in her explanation. DK smiled encouragingly and Gabby greeted her with a wide grin. The women looked expectantly at the array of vegetables in front of them, then stared at Ticia. The young woman shifted from foot to foot, and she looked to Roxy for guidance. Roxy smiled and gave a small wave to hearten the intern, remembering her own terrifying experiences with chefs long ago when she presented her ideas for a dish.

"Uummm, this is wonderful! What did you put in this?" DK spoke around a mouthful of food and stabbed her fork at Ticia for emphasis. Ticia got a big happy grin on her face and seemed to relax a little at the praise.

"It's vegetables, lots of different kinds. I had to use some from the commercial vendor because the local farmers don't have everything ready yet, but I wanted to see how they would taste together." She paused, then stood up straighter again and resumed her formal presentation.

"I grilled the vegetables whole for the most part, then I sliced them or chopped them, trying to present the best features of each ingredient. The herbs are a selection from the garden, and the dressing is extra virgin olive oil and white balsamic vinegar. I got those in town at the Oil+Vinegar store." She stopped as if running out of steam and looked anxious again.

"I love it! It's so tasty, and healthy too! Is this okra in here? I never would have thought to put that in!" Gabby smacked her lips appreciatively when she came up for air, then dove back in with her fork.

Roxy grinned and gave Ticia a thumbs-up. The woman wore a slightly dazed expression now, as if she couldn't quite believe she'd succeeded with her dish. The look of wonder on Ticia's face gave Roxy a warm feeling. She loved doing this, giving new talent a chance. She'd had less enjoyable early experiences, driven to work in her first big kitchen by circumstances she hadn't expected.

Mac. It all came back to Mac.

"You know we're not done with you yet," DK hissed in her ear. "We know you always say you don't want to date because you were hurt in the past, but what better opportunity to jump back into the pond than with someone who has an expiration date in town?"

Roxy waved a hand to shoo DK away.

She focused back on the kitchen as Angel approached the table with a swagger. He rattled the plates down in front of the women and stepped back to cross his arms over his chest and eye them. His knowing smile was probably intended to be seductive, but he came off as cocky and rude instead.

"Hey, my name's Angel and I'm from LA." He winked, and Roxy noted that Gabby's gaze became neutral and impassive while DK frowned slightly. Not a good beginning, but ultimately, it was the food that was important.

"I made a dish from my neighborhood, ya know, something with Latino roots but I put my own spin on it. It's hot, full of flavor."

Gabby had taken a tentative bite, chewed, and quickly reached for her water glass. "It's a little more than hot, Angel. In fact it's searing." She gasped out the last words as she gulped water with her eyes tearing.

"I know some people aren't used to heat, but they should get to be, ya know?" Angel seemed to be unconcerned with the reaction so far.

DK, who loved spicy-hot food, was chewing thoughtfully. "Ah, Angel? What's that flavor underneath, the bitter one?" She too reached for her water glass.

"Ah, it's some herbs and stuff I added in. Good, right?" His cocky stance hadn't changed, and in it, there was a challenge to like the food, or else. His expression was getting edgy and his smile was gone, leaving behind a grimace of mean that Roxy had noticed a few times before when he was challenged in the kitchen.

Roxy chewed and swallowed, considering the best approach to let Angel know that this was far short of decent. In fact, it was so full of mismatched flavors that the meat itself was obliterated.

"Angel, this is… interesting I guess you could say. But I don't think it's ready for prime time yet." Roxy wanted to let him down easy here, even if she would need to take him down a notch or two when they were in a less public setting.

"Aw, Chef, you're just not used to the food. I'm telling ya, people love this. I know how to cook! Ya just have to get used to the taste."

All three women looked at him, puzzled, and Gabby and DK then turned to Roxy to take the lead in the discussion.

His attitude needed work. He was starting to bristle now, Roxy noted, arms at his sides and hands formed into fists. She suspected that he was very insecure under his cockiness, but he was more willing to fight first than accept constructive criticism.

Angel looked ready to argue again but Roxy raised her hand and stopped him. "Angel, this isn't ready for the catering truck yet. But we'll work on it." When he opened his mouth once more, Roxy's sharp 'thank you' cut across whatever he was going to say and she pointed back to the depths of the kitchen. He mumbled as he turned with a final glare and stalked off, stamping his feet in his chef's clogs as he slammed a hand on a counter.

"Wow, that guy's got a 'tude, no doubt about it," Gabby said, and DK shook her head in agreement.

"And speaking of 'tudes, about this rule of not dating…" Gabby wasn't going to be dissuaded any more than DK. When she would have continued, Roxy broke in as if she hadn't heard the change in conversational direction.

"Yes, Angel's vocal about how great he is and critical of all of the others. Of all of them, he's my biggest concern right now." Roxy paused, ignoring her friends' frowns, before nodding towards the approaching intern and adding in a near-whisper. "And she's my biggest puzzle."

Jeannine placed heaping platters in front of each woman with a wan smile. She was pale and her face was pinched. Her chef's coat billowed out more than it should, but something else she hadn't been able to put her finger on wasn't quite right.

She'd tried over the last two weeks to engage the woman in conversation and learn more about what brought her to Flynn's Crossing. She had a stellar background and could probably work in first class kitchens in San Francisco or in any major city. After her initial teary outburst at their private interview, she'd clammed up.

Jeannine moved back to her presentation spot and turned to look at each of the women in turn. "Hello, my name is Jeannine, and you could say that being a chef runs in my blood."

DK was already diving into the food, and Gabby had paused long enough to take a picture of the dish with her cell phone, clearly delighted.

"I like to cook food that tells a story, and I love to grill. I picked a menu that represents the Pacific Northwest, a traditional salmon bake with fresh King grilled on a cedar plank, roasted sweet potatoes, grilled asparagus, corn on the cob, and relishes and toppings and such." She smiled as they were all digging in with gusto. "I hope that you like it."

Roxy didn't wait for her friends to speak first. "Jeannine, the flavors here are excellent, and the salmon is cooked to perfection, juicy and smoky. This would be an excellent menu for a celebratory dinner of some kind, even if we can't make it for the regular catering line. Where did you learn how to cook this?"

She undoubtedly had a life that included exposure to more than a single kitchen and technique, but Roxy didn't want to share more than Jeannine was willing to say.

"I spent a few months traveling around Oregon and Washington and British Columbia. I wanted to learn about indigenous cuisines to get new ideas for menus." She shifted uncomfortably on her feet with a downcast expression. "I, ah, haven't had a chance to practice what I learned very much."

Gabby opened her mouth to say something when Jeannine suddenly blanched as white as her chef's coat and put a hand to her mouth. As they looked on with concern, her skin tinged green and her eyes got wide.

"Chef? I'm sorry, I…"

And she ran out the kitchen's front door.

"What was that about? Should we go after her?" DK was already on her feet.

Roxy rose too and frowned at the still-swinging kitchen door. "No, I don't think so. She did this earlier this week too, and I followed her. She told me through the bathroom door that she was fine."

Gabby, still seated and munching another bite, frowned too. "If she's sick, she shouldn't be cooking, should she?" She trailed off before setting down her fork with a clatter.

Roxy and DK spun back to her, but they were interrupted by Bob's approach with his dessert plates. Roxy stood yet, undecided on what she most wanted to do. Soon, very soon, she was going to have to get some answers, and if Alej wouldn't confess why he felt the need to hire her, she'd press Jeannine for an answer.

"Hello, my name is Guanglie, but everyone calls me Bob." He loomed, hands behind his back, seemingly trying to make himself smaller with his head slightly bowed and shoulders hunched.

"I love your birth name, Bob, though I'm sure I'd butcher it." DK smiled up at him, trying to set him at ease. Gabby was grinning too.

The big man returned their smiles tentatively. "I'm first generation American. My parents, they were both born in China and immigrated here. And my mom is the one who taught me to cook."

"These desserts look incredible, Bob! I have such a sweet tooth!" DK was rubbing her hands in anticipation.

"I tried to appeal to a variety of different palates. There's a chocolate mousse, a savory sponge cake, and a fruit gelato." He turned to Roxy. "And Chef, I made sure that all of them could be prepared in bulk and held for a while, so they'll work on the catering line. I calculated the production costs too."

Inside this big guy was a talented chef and a good businessman. It wasn't only the care he'd taken with the desserts in front of them. He was always willing to step in whenever anyone needed a hand.

"These flavors are wonderful, and I'm not just saying that. I'm not usually a big sweets person, so the cake is really appealing to me." Gabby took another bite, chewed slowly in appreciation, and swallowed. "What did you put in it?"

Chapter 10

Mac played with the pen in his hand, flipping it over again and again on his fingers in a nimble move. Once it reached his pinkie, he flipped it back in the other direction. It was his only real sports skill. The motion was soothing, just as the rain pouring down could have been comforting, given the right conditions.

"The weather forecasters are saying that this storm will only stick around for a couple more days, but it'll bring about three inches of wet stuff. That'll mean that the big equipment can't drive into the fields, since they'll sink into the ground." Barry pushed his glasses up his nose and lifted his gaze off the tablet to look at Mac. "The location manager said the soil is like quicksand."

Great, just eff-ing great. Here he was, trying to deliver the movie on time and within budget, and now he'd lose precious days to the weather. Granted, they had insurance for this, but it was still a hassle.

And it left him with too much time on his hands, too much time to think.

The last two days had been painful, but the physical kind wasn't the worst of it. The moment he'd set eyes on Madeleine – no, scratch that, she called herself Roxy now, and why was that – the old raw feelings had risen to the surface. Through an exercise of will all those years ago, he'd pushed them down so deep that only on singularly rare occasions when he allowed himself to feel did he ever realize that they still blistered painfully.

She looked magnificent, at least from what he could tell in the waning light of that evening and the over-bright spotlights. Even at a distance, he remembered the cornflower blue of her eyes. Her hair was still ruler straight, something that pissed her off to no end way back when. And it was still the same natural blonde, the color of ripe wheat. He wondered if anything had changed, other than both of their ages.

And her lack of commitment.

"Boss, what do you want me to tell the crew to do tomorrow?"

Mac blinked hard to rid himself of the flaming resentment that roiled up inside, remembering he wasn't alone. Barry was staring at him questioningly, and he was sure it wasn't only because he wanted instructions for the cast and crew. Mac wondered what his face had looked like in these past few minutes, unschooled and uncensored as he remembered his weeks with Madeleine.

"Let's give everyone a day off," he said, dropping his feet off the table and sitting forward. The drum of rain continued, a perpetual nagging pitch that echoed off the tin roof of his rental house. "In fact, based on the weather, let's give everyone a long weekend. Hell, we can't film in the rain and we can't even get the equipment out there for a couple of days after it stops. That makes it Monday before we can resume."

"Right, boss." Barry rose and headed for the door.

"Barry, do me a favor, would you?"

The young man stopped and turned. "Sure thing," he said as he woke the snoozing electronics in his hand, ready to make a note.

"Order me dinner from Roxy's, and please ask them to deliver it."

"Anything in particular? You have a taste for something specific?"

Ever trying to please. Such a contrast from Martha, who had again mysteriously made herself unavailable tonight but who would have just ordered him whatever she saw fit.

"No, nothing specific in mind. Ask that Chef Roxy fix me something herself, something she deems to be, ah, appropriate."

Barry shot him an odd look.

"For the weather I mean." Mac clarified his point to hide his intention, and he kept the inner grimace of trepidation to himself. God only knows what she'd fix him.

"Sure thing, boss. Anything else?"

"No Barry, that's it for the evening. In fact, take a couple of days off yourself. I'll expect to see you on Sunday afternoon, but not earlier."

Glasses slipping once again, Barry nodded vigorously, and started a stuttered explanation of how he might spend his days. Waving him out the door, Mac threw out a final word. "Just remember to order my dinner."

The front door of the house closed quietly and Mac was left with the tumult of the falling rain and his own inner storm. He got up slowly, willing his aching joints to respond with minimal complaints for a change, and moved to the window to look down on the town.

The view wavered in the gray light and incessant downpour. His house was high on the hill, and the entrance and drive were on the opposite side, the uphill side of the slope. From his vantage point in the dining room, Flynn's Crossing spread out below him.

If he squinted his eyes in this weather, he could imagine how it looked in Gold Rush times. The buildings were for the most part historic and the bruises of modern times like flashy signs and off-color modern architecture hadn't been allowed to make an appearance. Some things didn't change that much.

Other things, though, changed a lot. He'd changed, and not necessarily for the better, though it wasn't by choice. He still believed in honor, in doing the right thing, in keeping his word and in others keeping theirs.

He flashed back to another rainy day, another northern California city that was so different, yet felt so much the same after the big reveal of this week.

She invaded his thoughts, memories that included a slow unbuttoning of a chef's coat stained with the day's lunch service, laughing protestations, kisses of insistence, the click of the door lock on his trailer. Hot young bodies that craved each other...

The ring of his cell phone interrupted his memory, so real in that instant that he thought he could feel the heat of her skin under his hand. The ring sounded again, louder this time as if demanding that he turn around and address the noise immediately. He closed his eyes and took a deep breath, but his thoughts of the past never drifted far below the surface.

*****

It was peaceful here, up in her aerie of a kitchen perched at the top of the building. The restaurant's kitchen below her was too crowded today, too full of people and their expectations and their needs. She had needs of her own. Preparing food was the one thing that always calmed her.

Roxy chopped methodically, each dice of carrot identical in size and perfectly cubed. Her technique was famous. She had mastered it over the years, practicing on bags of seconds that produce managers were going to throw out when they became a little too unpleasant to appeal to grocery store customers. Further honed to razor sharpness at the restaurants where she spent her time before founding Roxy's, she could skin and fillet a trout without leaving a single bone, break down a whole pig into perfect servings, and debone a chicken in scant minutes.

And that was only part of the reason why interns flocked to Roxy's to work after they finished their schooling. Yes, they learned the proper techniques, but it took years of practice to get this good. And this fast.

She wasn't rushing today, though. It was a relief to be doing something repetitious, something she could work on without conscious consideration, while her mind continued to whirl through the last few days.

Mac Smythe, after all these years. And her pain had not disappeared in the interim as she'd often told herself it had. Longing still churned through her.

The rain pounding her roof reminded her of San Francisco, fifteen years ago plus, the autumn. The end of one era of her life and the beginning of another, though not the one she'd expected at the time. He had blazed into her world, bigger than life with wild magnetism pulling her close. He'd convinced her that they could have something different, not a fling until the movie was completed but a full-fledged relationship, two people committed to each other and ready to explore the rest of their shared life.

So much for commitment, and so much for his so-called honor. He'd kicked her to the curb without so much as a goodbye, but that didn't stop the hunger from rising in her at the thought of his gasps of pleasure, his desire to please her, and the hidden world they'd created for themselves.

Moving the carrots to a tray next to her cutting board, she grabbed the celery next. The knife blade's crunch through the green stems was rewarding, kind of like the crunch her fist might make into his nose if she happened to run into it. Accidently, of course.

She grinned at the thought, then chided herself for the malicious turn her mind had taken.

"Rox? Roxy!" Alej's voice carried up the stairs from the kitchen below to her private lair. "You still up there?"

She sighed. No hiding away for the wicked.

"Yes, I'm up here chopping. It's too crowded down there."

Alej's head popped above the top of the backstairs. "Yeah, tell me about it. Having the movie crew off for a couple of days means all of the interns are in the restaurant. I'm going to send some over to the store to do prep in a little while. But in the meantime…"

"The movie's on hold?" She didn't even glance up when Alej hauled himself on to the end of the counter, sitting with his legs swinging.

"Yeah, Barry called, the director's assistant. He said that they're off until Monday because their locations are all under water and the ground's too soft. So we're free and clear there until Monday. Maybe we should give some of the interns a couple extra days off?" He shot her a questioning look as she raised her head.

"No, keep them on schedule for Thursday and Friday. They can spend time in the store kitchen instead, stock up on some prep that we'll can from the produce in the garden. We'll get a little ahead of the game."

Alej grabbed a stick of celery and she slapped his hand, happy that this, at least, was so normal. Fifteen years of friendship made him an adopted brother in her book.

"Oh, and Barry had a request from his boss."

Roxy's knife paused on a downward slice. "What did he want?"

"He wants you, as in the great Chef Roxy herself, to select his dinner menu for tonight. Something, as Barry put it, that would be appropriate for the weather."

Roxy paused mid-slice and lifted her head to look out the rain-streaked glass. He must remember how it had been outside the day they ended. He couldn't miss the irony, and he wanted to rub it in. Damn him!

"I'm happy, no in fact, absolutely delighted to select something appropriate. In fact, I'll make it myself. But on one condition." She couldn't help it, she was feeling just a little mean and spiteful. "You have to deliver it."

"Me? Why not you? It will be your menu."

"I don't want to see the man. Besides, Alej, you're the one he's used to dealing with. You won't have to do anything other than deliver the bags. I'll make the rest of it, ah, self-explanatory."

Chapter 11

She almost hummed as she put the finishing touches on the takeout containers. The aromas from the veal ragout were just shy of sinful. In fact, it made her own mouth water, everything in the flavors balanced and tasty. Homemade pasta was perfectly cooked, serving as a base for all of that spicy goodness. It was comforting perfection, particularly given the cold rainy evening ahead.

A folded box carrying garlic bread joined the mozzarella cheese sticks in the hot insulated bag. The endive salad with pickled red onion and rich blue cheese found its home in a separate stay-cool carrier. And for dessert? Something gooey, though she would have preferred he eat humble pie.

It was all designed to deliver dinner that mirrored a restaurant experience, and she expected Mac would be reminded of their final dinner years ago. The intimate restaurant in the Italian enclave of North Beach in San Francisco surrounded them with flickering candles and dimmed lighting. Roxy hoped the meal kept him up all night thinking of everything he lost, and not only in the culinary department.

It was mean-spirited of her, but he deserved it. It was hard to avoid thoughts of him completely over the years, since he was in both the celebrity news for his movies and the political columns for his stands against the wrongs of the world. 'An honorable man' he was called in so many circles.

Yeah, right. She'd had a different experience.

Early on, she avoided any mention of him, though she'd heard through random discussions of others about his wild days, his partying for a couple of years after their

San Francisco experience, and the insinuations that he wasn't a professional and that his crazy behaviors were effecting his ability to act in a less than positive way.

After a couple of years, he seemed to settle down, and he was then seen around town with a sequence of dark haired beauties, all amazingly similar and seemingly interchangeable. No one stuck around for more than a few months.

Romantically linked to every leading lady of his age, slightly older and considerably younger, his reputation as a confirmed bachelor never faltered. While the ladies in question never had a bad thing to say about him, there were also never rumors of wedding bells or true love.

That had given Roxy some hope in the early years that he might come looking for her. She'd even made attempts to get in touch with him, but after trying to run the gauntlet of assistants unsuccessfully, she'd given up. Besides, when questioned in interviews, he denied having deep feelings for any specific woman.

Final touches completed and packaging done, Roxy looked around the restaurant kitchen for Alej, ready to command him to deliver the bags as soon as the interns settled into their routines for the evening.

A rich octave of laughter echoed in the space, followed by a higher pitched giggle. Alej was working beside Jeannine at the grill, supervising her preparation of dishes slated for the dining room. Their heads were together, both enjoying the process a little too much. She frowned, making a mental note to remind Alej about appropriate supervisory behavior. Something had gotten into him lately.

Her restaurant sous chef Patrick was working with Ticia in the appetizer area. Bob was prepping food over at the store tonight. That left Angel, and he was filleting fish for tonight's restaurant orders. While it wasn't busy, there were still diners ready to brave the lousy weather and sit next to one of the roaring fireplaces in a main floor room. Maybe it was all of the water coming down, but fish seemed to be popular tonight.

Maybe the interns were ready for some one-on-one time with her after…

"Shit!" The voice rang out from the corner, and Angel dropped his knife with a clatter of metal on metal and grabbed his left hand. "Shit, fuck, shit!"

Alej, closer in distance, got there first, Roxy right on his heels. At first, it was hard to tell what had happened, since Angel was half-bent over with his hands tucked into his waist and hidden by the folds of his apron. But as they approached, he looked up wild-eyed.

"I cut my fucking hand!" He was hysterical, and Roxy's first concern was how deep a slice it might be. She grabbed a clean towel off the stack and pulled his right hand away.

"Let me see," she soothed, gentler than her usual gruffness.

He'd carved his left palm from just above the thumb all the way across. It was a bleeder, no doubt about it, but thankfully, muscles and tendons appeared to have escaped the sharp blade.

"Fuck, it's bleeding, shit!" Angel was pale and weaving. It didn't fit his street-wise image. But the slice looked scary. She knew, as she'd had a few of these herself over the years.

"Angel, we need to take you to the hospital and get you stitched up."

"Stitches? Oh shit." He glanced at the bleeding palm and he looked like he would faint. She pressured his arm until he raised it, hugging the injured hand to his shoulder.

"I'll take him," Alej said, stepping around Roxy and taking the young man's arm, keeping pressure on the hand and a towel changing color from white to bright crimson.

"No, I'll take him. Ultimately he's my responsibility." Roxy was already heading to the stairs for her keys and coat.

"No, he might feel, ah, better about being around a guy right now, you know what I mean?"

Alej stared at her intently, and she got his drift right away. If the kid needed to break down, better in front of another man and not the big woman boss.

She spun to the kitchen. After the initial excitement, everyone returned to their stations. Patrick had already removed the fillet Angel had been working on, and he was disinfecting the work surface. Everyone knew what needed to be done and they did it.

Roxy felt a small tug of satisfaction, knowing how much training paid off at times like this.

"Okay, you take him, and text me when you know how bad it really is. I'll call the emergency room and tell them you're on your way in."

Alej waved his acknowledgment and headed out the door, throwing a coat over a now pale Angel. God, she hoped he made it to the ER before he passed out.

Things returned to a low hum in the kitchen when the back door swung shut. Through the noise and the rain, she could hear the engine of Alej's SUV throb to life and head down the driveway. In the silence that followed, she glanced around again to see what needed doing and where she needed to step in.

And her eyes fell on the hot and cold insulated bags due at Mac's house on the hill.

Roxy ran through her repertoire of curse words silently, and felt the pounding of tension start in her head.

Chapter 12

He had expected dinner to be here by now, since the clock was pushing eight. His second shot of Scotch was burning a hole in his gut. He wondered if Barry forgot to call the order in. No, that wouldn't be like him. He could text the guy and ask though, just to make sure.

As he was searching for his cell phone under the papers on the table, Mac heard the harsh whine of an engine followed by sudden stillness. Shoving papers into rough piles to the side, he made a space for his meal. He'd loved the flavors and tastes of everything the catering company offered the crew for their daily menu, even if it hadn't helped his stomach one bit.

Tonight, though, was an exception. He couldn't help but be curious about how Madeleine had evolved as a chef over the years. He remembered some wonderful meals, the few times they could find a kitchen to use, and if the catering was any indication, her status in the culinary world was well earned.

An abrupt knock thumped the wood of the main door. With a start, he realized that he needed to get it himself. It was hard to bounce out of the chair, even though he wanted to. His insides might be tied in knots, but his taste buds still screamed for food. Rubbing his hands in anticipation, he headed down the corridor that divided the main floor.

"Coming!" He didn't want his delivery to disappear, thinking he wasn't home since no one answered right away. Stepping to the side, he wrenched the door open.

"Finally, I thought someone –"

And bit off the rest as he looked into grim cornflower blue eyes under a dripping oilskin hat.

*****

It wasn't the soaking roads, concern over Angel's hand, or leaving the restaurant kitchen in Patrick's capable control that made the fifteen minutes seem to take a lifetime. It was the man who would be receiving this dinner that had her jittery and mad. But even as Roxy ranted to herself, wiper blades making a vain attempt to clear her windshield, she felt the pooling of heat in her core as her thoughts drifted back to other deluges of water.

Mac in the shower was a memory she didn't want to call up, but unbidden, it came. His sleek muscled body with hard contours she'd known so well melted into her mind. So too did thoughts of them together, sharing that shower until the water ran cold, neither of them noticing. Falling into bed without bothering to towel off, heated skin evaporated what moisture was left.

No, she had to forget all of that, had to lock it up or she would give her thoughts away. It was and always would be in the past.

Roxy didn't want to be up close and personal with Mac the actor/director now, and she offered up a rare prayer that an assistant would answer the door. She was about to knock again, considering the ramifications of leaving the bags on the stoop, when the door was yanked open quickly and she was eyeball to eyeball with Mac Smythe, up close and personal after all these years.

Her first reaction was one of anger at him for causing these reactions and too-vivid memories. Her second, fast on its heels, was concern over how he looked today. It confirmed everything she'd thought she'd noticed on the set and on that podium.

The hair that was once thick and wavy hung without its former luster, and maybe it was the gray, but it seemed to pull all of his features down as well. His eyes were sunken and red-rimmed and his brown gaze was shocked and slightly hazy. The stoop of his shoulders would have been more appropriate on a man decades older.

Mac looked like hell. Sallow skin creased with lines had nothing to do with age. The pallor was out of place. He'd been out in the sun on the set for over two weeks now, and the last two days of rain weren't enough to dull the results in a healthy person.

On one level, Roxy did a mental fist pump because she was, she knew, still looking very hot, despite the intervening fifteen years. Take that sucker. Look at what you missed.

But her compassionate side was shocked and worried about him. Was he ill? Had something happened? There hadn't been any news in the press about any sickness or disease. But the proof of his failing health was evident at this close range.

He was staring at her, his eyes brighter and less foggy now. In them, she could see a hint of that old swagger, the challenge and the promise in melting chocolate tones making a shiver run up her spine in remembrance. The hunger in his gaze traveled over her face quickly in multiple passes. He didn't speak and hadn't moved to allow her to pass with the bags. Neither did he reach for them.

They both stood there, staring.

"Ah, may I come in? Or do you want to take the carriers and have your assistant return them tomorrow?" She gestured with the dripping insulated containers and held them forward, hoping he'd grab them so she could leave quickly.

His gaze changed in a blink to a stony wariness and his shoulders seemed to lift and straighten as if suddenly aware of his drooping posture. He motioned her in with a wave, then slammed the door with more force than necessary behind her.

The long hallway with its high ceiling stretched in front of her, and she waited for him to either provide directions or lead the way. If he attempted to pay her right now, like a pizza delivery kid, she would throw the food in his face.

But instead, he swept by, never touching her, and turned right at the end of the hall.

Assuming he meant for her to follow, she put the bags down and shrugged out of the dripping hat and coat. Even when she knew she'd put them right back on, there was no point in leaving a wet trail through the house.

By the time she reached the arch he'd turned through, he was seated at the dining room table, though right now it was stacked with a slim laptop, a tablet, papers, photos, loupes, and various other tools of the movie-making trade. A space was cleared in front of him, and he was in the process of moving a glass of amber liquid front and center in the beverage position. Then he looked up at her, steepling his fingers as his elbows rested on the arms of his chair. And he waited.

Fine, so this is how it will go. He doesn't want to talk. She didn't have to speak either. She could fume instead.

With more force than was necessary, she unzipped the hot pack and pulled out containers. Luckily, they were packaged so that plates weren't necessary, but silverware was another issue. She didn't see that he'd made any effort to prepare for his meal, no fork and knife lined up and ready to use.

"Do you have utensils? You know, fork and knife?"

Mac didn't say a word, only pointing to a door behind him and then returning to his steepled fingers and his unreadable gaze.

What the hell? Was this the silent treatment? Was he pissed with her for some reason? They had nothing but a contractual relationship in the present. And she was the one who deserved to be pissed off about the past.

She slammed through the door he indicated and found a contemporary kitchen. Rummaging through drawers, she came up with fork, knife and spoon, and grabbed a couple of paper towels off a roll to use as napkins.

Her temper was peaking fast, and she could feel the anger getting ready to blow. She placed the utensils and containers in front of him with exaggerated care, making her movements slow and controlled when all she wanted to do was dump the contents on his head. Two could play this game.

Finishing the hot placements, she removed the contents from the cold case and pushed them across the table towards Mac. And she turned for the hallway and freedom as if a stove was on fire.

He never said a single damned word.

*****

He sat numb and frozen as he heard the whoosh of wind and pounding rain right before the slam of the outside door. How long he sat, he wasn't sure. Struggling to get a grip on himself, he was thankful for his years of training because he'd just put on one hell of a great performance.

If he'd spoken, he was afraid he'd have given himself away, allowing the longing to overcome the anger and hurt of that final weekend long ago. She would see the desire in his eyes and the sorrow for what they'd lost.

And she would have known that she'd won.

"Damn it! Damn it all to hell!" His yell echoed in the empty house and his fist hurt where he pounded it on the table, making the food containers jump and the silverware clatter. He'd lost his appetite.

Why did it still hurt so much after all of these years?

She had changed, but in all of the good ways. Her hair was long, its casual loose bun revealed when she'd shed the hat and coat in the hallway. Her eyes didn't miss a thing, he suspected. She was probably wondering what was going on with him, since she'd examined his face closely with a deep frown.

The anger she'd shown had been barely concealed as she'd slapped the containers on the table. A couple of lines in her face that hadn't been there years ago, lines of determination and strength, lines of someone who had faced challenges in life and overcome them, only made her more attractive.

Mac was proud of her. If the stories he'd googled were true, she was a substantial success here in the local community and her reputation had spread across the country. Roxy LaFollette was listed as one of the top chefs to watch on numerous polls, and her restaurant was a destination for foodies from around the globe.

He wondered, though, what had happened in the intervening years. When did Madeleine become Roxy? There was no hint of her before she appeared as Roxy in Portland's unique foodie scene. What had happened? It was as if their time together had never existed.

He looked down at the aluminum containers, noting now the writing on the cardboard lids. 'No Comfort Ragout with Tender Pasta', and 'Chillin' for Days Salad', and 'Hot Stuff Garlic Bread'.

He grinned, amused at the double entendres in her words. Yes, they had been all of that and more to each other. So she hadn't forgotten that final meal in Little Italy either. Each dish was a replica of their last supper together.

Mac pulled the dessert container forward, eager to see what snappy phrase she'd used to wrap up dinner. 'Death by Chocolate'. They'd fed each other, fork by tasty fork between laughing lips, until every bite was gone. He frowned as a wave of desolation swamped over him.

Dying inside had been how he'd felt after she left him. Clearly, she needed to stab him one more time. He'd earned the right to be angry.

But why was she so angry with him?

Chapter 13

"Yes, I get to meet him, and no, you can't come along."

Dane was checking his camera equipment, taking each item off the dining room table and placing it in the padded bag. Serena paced the open living room, turning with a new argument on almost every lap. And the girl tribe smiled at the picture.

"Yeah, you guys get all the luck. Vince gets to interview him, you get to take the pictures. I'm surprised you haven't asked Rick along to haul equipment or carry water or something," DK huffed.

"Rick was busy grading final exams. Otherwise, he would be coming along. Relax, we'll tell you all about it when we get back." Vince leaned over and dropped a kiss on DK's head, and while she huffed again and crossed her arms in rebuke, he smiled anyway.

Roxy was worried. The guys were going to interview Mac for a lifestyle piece. They were supposed to talk about his hobbies, what he did with his free time, and how he liked the Flynn's Crossing area.

Of course, they didn't know about the past connection, and Roxy wasn't about to explain it to them. Maybe it would never come up.

"Okay, I've got everything," Dane confirmed as he hefted the bag over his shoulder. Before he picked up the giant tripod and lighting bag, he pulled Serena into his arms for an exaggerated and lusty kiss. She was still pouting when he let her go, but once she turned so that he couldn't see her face, she grinned.

This is what love is supposed to be like, Roxy thought. It didn't kick you to the curb without any explanation, without a goodbye.

Vince and Dane made a big production of leaving, with Serena and DK making equally big productions about complaining. When the door finally closed and they heard the distant sound of a truck pulling down the drive, Serena settled on her couch near DK and sighed.

"I really am one of the luckiest women on the planet." She smiled at Roxy and DK and snuggled deeper into the cushions.

"Ditto," said DK. "I'd love to make Vince out to be the bad guy, but he has a job to do and I'm sure it will be a great interview. With terrific pictures, I might add." She saluted Serena, who inclined her head in agreement.

Restless, Roxy stood and walked to the windows over the canyon. Serena and Dane had a gorgeous home perched on a cliff over a river coursing down from the mountains. The rains had finally stopped, leaving behind glistening foliage on the trees and shrubs. Grasses were growing so fast that you could almost see their minute-by-minute progress.

"I didn't mean to sound so snotty, Rox, sorry." Serena came to stand next to her and placed a hand on her arm. "You'll find yours and probably when you least expect it."

"I'm not concerned about that in the least." Roxy put a proud smile on her face and turned back to the room. "You know I barely have time to tend my vegetables before my long workday, so when would I get a chance to have a relationship anyway?" She brushed it aside with a wave of her hand.

Going for a casual tone, she added, "Did I ever tell you that I worked on a Mac Smythe movie before?"

"No! Really? When? I can't believe you never said anything. Tell!" Serena dropped to the edge of her seat and DK thumped her feet to the floor and leaned forward.

Roxy sat more slowly, and she played with the fringes on a pillow as she composed her story.

"It was a very long time ago. I was just out of culinary school and working for a catering company that had a contract to support a movie crew. The film didn't do very well at the box office, but Mac got Oscar and Golden Globe nominations out of it for his performance." In the silence that followed, she stopped fiddling and looked up.

Serena was looking puzzled and DK was smiling in rapt attention. When Roxy didn't continue, DK prompted, "And so?"

It was Roxy's turn to frown now. "And so what?"

Huffing almost as loudly as she'd done with her fiancé, DK urged, "And so did you meet? What was he like? Did you get to see him often?"

Because she wanted to answer as truthfully as possible without giving away the depth of her secret, Roxy spoke carefully. "I was working on the catering line, like my interns are now. He came through the line, cracked a lot of jokes, and got to know everyone's name." She stopped, realizing that she might have already said too much, but it appeared that DK and Serena weren't thinking anything was unusual.

"And so?" Serena waved her hands to move the story forward.

"He was very handsome, very charming, very... engaging I guess you'd say. Every woman working on or near the set, even the grannies, had a crush on him. And he was very polite with all of us and made sure he didn't hurt anyone's feelings or single anyone out for too much attention."

Except her, and then surreptitiously so that they weren't an obvious couple. But his special attention was what made the ending so confusing and hurtful.

"What did he look like back then, up close?" DK's eyes were wide from the brush with celebrity, even though she herself was a celeb in art circles.

Roxy stirred, afraid to think back to his sleek good looks and warm charm, the same deadly charm he'd exercised on her so effectively.

"Forget back then. What about now? I'm sure you're getting plenty of time to hobnob with the stars now that you're the head of their catering company." Serena leaned forward, eyes intent on Roxy's with more questions than her words had let on.

Trust Serena to pick up the scent of something amiss, Roxy thought with an internal groan. But she could brazen it out with the best of them.

"He looks different from then, that's for sure. Granted, I'm not spending any time with him and I've only seen him a couple of times, but don't you think he looks, I don't know, sick?"

"Yeah, come to think of it, he looks skinny, and not in a good way. And pale, like he's never out of a basement." DK bit her lip and concentrated.

"I don't know. Other than seeing him at the Main Street celebration and then it wasn't up close and the lighting was bad, I wouldn't be able to say. Maybe he's a little sunken or something." Despite her comments, Serena was still watching Roxy intently.

"I haven't heard anything about an illness in the media, and they usually follow him closely. You know, who he's dating, how serious it is, what cause he's championing, when he breaks up with someone, where he parties to lick his wounds, that is, if he has any." DK laughed at this, and Serena joined in. Roxy smiled, but she knew it was forced.

Serena regarded her again thoughtfully. "Roxy, is there something you're not telling us? You seem out of sorts with all of this."

Shit, she knew it. Roxy exaggerated a grumble and a sigh to cover the rest of the story, confessing, "It's just that there's a lot going on right now. Four interns, the new catering business, demanding movie clientele, and the restaurant and store to consider."

She looked at her short cut nails and realized that she was so not a Hollywood type.

"I'm just… busy. And delivering meals to the big man himself took a chunk out of my day."

"Oooh, delivering meals? Why haven't we heard about this?" DK was so near the edge of her seat that she was at risk of falling off the couch.

Realizing she might have made a tactically error, Roxy decided that retreat looked honorable right now. She waved a hand.

"Just dinner once, the other night in the pouring rain when Angel sliced his hand and Alej took him to the emergency room. I played pizza guy. It was nothing."

When the women would have quizzed her further, her cell phone buzzed.

"Yes, what's up Alej? Oh really? On Monday as in tomorrow? Well, we can't get the truck in there… hold on."

She put the phone down and said, "Emergency, in the catering business of course. The demands of the movie crew never cease. I need to go. Love you both!"

Roxy looked over her shoulder to see Serena and DK staring at her in consternation. DK put up her hands as if to say, you're leaving us hanging in the middle of the story. And Serena frowned with question marks evident all over her face.

Chapter 14

"Thanks for seeing us on a Sunday, man. We appreciate it." The tall writer moved towards Mac, and he knew he should be prepared for a man-hug, one arm around a shoulder and a slap on the other arm, body distance maintained.

Except he was worried that it would bowl him over to the floor.

Still, he endured it and didn't collapse. "Cassidy, good to see you too, man. What's it been, two years, Monte Carlo?"

Released, he tried not to fall on his ass and start the interview off with a bang. The other man, his own height and age with a long scar slicing down his cheek, was watching him closely. Mac feared that his eyes didn't miss much.

"Yeah, I think you're right. I want you to meet a friend of mine, Dane Matthews Ashland. He'll be taking a few photos of you today for the article. Hope you don't mind, since your assistant Martha cleared it."

Damn Martha! She'd said nothing about photos to him, and she knew how he needed to be prepared for pictures now. He wasn't looking good enough to pass for a homeless guy most days without make-up and hair and a whole lot of good lighting.

"Wait, Dane Matthews, I know that name. Are you the one who takes those incredible wildlife shots? And you did a series recently on vets too, didn't you? Awesome work, man! You have an amazing eye." Mac moved over to pump Dane's hand with honest enthusiasm, and he noted that the man came out of his watchful pose and smiled.

"Good to meet you too. I admire the work you're doing in Southeast Asia in the old war zones, and in Africa. And yes, guilty as charged on the vets shots. My wife Serena needed me to come out of retirement for them and I've never been sorry."

Mac saw a range of expressions flash across the man's face and knew that there was a story there, a personal interest of some caliber that would probably make a good short film. He was always on the lookout for a good story.

"Ah, Vince? I'm going to set up over here. I assume that's okay with you, Mr. Smythe?" The photographer motioned to a chair set in the window of the living room overlooking the town. The light was gentle there, and Mac breathed a sigh of relief.

Maybe the man could see how much he needed gentler light.

He turned back to the interviewer. "Vince? I thought you were always Cassidy. Since when?"

The tall man laughed and moved to the chairs facing each other in an opposite corner. "Since I came here. Since I was keeping my identity a secret when I first arrived. Then I met DK, my fiancée, and the rest of the town. To them, I've always been Vince. Not Cassidy, the world-renowned lifestyle writer, though they know that part now too." And he chuckled.

"Yeah, I got sucked in myself two years ago, bought some land, built a house, and while I was building the house, Serena showed up." The photographer stopped while extending the legs on a tripod. "This place is magic." And both men laughed.

For him, Mac thought, it was simply painful. First, this mystery disease advancing so quickly, and now, Madeleine.

For public consumption, he put a good spin on things. "Yeah, the film is turning out to be quite incredible, I can tell you that. The locations are terrific, don't have to do much of anything to them to use them, and the people have been great, helpful but not too pushy, if you know what I mean."

"We take care of our own, and that includes respecting distance and privacy," Dane stated. "And now, Mr. Smythe, could I get a few test shots of you to set the frame and lighting?"

"Please, call me Mac."

*****

Two hours stretched into three, and three stretched into the balcony overlooking the town, formal interview and photos complete and a drink in each man's hand. Mac hadn't felt so relaxed in, well, he wasn't sure how long it had been.

"No, I'm telling you, the browns that you catch at Wilson are the biggest you'll ever see. They stock the lake but they're fighters just the same. There are feeder creeks all over the place, and you can walk for an hour and not see another human being." Dane took a pull on his beer.

Mac leaned forward, intrigued. Fly-fishing was one of the few things that took him so completely out of his head it was a pleasure, even if he couldn't walk far or do it for very long anymore.

"It is a beautiful spot," Vince concurred.

"That it is." Dane leaned forward and turned a sharp eye to Mac. "We'd love to have you out to the house and give you a tour of the area, if you're interested."

Mac contemplated the implications of this. Maybe he could wrangle a dinner at Roxy's restaurant out of the plan. That would make it all worthwhile.

"Yeah, that would be a good idea. DK's an artist – you probably have seen her work. Serena runs a nonprofit. Gabby's a writer and her other half Rick teaches at the university when he's not busy building the Panama Canal – no seriously," Vince added when he saw Mac's skeptical look. "Marguerite's a winemaker – you've gotta try their stuff – and you already know Tess and Roxy." He stopped.

Mac wanted to tread carefully, afraid of giving too much away. "Roxy I know, and I've even met her in person now. Tess?" He looked between the two other men.

"She owns the flower shop at the bottom of this hill, at the end of Main, Buds and Blooms. She's providing the displays for your shoots."

Damn his memory again. He knew there was a local flower shop supplying something, though he was vague on the details.

"All of those women – how do you guys get any rest?" He tried humor to get out of his corner of haziness. He was so tired.

The two men glanced at each other, grinned, and turned to Mac. "They call themselves the girl tribe," Vince explained. "They've been close for a long time, long before we were on the scene."

Dane added, "And they stay that way, even though we're on the scene."

"So they're close? These women? Like tell each other everything close?" Mac wondered what they knew about him and about the past, and what that would mean for his reception at any upcoming dinner.

"I'm guessing yes, thought we're not necessarily privy to those conversations, loves of their lives or not," Vince continued.

Mac considered, then dove in. "Yeah, women are like that. They tell each other everything, but nothing to us guys." He laughed more heartily than he was feeling.

"But seriously, guys, how about some fishing time before I have to leave? Can you swing it?"

Chapter 15

"Come on, Chef, I can work! It's just a scratch! See, I can take these bandages off and…"

"No!" Roxy and Alej yelled at Angel in unison, though Angel had been trying to convince Roxy for the past fifteen minutes that he was fine. He'd been doing the same with Alej before that.

She tried for reason. "Angel, the slice was deep enough to need stitches. You can't work when you have an open wound, it's not sanitary, and the doctor told you to take it easy. But there are plenty of non-cooking things for you to do."

The young man bristled and opened his mouth to argue again, but Roxy put up a hand and stared hard at him. At times like this, it was best to bring out Chef Mean and Nasty and stare him down.

Angel subsided, though his shoulders were tight and he sent her a stubborn glare.

"We have a lot of planning to do for the catering truck. How much meat do we need? What must be prepped before, what doesn't? How do we plan the rest of their menus for the final four weeks?" She softened her gaze and tried to appeal to his need to be special. "I need someone I can trust to do the calculations for the portions, translate that into the product we need, and write out menus. Can you do that for us, Angel? It would be a huge help."

He switched from angry man to eager boy, and his unbandaged hand unclenched from its tight fist. "Yeah Chef, sure! I did the same thing at my mom's restaurant all the time. See, it was like this…"

Roxy nodded, tuning out his story. The rain had delayed the movie by a week, which meant that she would have to endure Mac being in town for one week longer. Granted, she didn't need to see him under normal daily circumstances.

But that was before the summons, as she thought of it.

It had begun innocently enough with Alej taking a call from Mac's assistant, Barry. Except Barry didn't want to talk with Alej. He wanted to talk with Roxy.

"Hello, Ms. LaFollette? Or – I'm sorry – Chef LaFollette? I'm a big fan!" His enthusiasm raged over the phone connection, and he started to tell her the story of his dining experience at her restaurant when he'd been scouting the location.

"Barry, sorry to interrupt you. I'm really pleased that you had such a wonderful time at Roxy's, and I hope you come back a few times before you leave and bring others on your crew. And please, ask for me or Chef Alej any time you come in. Please call me," she paused, considering boundaries, "…Chef Roxy."

Long story short, Barry was calling at the behest of Mr. Smythe, who evidently, Roxy thought snottily, was too damn busy to call her himself. Mr. Smythe wanted to order dinner in any night that they were not shooting late.

No big deal. Alej could have handled this.

"And Chef? He has a special request." She waited, wondering what sort of food hoops Mac wanted her to jump through. The starlet's requirements were enough to make people weep, and a few of the crew had now added to the list.

"Yes Barry?" She listening to his heavy breathing on the other end of the phone.

"Mr. Smythe would like you to prepare and deliver the meals yourself. A special and unique menu just for him.

Not Chef Alej, not anyone else working on it." He paused, as if expecting an explosion. "Just you."

*****

"My office." She stood directly in front of Alej and ground out the words, then spun on her heel and headed across the kitchen. She noted with grim comfort that the staff and interns were all watching her warily.

Of course they were. While she could get a real temper going if the need arose, it didn't happen often. So when she threw the kitchen phone across the room, narrowly missing the grill, Angel whistled, Jeannine applauded, and Bob and Ticia turned pale.

Alej too, for that matter.

She stomped across the space, now silent except for the hollow thump of her chef's clogs slapping on the tile surface. She dropped into her chair facing the desk and slammed her hands flat on its surface. At ten seconds – she was counting – Alej appeared in the door.

The man was seemingly unperturbed now, examining him nails and then flexing his hands, as if admiring muscles and tendons making their subtle movements. He slouched in the doorway, and when Roxy didn't say anything, he looked up. Still moving slowly, he stepped forward, closed the door quietly, and sat down across from her.

Her face, she knew, was a picture of anger. There was nothing she wanted to do to control it. She was damn mad. And she wanted Alej to know it.

They both waited. From experience, she knew he would cave first. And here he came.

"So, the interns are working out, don't you think? Even Angel, though granted, he's got some anger management issues," he shot her a quick glance, "and Ticia's shy, and Bob's got to get his confidence up. Jeannine, well Jeannine is, she's…"

Roxy inhaled sharply, blew out a big sigh, and started in. "We're not here to talk about the interns." She slapped a palm on her desk, and to his credit, Alej didn't jump.

"And we're here to talk about...?" He waved his hands in the air, then subsided into the indolent posture of relaxation that Roxy knew was staged to hide his anxiety. She rarely ever, ever got mad at him.

"What did you do to piss off the movie crew?"

Alej's chin pulled in and he shot her a what-the-hell look that said he had no idea what she was talking about.

Just as she suspected. It had nothing to do with the team and everything to do with her. A simple request, which was probably an ego trip by the man so that he could lord it over her, making her answer to him even after leaving her on the street all those years ago.

Just because he could.

Chapter 16

She wrapped the chicken and house-made noodles with care, making sure that the delicate sauce didn't break in the process. At least there was a kitchen to repair things if they didn't travel well.

Roxy looked around the restaurant kitchen space and noted that everyone had their head down and intent on the work in front of them. Their edginess hung in the air thicker than the rich aromas from the sauces and soups. Earlier, Alej held an impromptu chef staff meeting during which everyone to a person turned to stare at her.

"Chef? Do you have a minute?" The intern Jeannine stood to the side, anxiety on her features.

Roxy sighed and nodded, realizing that nothing could delay tonight's command performance for long.

The night before last, the first night under this weird new arrangement, he'd been silent as he answered the door and turned quickly back down the hallway. He dropped into a chair in the dining room, staring at her without comment, his table full of papers. She waved at them, no words necessary, asking where she should set things.

And her staff noticed that something was unusual about this dinner gig. As Roxy picked herbs and vegetables from her restaurant's garden for yesterday's menu, Ticia had come to stand silently beside her, basket at the ready to accept the produce. She didn't ask any questions, instead noting with keen interest every item Roxy selected.

Finally, when the quiet observation became too much for even Roxy to bear, the intern spoke.

"Is this all for Mr. Smythe?"

"Yes, all of this and more. I'm, ah, trying out some new menu ideas on him. Since I'm cooking for him anyway, I may as well use the time for some things we need at the restaurant too, right?" Roxy smiled, though she was sure that she wasn't fooling the woman. Tension hung in the air like a lingering mist.

He'd been silent again last night. She'd rapped on the door. He'd answered and motioned her in, waving to the dining room/office. This time, the table was cleared. Neither of them said a word as she set his place and packed up the cases. The front door clattered shut behind her.

Edgy, hell. She could slice an overripe tomato with her tension.

"Ah, Chef?" Jeannine stood to the side, leaning slightly with hands together and her posture bent. Her chef's coat no longer billowed and Roxy noted that things seemed to be getting tighter, even as Jeannine's face was becoming more drawn.

"Yes, Jeannine. Give me one minute." Putting the containers in the carriers and zipping the bags, she turned. "Yes?"

The woman hesitated. "Could we have this conversation in your office?"

Roxy frowned. It was rare – no, scratch that – never before had an intern requested a discussion in her office. It was most often considered a scary execution chamber where interns went to – well, die – but more aptly, be told to move along to a new position. They rarely entered by choice, and never by their request.

Seating herself behind the desk, she waited as Jeannine closed the door and dropped into the molded chair across the narrow expanse. She seemed unfazed by the privacy that the office offered or the speculative glare that Roxy was now giving her.

She turned a few papers over for show, then moved a folder to the side, folding her hands on top of the remaining pile. "Yes, Jeannine?"

The woman regarded her with a mixed expression. Roxy saw anger, resentment, and resignation dash across. Jeannine's shoulders slumped back into the curve of the chair and she drew a shaky breath.

"You asked why I was here." Jeannine waited after her words, clearly not expecting an answer.

Thinking back, Roxy tried to recall the craziness of her first few days of the interns when she'd returned from Serena and Dane's wedding. Jeannine's wail about needing a safe place to come to had lapsed into silence, broken only by an occasional hiccup of a well-controlled sob. No further mention of it was forthcoming on this woman's part.

And Roxy had been distracted.

Leaning forward, Roxy fixed her with a stare that was meant to make her intern squirm. It seemed to have no effect, however. Jeannine was fighting a private battle that had nothing to do with the glower directed at her by her boss.

"You remember my father?"

Roxy nodded. Oh boy, did she remember him. Bartholomew Paush – Bart to his friends, of which he seemed to have very few – was the epitome of the arrogant, irate and angry chef. He lived life at full volume, whether the occasion called for it or not. He had made Roxy's life a living hell for that first year in San Francisco.

"He is just about impossible to forget," she responded wryly.

Jeannine shifted in her chair and stared at her feet. "He and I don't see eye to eye." She paused, selecting her words carefully. "In fact, I don't think we ever will again."

Roxy was surprised. When she'd worked at Paush's restaurant, this woman, then just a newly minted teenager, was around all the time. She visited almost every day, and she was the only thing that made her father slow down, take a breath, and speak at a normal volume. She made him laugh, a sound so rare that all work stopped in the kitchen when it rang out. He doted on his daughter.

"Did something happen between the two of you?"

Raising her eyes to meet Roxy's gaze, Jeannine's mouth quirked into a grimace. "It's been happening for a while, I think." And she got up to pace the small office.

"You see, I wanted to follow in his footsteps, make a name for myself in other restaurants, and then return with seasoning and experience to offer as a partner to my father. But he didn't like that idea. He wanted me to come home as soon as I graduated from culinary school. He wanted to train me himself, he said. It would all be so wonderful, working side by side, the Paush culinary dynasty." Jeannine barked out a sharp laugh.

"I traveled between kitchens for a while, learning new techniques, before I came back. Of course, working together was impossible. There was only one way to do things, his way. There was only one menu and one selection of appropriate dishes, his choices. There was only one true chef in the kitchen, despite my training and skills, and that was him." She flopped back into the chair.

"It must be hard to be the child of someone so famous and want to follow in their footsteps," Roxy suggested gently.

"Hard doesn't even begin to describe it. So I'll cut to the chase. He didn't want to take my suggestions for menu updates, even when I could prove to him that the customers loved the dishes." She sucked in a loud mouthful of air before continuing, her eyes on her tightly entwined fingers. "And then I met a man, another chef who worked at a nearby restaurant, and my father did not approve of him. I think it was more like jealousy and rivalry than anything else. Things got even worse after that."

She paused now and searched Roxy's face. She must have felt comfortable what she saw because she hesitated only a moment before carrying on with her story.

"One thing led to another, and the more involved I got with the guy, the more my father raged at me. Finally, he threw me out of the kitchen, told me never to return, and wouldn't even take my phone calls afterward. That was a little over two months ago."

"I remember that your mother died when you were very young and there isn't any other family, right?" How could anyone throw their only daughter out of their life?

Jeannine nodded. "Both my parents were only children and their parents died young as well. And Jerry? That's the guy I was seeing. He seemed to lose interest too." Tears were threatening, glistening on the edges of her long lashes. "I guess all he really wanted was an inside track on the competition."

"Men are beasts, the scum of the earth," Roxy stated, flashing on her own youthful experience, earning a watery smile from the other woman.

"Jerry wasn't like that, or at least I didn't think so before. But you see, there's one other thing, something I told him right after my father threw me out."

Roxy waited in silence as Jeannine opened her mouth to explain, shut it again, sighed, and started one more time.

"I'm pregnant, Jerry's the father, and he's not interested in the baby. Not at all. And my own father could care less."

Chapter 17

She sat in the driveway on the hill, the view of Flynn's Crossing blocked by the house in front of her. Roxy pondered what Jeannine shared. When her father had blackballed her from working in any kitchen in San Francisco, she'd remembered Roxy and Alej and their Flynn's Crossing businesses. Begging for a job, she'd sworn Alej to secrecy until she could explain to Roxy herself what had happened. A holiday baby, maybe even a Christmas baby, was on the way.

How she ended up with these situations, Roxy wasn't sure. First Angel, with his attitude and his injury. Now a pregnant intern, except as something of a chef-celebrity in her own right, she really wasn't an apprentice anymore either.

If Bob started speaking Chinese and requesting a wok for the kitchen or Ticia whipped up chicken fried steak with gravy and called it health food, she wouldn't be that surprised. It seemed that nothing was going smoothly these days.

Which led her back to why she was sitting in this driveway in the first place, hesitating before she entered the house because she wasn't sure what she should anticipate tonight. She was tired of this diversion Mac was acting out, the silent treatment and pantomime of dinner presentation. And she was damn sure that it was simply a power trip to him.

Not any more, she fumed, and pushed open the door to get out. Opening the back hatch of her SUV, she grabbed the insulated cases and slammed it shut hard enough to rattle the license plate. It felt good to give in to her anger and frustration.

Knocking loudly, she waited. Then she pounded. "Mac? It's dinner time and I don't have the patience for games, so open up and let's get this over with."

No answer. Did he go out and forget to let them know that he wouldn't need dinner tonight? That would be just like him.

Patience expended, Roxy whirled on her heels and returned to the SUV, hand on the door handle of the backseat preparing to put the food carriers away. Ready to yank it wide, she heard the front door of the house rattle open. Spinning with her mouth already open to berate him, she stopped suddenly when she caught sight of the man.

Mac hung on the frame for support, panting and paler than the trim around that door.

"Madeleine, I'm sorry I kept you waiting. Please, come in."

*****

He'd barely made it to the bathroom in time, and the violent illness cost him his lunch and probably some of breakfast too. While eating again was the last thing he could tolerate right now, he wanted to see Madeleine.

Scratch that, needed to see her. She was his only solace in what had turned into a miserable time in his life.

He breathed in with painful effort leaning against the doorjamb, held it until the next wave of nausea passed, and blew it out on a gasp.

"It's Roxy now. Madeleine died a long time ago. I don't have time to be delayed with these special deliveries, so I'd appreciate it if you could be more prompt when you answer the door. I can't wait forever." She stopped and peered at him more closely. "What's wrong with you?"

He spun abruptly and trudged slowly down the airy hall to the dining room, using the time to get his breathing under control and adjust his features to neutral indifference. She couldn't be allowed to notice how bad he felt.

"Mac, are you all right?" She followed him into the room, standing under the arched entrance with an insulated bag in each hand. Even packed away, he could smell tempting aromas that tickled his taste buds and made him curious about what treasures she'd brought him today, all while his stomach rolled in revolt.

The concern on her face got to him. "Look, I'm just having a few issues, okay? No big deal and nothing to alert the press over. We all have bad days."

Still frowning but no longer watching him, she advanced across the space and started talking.

"Yeah, tell me about bad days. My bad boy intern sliced his hand deep enough to need stitches and now I'll be finding him busy work until he's healed enough to serve on the line again. Another intern – except well, she's probably not really an intern – is having other kinds of problems. Going from rain in torrents to this heat wave means that produce is coming in so quickly I can't preserve it fast enough to keep from losing some to spoilage. And the store…"

She was frowning and rambling on, and she looked so cute in her tank top and chef's pants. The outfit, he knew, would be topped with a sparkling clean chef's coat when she was on duty. This was the first time she'd shed it before making his delivery.

Her curves were still lush, and he remembered with electrifying vividness what they felt like wrapped around him.

Mac had to do it. Maybe it was this sickness lowering his resistance, but he needed to feel her pressed against him, just to see if it was only an imagined memory that haunted him.

Her hands were full of the bags, and as she passed him, he put a hand on her arm to turn her. Madeleine stopped talking abruptly, eyes moving rapidly between his hand and his face, sharpness in her expression and her mouth open in what would probably be a protest.

Before she had a chance to say a word, he pulled her into his arms and pressed his open lips to hers.

He didn't intend to be subtle or timid, couldn't be anything but greedy. His tongue met hers, and he felt the shocked stiffness in her body even as his mouth teased hers. All those years ago, it had been like making love with her, mouth to mouth, and it still was.

She didn't struggle, which surprised him. Her anger with him had been all too obvious in the past couple of weeks, but she wasn't resisting. In fact, he could swear she melted closer as her tongue began a tentative exploration of its own.

Her curves were as luscious and rich as he remembered. She fit against him perfectly, their bodies a flawlessly orchestrated combination. His hands wandered up her back to pull the fastener from her hair so that it tumbled over his knuckles. It still felt like the finest silk.

Abruptly she dropped the bags and shoved him back. Two paces away from her was too far, Mac mused with what little was left of his brainpower, and he started forward with hands outstretched. But her posture was anything but welcoming.

"What the hell do you think you're doing?"

Madeleine was yelling at him, hands on hips and her eyes blazing. How could blue get that bright?

"What kind of game is this now, Mac?"

Retrieving the bags and ripping the zippers open with enough force to tear the contents in half, she slammed containers down on the table.

"Here, is, your, supper!" A smack of container to table emphasized each word.

"Made- I mean Roxy, please, can we talk?" He reached a hand out to touch her again but she swiveled away and put the table between them.

"Talk, you want to talk? Is that what they call it these days? Who gave you the right to lay a hand on me? What were you thinking?"

How did he answer that one? "I was thinking about us, about how good we were together, about how well we fit each other. I just wanted to see if it was real, or something my mind imagined."

She stared at him, and he noticed her breathing was ragged, as much of a pant as his. Hands gripped the back of a chair tightly, so hard that her knuckles were white. And that golden silky hair cascaded around her face as she shook her head in protest.

No, she was not unaffected by their kiss. Mac knew the signs. But in the past, a kiss like that would still be going on, or they'd be on the nearest horizontal surface it, or, hell, he'd be pushing her up against a convenient wall and her legs would be coming around his waist and…

"The past is just that, the past." Her voice was quieter now, but her breathing hadn't slowed. "I needed to move on, to build my life and my career and my business. For myself. By myself."

It hurt him to hear that. So she had wanted to leave him, even when she'd been making promises of love and commitment. They hadn't meant a thing.

Martha had warned him, but he had been too love-struck to listen.

*****

The kiss changed nothing and everything for her. Her heart was pounding and she was afraid to let go of the chair. She might keel over.

Nothing had changed. The feel of his lips, his persuasive touch, ranged over her like fire, the sizzle of cold meat meeting hot grill and the sparks that flew off the flame. She was shaking on the inside, her stomach flipping over even as her core throbbed. Memories be damned – the real thing was a whole lot better.

And everything had changed. They were two different people now. She was honed to a fine knife's edge, but then the life she'd had to build by herself created that. And he was more famous and more in demand and more focused on his own needs.

"You have to understand, Roxy, how it was for me back then. I had a career that was accelerating so fast I wasn't in control of it. If anything, it's even crazier now, with directing as well as acting and my foundation and the production company and…"

Yes, his own needs were most important, so he had walked away from her on that rainy morning.

Part of her had wanted to believe that the woman he'd sent to evict her was wrong. For a few months, she kept waiting for him to find her, to pull her into his arms and say it was all a big mistake, that he'd been searching for her endlessly.

But after a few months, that dream died. The grueling days in the kitchen at Paush's restaurant zapped her optimism that love would conquer all, and she'd come to realize that Mac was on to new and better adventures that didn't include her. In fact, she was probably no more than a tiny brief blip on his radar, a convenience of consequences to pass the time on the set.

She forced herself to wave a hand in nonchalant dismissal. "I never played the violin and I'm not going to learn now, so save the sob story about your rough life for someone who cares. I don't."

He blanched, and she noted again the strange green pallor and deeply carved lines in his face. He'd changed in other ways too. Mac was no less handsome or charming, but time was taking a heavy toll on him beyond the passage of years. She slammed shut the window her heart peeked through, hurting for him.

Straightening her spine and moving back to the tote bags, she bent to lift them and zip them closed with more gentleness than she'd used before. One stuck, the zipper's tab jammed so tightly into the fabric that it refused to budge. Roxy felt tears prick her eyes in frustration.

"Aahhhh!"

She looked up in surprise at Mac's cry. He was doubled over with an arm wrapped across his stomach. This was hardly the time for a game, and anger waded in over the tears and took over.

"Mac, I don't have time for some new act, okay?"

But he wasn't paying attention to her. His eyes were closed and the agony on his face was horrible to look at.

Maybe he wasn't acting.

His eyes opened, barely, and he reached blindly for a chair, missing the arm and nearly falling. She jumped forward and grabbed him around the waist, pulling out the chair as she did and easing him down on the edge of it.

"What's wrong? Mac?"

Roxy knelt in front of him and tried to get his attention, but he was far away in the throes of some pain she didn't understand. Then just as suddenly as it started, he collapsed back into the chair, sweating and panting and letting his arms fall to his sides. His head hit the chair's back with a notable crack and his eyes stayed closed.

"Oh god, it just keeps getting worse."

"What keeps getting worse? Mac, should I call you an ambulance?"

He shook his head vehemently, red stains appearing on his cheeks in stark contrast to his ashen skin. "No ambulance, no doctors, and no media. Remember that, okay? Absolutely no media! Don't talk to anyone about this!"

Fear replaced her anger.

Rising and moving quickly to the kitchen, she found a glass and filled it with water, bringing it back to Mac. She touched his arm and put it in front of him, and he needed both hands to close around it and lift it. Whatever it was, it was sapping his strength. She kept one hand on the glass to steady it as he gulped greedily.

"What is wrong with you?" Her question was gentler this time.

He held on to the glass, bracing it on the arm of the chair, his head back and eyes closed again. Slowly, he shook his head.

"I don't – I don't know."

"Well what do the doctors say? You have been to a doctor, right?" She pulled out another chair and put it at an angle to his.

He waved a hand as if to shoo away the idea of medical help, eyes staying closed.

"Been to them, and they all say about the same thing. 'It's lifestyle, Mac.' And 'you need to lay off the food and the booze, Mac.' And 'maybe you have some food allergies, Mac.' Blah, blah, blah."

Finally, he opened his eyes to narrow slits and stared into hers. "I tried what they told me, tried to eat a vegan diet even, tried raw foods and slow foods and whole foods and god knows what else." His face was bleak. "It's getting worse, not better."

Chapter 18

He'd sworn her to secrecy. He couldn't afford for this to leak out, not when there were already questions about his appearance starting to nibble at the edges of his public image.

"But you have to go to the doctor! Something is very wrong! Why won't you take care of yourself?"

Searching through the containers she'd brought from the restaurant, she declared each dish wrong. She paced in the dining room as he drank some packaged broth she'd deemed acceptable from a stash in a kitchen cupboard.

But those noodles in cream sauce sure smelled good as she dumped them down the disposal.

"I am not going to the doctor. I told you, I've been to the best, specialists and everything. I have to change my whole lifestyle, and if I start eating the way they want me to, I may as well die now." He shivered at the thought of so much rigidity. "That's no way to live."

"But how can you go on like this? I've only seen you for the past few weeks and even I can tell that you're worse." She sat in front of him, pulling the chair forward until they were almost knee-to-knee. "I have a proposition for you."

He almost laughed then. Here he was, too exhausted to raise his head from the chair back and she wanted to proposition him? Talk about timing. He tried to give her a wolfish grin as his thoughts returned to the taste of her mere moments ago.

"Not that kind! Yeesh." She frowned at him, then gave him a grudging smile of her own. "I guess you're feeling a little bit better now."

Better, but not well enough to lean forward and plant another kiss on that earnest mouth. "A little better," he agreed.

"Okay, so here's what we'll do. We'll prepare you a healthy meal minus any common food allergens, since you don't know what might be bothering you, and we'll have that available for all of the catered meals on the set. And I'll bring over some breakfast food that should work too. Easy stuff."

He knew that it was a good idea, but he shook his head before she even finished. She frowned at him and opened her mouth to protest but he raised a shaky hand.

"This can't be made public, I keep telling you. There's no 'we'. You can't have your staff preparing anything different for me because then they'll know. And if the crew sees that you're feeding me rabbit food or something else so bland it defies description, they'll start asking questions. And that will lead to the media asking questions. Pretty soon the news of my imminent death will be on the cover of every tabloid at the supermarket checkout line."

Madeleine flopped back in her chair and crossed her arms, mutiny written all over her face. When she would have argued again, Mac raised a hand to stop her.

"I appreciate your concern, but this needs to stay a secret between you and me. I can't have this getting out."

She wasn't looking at him now, frowning slightly and staring at a spot on the carpet halfway between them.

"Okay, here's an alternative. I can make your meals myself. I'll send them over each day with one of the interns or with Alej. They don't have to know what's in the containers. They'll just delivery them and leave."

"How are you going to prepare them without them seeing you?"

Resignation crossed her face. "I can do the work in my own personal kitchen."

He paused, intrigued that she would offer to do this, glancing thoughtfully at the door across the room. "Anything wrong with the kitchen in this house?"

A frowned creased her brow again, and he noticed faint lines there that hadn't been there fifteen years ago. "No, but then I'd have to come over here."

"This is between you and me, remember. Alej or an intern might start to ask questions." He paused, wondering if this thing he had was making him certifiably crazy. It would be a tumultuous combination of heaven and hell to have her so close every day. And her lips had tasted better than any fine treat he'd eaten in years.

"Here's my counteroffer. I'd prefer it if you cook here, unless absolutely necessary. Become my personal chef, here in this house, for the duration of the movie filming."

"Mac, I can't take all that time away from my businesses – "

"I'll make it very worth your while," and he named a figure that had her eyes going so wide, white completely ringed the cornflower blue.

"Geez, that's a lot of cash for some produce and protein. Just how rich are you?"

He laughed, feeling the hollow sensation that the pain always left behind fading as he took in her amazed expression.

"Rich enough to be able to pay you to help me survive."

*****

Was she crazy? Exactly what had she agreed to? She could still get out of this, but she couldn't stand the thought of Mac in so much pain. It was only human compassion, she'd been assuring herself since she left his house last night. She would do the same for anyone.

Not exactly. His mouth had the same taste and texture, the same roughness that appealed to her in the past. Hadn't she learned anything?

"Ah, Roxy? Got a minute?" Alej poked his head into her office door as she stared unseeing at her computer screen.

She waved him in, ready for her role. "What's up? Please tell me there isn't more drama on the intern front."

Alej slouched into the guest chair and shook his head. "Nope. Angel is still chomping at the bit to get back to work – probably later this week according to the docs. Jeannine has stopped throwing up, so I guess that means she's in her second trimester. God, can you believe what her father and that guy did to her?"

Roxy shook her head. But it reminded her of something she needed to say.

"Alej, you need to be careful around Jeannine. She could get ideas, you know? Just make sure you aren't too, ah, personal with her, okay?"

He frowned and opened his mouth, then seemed to think the better of it and shut it again, glancing out the door into the kitchen area. She followed his gaze to see that it landed on the woman in question. Something softened in his expression, gone so quickly Roxy wasn't sure it had even been there. His game face back on, he swung around to her again with great seriousness.

She knew what was coming, since she'd primed the pump herself. But Alej had to lead up to it because in his mind, this was going to be something she fought.

"Anyway, Bob and Ticia are working out nicely, though I'd love to give Ticia a confidence vaccine. I have an idea." He leaned forward.

"And it is?" Roxy leaned back, preparing to be appropriately surprised and indignant.

"We have this little situation. Barry, the director's assistant, called, and the big boss requested that you prepare his meals at his house, in the kitchen there. Something about wanting to see your technique and learn from a pro." He actually cringed, expecting her to blow up.

She added intensity to her gaze and forced herself to look angry, leaning forward now as if she'd jump across the desk.

Alej continued quickly, "But that's not all. He wants breakfast and lunches too. Says he wants to try out the full range of your culinary talents, a personal chef for the duration of the filming." He raised a hand to stave off what he expected to be her protests. "And he's willing to pay top dollar for it." He named the figure.

She let her mouth fall open in feigned astonishment and allowed surprise to rule her features. Then she frowned in mock consternation.

Mac wasn't the only one who could act, she thought with grim satisfaction.

"I was thinking that this might be a good opportunity to let the interns step up, take on more responsibility. Ultimately it's your decision, of course, but here's how I think we can handle it…"

Alej outlined responsibilities, schedules and juggling that would occur to allow her the time required to fulfill this new contract. The money was great, enough to pay off the catering truck a whole hell of a lot faster than they had anticipated.

Of course, he didn't know the back-story and in his mind, he was doing the convincing.

"…so you see, we can make this work. And think of the prestige and the contacts for the restaurant and the catering line, being a personal chef to a man with his influence and connections. It's a win-win."

Roxy let herself nod in agreement, though in her mind, there was even greater satisfaction in knowing that the plan she and Mac had hatched to preserve his cover had worked.

She sighed deeply and frowned at her short fingernails. Not Hollywood in the least.

She argued out of principle, because Alej would expect it. He countered with all of the reasons and rationales she'd anticipated.

And then she allowed herself to agree.

"Great, that's great! I'll call Barry right now and let him know that you're on board. He wants you there tonight, by the way. The big boss I mean." He leaped from his chair and strode to the door. "I'll get the staff together so that you can tell them all about this." And he walked out.

On board, yes, but at what cost? The pull of attraction was still there, and if anything it was even stronger than before, buffeted by years of success and maturity that assured her she didn't need him to survive. But why was she putting herself in hours of daily contact with the man who had broken her young heart?

Chapter 19

"But why now? You've turned down people with the same request before. What makes this any different?"

Roxy stared around her kitchen, examined the pictures on her living room walls, traced the crumbs on the plate in front of her with her finger, and even tried to read the tealeaves in her cup. She looked everywhere but at Tess and Serena sitting across from her.

How could she explain something to them when she couldn't even explain it to herself?

"When I delivered plants to the set yesterday, some of the crew were talking about it. One man who's worked with the director before said it was highly unusual for Mac Smythe to hire a personal anything. Usually he uses the same services as the rest of the crew on a set." Tess paused and smirked. "Of course, he also said that the chefs are usually portly and male and not at all Mac's type, so maybe that was it."

Serena chuckled and Roxy felt herself blush. She rarely ever blushed. In fact, the last time she'd blushed with any regularity was fifteen years ago, and look where that had landed her.

"Come on, Rox, even you can't be immune to the man's charm and his good looks. Even though he's looking a little less than stunning right now," Serena added with a small frown. "I wonder why that is. Maybe he's sick. Has he shared anything with you?"

She willed her body not to twitch. Serena had come a little too close to hitting the nail on the head. Roxy needed to get the scrutiny off herself and Mac.

"Look, the money's terrific, okay? I mean, really terrific." She forced a huge smile to her face. "And in today's economy, that's nothing to sneeze at. We have payments on the catering truck, and if Cal Fire doesn't need us during the summer, once the movie's done, we're quiet for a while in that line of business. This way, I can get ahead on those payments and not have to stress about what the season brings."

She rose and picked up her mug, motioning to those in front of Serena and Tess. "You two done? I have to get to the store."

The women set their mugs on the counter and followed Roxy down the front stairs and out the restaurant's main entrance. It made for a very short commute when you lived above one of your businesses and next door to the other. It also made it very tough to escape them.

"I still don't get it. Are you telling us everything? I know! You've got a movie star crush going and you don't want to 'fess up." Serena clapped her hands, convinced she'd found the reason for Roxy's interest.

Crush didn't even begin to describe it, and Roxy remembered the sudden heat flaming through her body when Mac had her in his arms. She needed to travel around with a fire suppression unit right over her head when she was near him, and she wasn't sure the big one in the hood over the professional grill in her kitchen was even up to the job.

"No crush, and I mean it." She turned to give Serena a sharp glare, though it had no effect on her friend's mischievous expression.

"Ms. L.?" The freckle-faced checker tried to get her attention as the women entered the front door of Roxy's Gourmet Grocery.

"Yes Shawn?" Saved by her staff from going further on that conversational path, she waited to see what he needed with a whole lot more eagerness than the situation called for.

"That special olive oil you wanted came in today. It's in one of the big tanks. Thought you'd want to know right off."

She smiled her thanks and made a beeline for the area where the store stocked specialty olive oils and vinegars in bulk. Tess and Serena trailed behind, intent on a quiet conversation. When Roxy reached for an empty bottle from an adjoining shelf, they stopped whispering and stared at her knowingly. Damn.

Backpedaling for an idea to distract them, she dove for two more empty bottles. "Would you like to try some of this? It's something new that we're carrying."

Tess moved forward, temporarily letting her off the hook. "A new olive oil? Arbequina, a little Spanish influence. What're you making?" Tess accepted the filled bottle as she eyed Roxy carefully.

Before she could respond, Serena came up to join them, an olive speared on each of three toothpicks. "Maybe you need some olives to go with that. Variety, you know, to go with the bread and olive oil for that antipasto plate you'll be making for the big director, in his big kitchen, at his big house, just the two of you."

Serena and Tess giggled.

If they only knew the truth. There would be no bread and no antipasto plate. There would be lots of fresh vegetables and some fruits and pounds of lean protein. But that was between her and Mac.

And that was all that was between them. Really.

She tried for bravado. "Yeah, and I'll serve it right between all the courses of hot sex we'll be having. I'll make sure to write up the menu and all of the recipes for you." She gave her friends a lecherous wink.

The rewarding laughter bounced off the aisles of gourmet products in her store. Now if she could only fend off her feelings about Mac as easily.

*****

"I still don't know how you can be immune to him. I know you saw him when you worked on his movie years ago, when he was raging hot. Even if he's older, he's still a gorgeous man, and the causes he fights for only add to his allure." Serena shook her head as they walked back to the parking lot.

"We don't click, so there's nothing to imagine happening." Roxy couldn't seem to get Serena off the subject. It was a good thing Tess had already left, or they'd both be interrogating her.

Her friends didn't know about the dark side of her history with Mac. They didn't connect Mac with her own often-stated belief that a relationship wasn't in the cards for her. She'd never told the girl tribe the identity of the only man who had engaged her heart, only to smash it into crumbs.

"So who does make you click?" Serena put the last word in air quotes as she juggled her purchases from the store.

"Listen, I don't have time to click with anyone right now. I have the restaurant to run, four interns to train, the store to oversee, and now the catering business. I'm a busy woman!"

"You've found enough time to take on a personal chef client."

She felt her friend's intent stare but refused to be drawn into a direct connection.

"Just a man and his money, soon to be parted courtesy of my astonishingly excellent culinary talents." Her laugh sounded forced even to her own ears.

"You were gung-ho about the movie-catering contract until you learned who the director was going to be. You didn't want to visit the set and see the big man himself, according to Alejandro, even though you've seen him before, and you're more than willing to throw the newly minted interns on the line for this new business line. None of it makes any sense."

They'd reached their vehicles and Roxy beeped hers open and yanked the door in an attempt to stop the direction of their conversation. Serena lifted the trunk on hers and loaded in the bags, turning back to the other SUV. Fumbling the key in the ignition, Roxy thought that escape seemed like the best response.

"I'm not going to drop this, you know," Serena said, putting a hand on the door and getting in the way of Roxy's attempt to close it. "Something's going on, and eventually, when you're ready to talk about it, I want to hear what it is."

Chapter 20

"Here, let me feed you for a change," he said, taking his fork and cutting a tender slice of steak, adding a dab of truffle-oil mashed potatoes, and putting it to her lips.

She couldn't tear her eyes away from his.

As she chewed, he added, "You're always feeding me, cooking me these magnificent meals, and I have no way to repay you." He smiled slyly.

Remembering to continue to chew was hard, given the lump that suddenly rose in her throat at his innuendo.

She swallowed with difficulty, then replied, "Repay me? You are paying me. What do you mean?"

His eyes flashed. "Ah, but it's the special care you take of me, Madeleine. Please allow me to show my gratitude."

Setting the fork aside carefully, he floated forward and put his hands gently on her shoulders. His face tilted closer and his lips were just a breath away from hers.

"I wanted you then, want you still, and always," he murmured.

And then he kissed her. It was the softest kiss, as light and sweet as the finest marshmallow, spun sugar on her tongue.

His hands began to roam, and things accelerated too quickly for her to comprehend. How did they end up in her home, in her bedroom? They rolled around the big king bed until he was looming over her, buried deep inside, and they were both moving at a frantic pace.

"I will never leave you again, Madeleine," he promised, his chocolate brown eyes burning with dark emotions as he placed a searing kiss on her mouth. One hand at her nape pulled her closer still, and with the other, he locked fingers with hers in a grip tight enough to prove his declaration.

Her orgasm was just out of reach, the release a few precious seconds away, and she increased their pace. Something was pounding a primitive rhythm, something that kicked up their hearts and their sprint to completion.

Something was pounding, pounding out of kilter and ruining the moment, and she squeezed her eyes shut tight to ignore it.

The noise ceased abruptly. She felt oddly incomplete, and she tried to reach for Mac and find the combination of emotion and physicality that meant they were both going to explode any second.

But he wasn't there.

Roxy sat up and looked around her dark bedroom, panting and confused and undeniably aroused. A dream. She'd been having an incredibly erotic and kick-ass dream, and it was all about Mac.

Falling back to the mattress, she tried to control the pace of her pulse and the rage of disappointment that filled her heart. It had been Mac, tender and caring as he'd been back then, but the story line was all in the present. He was paying her, all right, and repaying her at the same time for the pain of love she thought they'd shared before.

Crap. She should never have agreed to this weird arrangement, and the secrecy was going to drive her crazy. According to his rules, there wasn't anyone she could talk with about this, except Mac himself.

That would be a recipe for trouble if ever there was one.

And his proximity was making her horny and sad. She'd like to work herself back up to a good buzz of anger, because that at least would protect her heart. But it was almost impossible, given the pain Mac was suffering. A part of her that she didn't want to examine too closely wanted to comfort him, and the only way she could do that was with food.

The pounding started again, only to stop almost immediately. Roxy frowned. The big bread mixer in the store next door had suffered a major breakdown, and they were forced to use the restaurant's smaller machine until the new replacement arrived in another week. It must be about three in the morning, the time when her baker came in to begin her work.

Groaning, Roxy pulled the covers over her head to count to twenty, and at fourteen, the pounding began yet again. It sounded like a jungle rhythm coming through the floor and up the back staircase. If the dream didn't have her world completely on edge right now, the mixer would have driven her insane anyway.

She may as well get up and start her own day. As the sheets slid down her body, the memory of the dream shifted through her mind. The scent of his skin and the taste of his mouth. Mac of the past juxtaposed with Mac of the present.

But there was no future here, none at all.

*****

Faint music played in the background, a gentle island song that brought to mind Hawaiian sunsets and tropical breezes, lazy days spent in the ocean waves or on the edge of their own private pool. The tiki drinks helped set the mood, and their fake thatched hut corner was dark with the tables around them deserted.

He studied her in the dim shifting light, her eyes sparkling with mischief and her hair hanging free in a curtain down her back. The sundress left little to his imagination, and that was just the way he wanted it. He didn't need any imagination to know what it was like to caress her curves or bury his face in the richness of her breasts. Luscious, that was the word for her.

Sure, there were a couple of lines in her face now, but that spoke of the character she had to have to succeed in her cutthroat culinary world. It hadn't destroyed her, and to prove it, she picked that moment to laugh, her voice richly trembling, and pushed closer to him.

"Maybe we can go to Hawaii for our vacation, once the movie is over." He whispered in her ear, loving the way she leaned against him, and he dropped a lingering kiss on the pulse below her earlobe. "Or a beach in Greece or Italy. You'd like it there, Madeleine."

"I'd love it anywhere, as long we're together, Mac." Without a glance around the restaurant, she straddled his lap, the skirt of her sundress lifting and settling around them.

Her tongue invaded his mouth as her hands roamed his chest and lowered to the belt of his slacks. Undoing the buckle, her fingers found the zipper and began to pull it down. She pushed back on his shoulders and he fell into the cushions behind them.

"I want you, right now," she all but purred, the huskiness of her voice reminding him of a tiger's low growl.

"Wait, let's go someplace a little more – private." He could barely spit out the words, but somehow, they had a magical effect. They were suddenly in a hammock swinging between two palm trees, and the night air was dark with secrets. Warm breezes brushed over bare skin, his and hers, as their clothes melted away.

"I want you, Mac." And she began to drop herself over his erection, sliding inch by delicious inch until he had to ball his fists at his sides to keep himself from hurrying her along. She rocked then, taking him deeper still, and he felt the rising need overwhelming him too quickly. Falling forward to kiss him, her hair curtained them both in a private sensual world.

"Madeleine, please, let's take this slower. I want time to pleasure you, to enjoy you." He knew he was begging, but he didn't care. All that mattered was staying locked together with this incredible woman for as long as they both could stand it.

"No Mac, this is the only way, and you'll feel better, I promise."

Shit-yeah, he thought.

She continued, "Sometimes, sacrifices have to be made." She rocked harder, and his mind was shorting out with the rising tension.

"I can't take much more of this, Madeleine. It's been a long time, too long." He reached out to grip her hips and slow her movements, but he couldn't seem to find her. His hands passed through air, even though he could see her.

"Mac. Mac?"

He frowned, because her lips weren't moving. Her voice didn't sound right either.

"Mac!"

He blinked his eyes and she was gone. Instead, he stared into the concerned gaze of Martha, standing in the doorway of his bedroom on the second floor of the rental house. He looked around in confusion.

Madeleine, or rather Roxy, wasn't there.

That was one hell of a dream, arousing and erotic and so real that he swore he could still feel her skin under his fingers. The hot touch of her, wrapped around him and glorious in her possession, was even on his now-throbbing erection.

Damn, it was a good thing he was laying on his side. Old Martha would be surprised to see the tent he could make of the covers this morning. In fact, he was shocked himself.

"Are you finally awake? I called you on the phone and you didn't answer, and then I knocked and knocked and you still didn't answer. I was worried, so I used the key you gave me. Are you all right?"

Her concern sounded genuine enough. She looked uncertainly around the room. "Am I interrupting something? I heard you talking when I came up the stairs, but I couldn't tell what you were saying. And you didn't respond when I knocked on this door either."

Yeah, she had interrupted something, an incredible dream where Madeleine wanted to do nothing but bring them both pleasure, and she had looked so powerful doing it that he almost drifted back to the erotic sensation of her on top of him, Martha or no Martha.

It was simply that, though, a dream. The reality was Roxy was going to feed him and hopefully help his health get a little bit better. Today was day one of their little experiment.

"I'm fine, Martha. Just running through some things out loud, that's all."

"Are you sure you're okay? You look, I don't know, weird."

Yeah, he felt weird. He couldn't shake the sensations of the dream, and it wasn't only the sex. That had been, metaphorically speaking, incredible. No, it was the wonder that was Madeleine, or rather, Roxy, coming into her own as a strong and powerful woman.

But she was never going to draw him into her again, making him feel so complete that no other sexual encounter he'd had in the past fifteen plus years had ever been quite right. Physically satisfying, yes, but never complete.

Mac sighed. "It's fine, Martha. Nothing's happening." Except the hard-on that didn't seem to want to disappear. "I'll be downstairs in a few minutes and we can get started on the correspondence for the day."

Her frown still in place, she clicked the door shut quietly behind her, and Mac stared sightlessly at the sunlight growing stronger behind the window blind. It hurt to want Roxy this much. She had done this to him without even touching him. Scratch that, without even being in the room.

He glanced down at himself in silent consideration. It had been a long time since he felt this ready for action, rock hard and throbbing even though the day intruded and the dream was now only on the fringes of his memory.

What would Roxy make of this, he wondered. Was this part of her cure?

Then he smiled. Maybe at some point he needed to tell her about it and find out.

Chapter 21

"CUT!"

He was cranky and irritable and itchy with nerves. She'd cut out his caffeine, and it pissed him off. And he was ready to take it out on anyone, reason or not.

"Justin, I told you, you need to move right and expect that the bad guy is going to come at you from the left. If we don't block this properly, you're in danger of serious injury." Mac put hands to his pounding head and wondered if it would explode any time soon.

At least that would release the pressure.

The actor getting his head chewed off looked affronted. "I know that, Mac. I know all of that. I want to get through this so we can do the real action sequence." He rubbed his hands together. "I love the idea of doing my own stunts!"

Mac couldn't be any less excited if he tried. The risk of a yahoo like Justin, big on ego and small on sense, hurting himself badly enough to delay the picture was very real. But Justin was determined to do his own action work, and he'd stipulated that as a condition of signing his contract.

"Okay everybody, from the top. Justin, be careful. Action!"

With an eye on the scene unfolding in front of the cameras, Mac massaged his temples and wondered how long he would last under Roxy's culinary care. She'd eliminated so many things from his diet that it was easier for him to remember the short list of what was left. Coffee, sugar, anything made with a flour of any kind, his favorite Scotch, dairy even, all gone.

"It's for your own good, Mac. Have a couple of weeks of easy, predictable food, and then once your system has settled down, we'll start adding things back in to see how you react."

He'd been skeptical. "Have you ever done this kind of thing before?"

She paused to smile at him with supreme confidence and returned to discarding things from the fridge. What she put back in was miniscule by comparison. He thought he detected perverse satisfaction in her actions.

And even as he grumped at her, he admired the line of her neck and the arch of her back as she moved, graceful as any dancer.

"Yes, as a matter of fact I have. I was personal chef to a family in Seattle for over a year. Every single one of them, parents and kids, had food allergies. Believe me, it was a challenge to figure out what to make for them since each set of needs was different."

This was crazy. Hell, he was crazy. To think that he could be in close orbit to a woman who after all these years still caused his heart rate to pick up and his groin to tighten, sick or not, was nuts. It was a disaster waiting to happen.

The first dream had turned into many, waking him time and time again each night. If he could convince her to have sex with him for real, maybe he could get her out of his system. As it was, there was no way he could be this near Roxy on a daily basis and not act on it, even if she'd walked out on him years ago.

A yell and the splinter of breaking wood flooded into his reverie with a wallop of sound. In the scene, Justin had again forgotten where he was supposed to be on the porch of the house. Now he was down on the ground, straddling a water trough. And he was screaming.

"My leg! Fuck, I think I broke my leg!"

Crewmembers were running to his aid. The nurse they hired to take care of the minor cuts and scrapes typical on a movie set was also hustling across the open yard with her medical bag in hand. Mac made an effort to launch after them, but he was weak and shaky.

"Step back, give us some room so we can see what's happened." The nurse's no nonsense tone moved people back even as Mac approached with the intention of ordering them away. She knelt next to Justin. "Let's take a look at this, okay?"

But Mac could already tell it was bad, since something that shouldn't have been showing protruded through the denim of Justin's jeans. Blood seeped around ivory, and the leg was at a weird angle to the rest of the actor's body.

"We're going to need an ambulance," said the nurse, searching through the faces until she found Mac. Turning, he stared at Martha and Barry behind him, Barry already on the phone.

"I'll get his wallet and essentials from his trailer. They'll want that at the hospital." Martha turned in the direction of the actors' dressing rooms while Barry relayed the circumstances and reported back, "The ambulance is six minutes out."

Tears coursed down Justin's face, with the nurse making a vain attempt to calm him through quiet words while she checked his vitals.

Great, just great. His leading man had done major damage to his leg, and they had three weeks of shooting left on the film. Right in the middle. No changing actors without re-filming a lot of what they'd already done. And no going forward for most of it without Justin.

He didn't think the pounding in his head could get any worse, but it did.

*****

Roxy opened the rear gate of the SUV and eyed the boxes inside. She was more than capable of hefting them up and inside the house, but she was debating once more if these gifts of atonement for messing with his menus were a good idea. There were consequences for everything.

She'd consulted with Marguerite, and the winemaker had immediately compiled three cases of selections from her winery and others to provide a sample of the tastes of Flynn's Crossing wines for Mac's pleasure. The reds the area was famous for along with a few whites could go a long way towards calming her client.

Maybe.

"He will appreciate all of these, I am sure. And you can build your menus around them, since you know them yourself so well. How is it working out, being the personal chef to the internationally known and incredibly handsome Mac Smythe?"

Roxy gave Marguerite a mixed and measured look. "It has its benefits, I guess you could say, along with a whole lot of challenges."

Like dealing with a grumpy client who complained about everything, and they were only three days into this. She came over and cooked, closing the door to the dining room to block her noise from Mac as he worked at his dining room table. She wished it could be as easy to block thoughts of him from her mind.

No one considered it strange that the director requested she become his personal chef for the duration of the movie. In fact, everyone in her circle of friends thought this was the coolest thing ever, even if they were more and more vocal about their suspicions of her motives.

"How can you be close to him day after day and not be attracted to him?" DK's lack of comprehension on this was evident even over the phone.

"Is it terribly romantic, playing house with such a gorgeous guy? I mean, you cook your incredible meals, he eats and praises you, and then you move to the living room and dot-dot-dot we all know what comes next!" Gabby's romance writer's mind was whirling into overtime on that one.

And Serena kept asking her more pointed questions, which wasn't a good sign. Perhaps this wasn't the best idea she'd ever had, and his counter proposal was the long step off the short pier of her emotional journey.

If her dreams were any indication, it was going to be a tough month ahead. They'd become even hotter, strangely erotic and more explosive, until she'd found herself tied up in sweaty sheets with an ache of unrequited lust this morning, frustrated and ready to cry. And she rarely ever cried, considering it something else that she gave up once she realized Mac wasn't going to return for her.

Except he was back now, not specifically for her, but with her and around her nonetheless. And she had to deal with it. Mac could never know.

Sweeping aside her concerns, she lifted the first case of wine into her arms. She propped it on the door handle and pulled out the key Barry had given her, expecting to juggle the case back up as soon as she had things unlocked. But to her surprise, the handle turned and the door swung open into the hallway.

Very strange, since she was here two hours early to get food preparation started.

"Hello? Is anyone home?" Maybe Mac had forgotten to lock the door when he left this morning, since he often seemed to be forgetful. Or maybe one of the assistants had come over for something.

Shifting the case of wine to her hip, she moved forward cautiously. There was no point in getting blindsided by over-anxious fans who'd somehow broken in to lie in wait for the great man himself.

"In here." A rough male voice grated from the living room, and turning into the kitchen to put the case on a counter, she moved through the house to follow the sound.

Mac was lying on the sofa, the drapes drawn shut and a towel on his forehead. His eyes were closed, but slits appeared and he stared at her across the room with resentment. Sighing deeply, he closed his eyes again and pulled the towel over them.

With thoughts of the dream pounding suddenly in her head, she allowed her traitorous ideas to rage for a moment as she took in the long, lean sight of him. He appeared more powerful in a horizontal position. She wondered how his butt would feel in her hands.

Fuel for another round of sex-starved nighttime wakefulness.

"Gee, you're home early. Rough day? Have you been sick?" She peppered him with questions, in part to hide her own agitation.

He didn't move, and his face remained hidden. "Yes, I am home early. I had Barry drop me off after we left the hospital."

She cringed. "Hospital? Is it that bad? Why are you back here and not in a hospital bed?"

He stopped her rant with a wave of his hand. "It was a rough day because Justin fell off the porch of the set doing his own goddamned stunt and he has a compound fracture of his leg that required goddamn surgery. He's getting put back together, and then the doctor will call me with whatever news he can provide. No matter what, Justin's not going to be working for a while. Shooting is delayed until we can figure out how to proceed."

He sighed so deeply, she was surprised there was air left in the room for her.

"Maybe I should change the title of this movie to 'jinxed'."

Maybe he wasn't trying to be funny, but his remark caught her unprepared. She laughed, from nerves or relief she wasn't sure. He raised the corner of the towel to look at her with one accusatory eye before he dropped it back into place and covered it with his hands. It looked like he was trying to suffocate himself.

The idea sobered her immediately. He wasn't trying to be funny in the least.

"How do you feel?" She moved a little closer and searched what she could see of his face for signs of the gray pallor and fatigue that she was so used to finding there.

Mac's hand went to the towel again, and he flung it across the room. "How do you think I feel? My fucking movie is delayed again for god knows how long. Meanwhile, the cash clock is ticking away. Tick, tock, tick, tock. Can you hear that? How the hell do you think I feel? I'm pissed!"

Sitting up, he propped his elbows on his knees as he dropped his head into his hands. It hung there, unmoving. After the outburst, the stillness was scary.

Roxy moved to stand next to him. Being this close, she could smell the soap he'd used that morning, the scent that had been appearing in her dreams all too often as well. But this wasn't about lust and it wasn't about desire. She had a job to do, and the sooner she remembered that, the better.

"I'm sorry you had a really crappy day. But how does your body feel?"

Chapter 22

Until she'd asked him, he hadn't thought about it. His day had been spent dwelling on the pounding in his head, which she'd assured him was just caffeine withdrawal that would pass quickly. And then the stress of Justin and the hospital.

But through it all, he'd forgotten about the gut pain that had been his constant companion.

He looked up at his Madeleine, standing tall and silent next to him, waiting for his response. A braid held her glossy wheat hair back, leaving her unadorned face open to his view. That face was unreadable and he wished he could tell what she was thinking. Back in time, she'd been an open book, and he'd taken great pleasure in surprising her with small gifts to see excitement chase across her features.

No more. That woman was lost under the brisk no-nonsense exterior of the business mogul she'd become. The face, though, was as beautiful as it had been years ago. In fact, even more so.

"My stomach is fine, no pain, so I guess your cure is working." He got up, impatient for some small relief from the concerns of the day. He flashed on his body's traitorous reaction to the dreams of her that kept invading his nights. That wasn't the relief he could seek out right now. "Where'd you put my Scotch?"

She frowned at him. "That's not on your approved list."

"I don't damn care if it's on the damned list or not. I told you to hide it from me. Now I'm telling you to unhide it."

Roxy flipped her braid in what was probably dismissal and walked out of sight around the corner. "You can't have it."

Impatience gave way to anger. "I don't care what I can or can't have in your opinion. Now where'd you put it?" He was yelling now, which he knew was ridiculous given the circumstances. He always prided himself on his control, but it failed him whenever this woman was around.

"I poured it down the drain."

Unbelievable!

"You did what?" The neighbors could probably hear the shouting, even though they were some distance away. "That was premium single malt that I have imported. How could you pour it down the fucking drain?"

Mac rounded the archway to the hall, intent on his revenge. He'd shake some sense into her, and then he'd borrow her car, head to the nearest liquor store, and replace it with whatever kind of swill they had.

Or more likely, he'd act on his memory of those erotic dreams and grab her in his arms and…

She came out of the door that guarded the kitchen with her hands full. A wine bottle, dark green with a swirly kind of logo, and a wineglass. Scratch that, two wineglasses.

"Here, try some of this instead."

He blinked at the bottle, trying to make his mind focus on what his eyes were seeing.

"Wine? Is that on my program? You think that's going to make me feel better?"

She waggled the bottle back and forth. "Yes, wine. And yes, I think you can safely have it, just not a lot of it. And the only thing that's going to make you feel better is to let go of the things you can't control. Which are most things, by the way."

She sashayed past him with her braid swinging, and never once looked behind her to see if he followed.

Wine wouldn't take the edge off, he was sure of it. And that edge just got sharper with the gentle sway of her hips as she passed him. It was a damned fine sight, her backside snug and tempting today in well-loved jeans as she walked down the hall.

Mac felt the unfamiliar bolt of desire, a sensation that had not been in evidence these past few months as the pain had become worse. It ran down his spine to his groin and his pulse picked up a jungle beat. All she had to do was walk by him, and he was ready to take a chance on seeing if they could spark the old familiar heat between them. If his dreams were any indication, his tinderbox was definitely ready.

The seductive pop of a cork leaving a bottle spurred him to follow her. As he turned under the arch to the living room, she was standing at a side table by the now open bottle, twisting the cork off an opener with practiced ease. She waved him to the sofa and picked up the bottle.

"This is a very fine Petite Syrah Reserve from one of our local wineries, Witch Hill. My friend Marguerite is the winemaker there. You should take a ride out to experience it – the building is fantastic and a picnic on their terrace would go a long way towards reducing your stress."

She poured a small taste, swirled, sniffed, and sampled, and smiled with an affirmative shake of her head. "Yup, always terrific. This is their first vintage of this grape varietal. Four years ago, they harvested it from the vines they tended back to production, though surprisingly, there wasn't much tending that had to happen. Something about the ghost of the witch tending the vines, according to the legend, Marguerite said. It will be fun to see how this ages."

After pouring wine in the other glass, she handed it to Mac. Her fingers brushed his for a second, and he felt a tingle shoot through him. She felt it too, if her face was any indication. Shock made her eyes widen before she turned her back to block his view. The braid continued to sway when she stopped. It was beckoning him, even when the set of her shoulders told him differently.

"So you thought to bring some wine tonight? Is this to go with dinner?" He sniffed and immediately loved the velvety aroma that reminded him of blended berries. The first sip made him realize that this was a unique and special wine. Yes, he needed to visit this winery.

Madeleine had the empty tasting glass in her hand, and she walked across the room and away from him, heading for the nether regions of the kitchen. After everything that had happened today, she was leaving him alone.

"Stay here for a while. Talk with me. Have some wine." He thought to try a persuasive smile, but that might chase her away. He didn't think seduction would work.

She hesitated, and he could see indecision race across her face before she carefully schooled her features into neutrality. She considered him, and gave one quick shake of her head to agree. Returning to the side table, she filled her glass.

She dropped into a chair on the wall opposite from the sofa. She couldn't get any further from him and still be in the same room. That was okay with him, for now. The way he was reacting recently, he was better off keeping distance between them.

"Actually, I consulted with Marguerite about selecting wines from the area for you to try, and she got a few of the other wineries to chip in samples too." She paused and took a short sip. "There are three cases, which reminds me that I left the SUV open and two cases still in the back."

When she stood, Mac did too, setting his glass aside and getting ready to follow.

"No, sit. I can handle them by myself." She waved him back to the sofa.

"I'm sure you can, but I can help too, and then it's only one trip." He wasn't sure why her cavalier attitude about his assistance aggravated him, but it did.

"You don't have to, Mac. Besides, I think I'm stronger than you are these days."

He was sure that the gentleness of her tone was intended to defuse her words, but it only gave it a sharper edge to his ears. He brushed by her and stomped to the SUV, determined to lift not only one but both of the cases and carry them into the house himself, and in one goddamned trip.

Of course, the minute he hefted the first one into his arms, he knew he'd made a mistake. It was heavy and its size and shape were unruly. Things shifted around inside the box and he felt himself boggling it even as Madeleine's arms joined his around the case.

"What do you think you're doing? I told you I'd take care of it. You are the most stubborn man I know. You don't have to prove anything to me." Her hard tone contrasted sharply with her eyes, soft with understanding as he grimaced in relief with the sudden lessening of weight her help provided. "You and I are way past that by now, don't you think?"

*****

He was being stubborn and obstinate and determined to prove that he was, in fact, just fine. She could understand his need to prove to himself that things weren't that bad. But if he was trying to impress her, this wasn't the way to do it.

She shifted the case of wine to her arms and Mac dropped his hands to his sides. He still looked angry, but the undercurrent of pain and exhaustion was there too. She could have some sympathy for him, but only a little.

"Just go back in, sit down and sip your wine, and let me put these bottles away. Then I can work on dinner."

He stayed at the SUV's side when she moved into the house, setting this case next to the other on the kitchen countertop before returning for the last box. When she grabbed that one, he closed the SUV's hatch with more of a slam than was necessary, and trailed after her into the kitchen.

Mac began poking around in the cases, pulling out each bottle and examining the labels. "These are all from around here?"

Roxy smiled. "This is just a sample. We have over sixty wineries in our county alone, and then when you count the neighboring counties as well, we rival Sonoma and Napa these days. And the wines are excellent."

He smiled at her over a bottle. "Remember when we used to drink jug wine, the pink kind, and thought that we were very sophisticated?"

His sudden sentimentality surprised her. In all of her years since as she'd learned about wines and discovered that expanded world, she'd looked back on those days with blanching embarrassment. Her tastes were so limited then. It was funny that he would consider it fondly.

"We did a lot of things back then that didn't make a lot of sense, because we were young or... whatever." Like fall in love, she thought suddenly, glad she zipped her lips in time.

He turned to stare at her, seeming to arrive at a decision. "But they were good times, weren't they?" His voice was quiet and she thought she detected a note of pleading in it.

It had been good, great in fact. It was everything that a young woman would want, the attentions of a hot man who was building a skyrocketing career, the beginnings of her own meteoric rise. She supposed she should be grateful he kicked her to the curb, because she had then been forced to work without a safety net.

"Some of them, yeah, they were good times."

Roxy didn't want to add that they'd been good together in so many ways, the nights they'd talked and laughed and made love until dawn, the care he'd taken to make her happy, the feel of him against her. Those parts came to her in a flash. But she couldn't think about that now, because then she'd let go of the anger and be right back where she was when she had to rebuild her life all those years ago.

In love again, if she'd ever fallen out of it in the first place. The idea made her shiver in the warm kitchen. She was a different woman now, a success in so many ways, and she didn't need him to complete her or satisfy her or make her happy.

Or did she?

He continued to stare at her, a mask hiding his expressions. When she thought she might start to fidget under that gaze, he spun around and walked out of the room abruptly.

Just as well. Now she could get on with the making of dinner, and once it was in front of him, she could return to her own world, her kitchens and the empire she'd created. And in its silence and peace, she could think about how much he still affected her.

"Here's your wine." Mac put the glass on the counter next to her. She hadn't even heard him come up to stand beside her. He waited next to her, his glass raised for a toast. She looked at him uncertainly, finally wrapping her fingers around the stemware.

"Here's to good times past and better times present. I'm glad that you've made a success of your life." His gaze was serious with an undercurrent of something she thought might be regret. He added, "I always knew you would, Madeleine."

That surprised her. The soft clink of glass was the only sound in the room. His sad eyes didn't leave hers. Roxy felt the need to make that emotion disappear and leave a laughing and happy Mac in its wake.

Where did the sudden urge to wipe away his gloom come from? She didn't want to give in to it, so she snapped at him instead.

"Stop calling me Madeleine!"

Chapter 23

"How many of these I gotta do, Chef?" Angel methodically pulled the shells off the large prawns and deveined them. It was taking him a minute to do about three, Roxy calculated. At that rate, he'd be busy all morning and into the afternoon.

"All of them."

Angel looked up in horror. "All of them? Really Chef? Can't we, ya know, skip some and give them something else?"

Roxy hid a smile. Angel had been so excited about the menus he'd designed while his hand healed, and when she had gently tried to focus him on how much work some of the preparations would require, he'd waved off the concerns and said that he'd handle it, no problem.

Well, now he had to handle it. And he'd get a better sense about how important is was to listen to the boss when the boss tried to guide him. Or so she hoped.

"I thought we bought 'em without the shells and deveined and stuff." He eyed the big pile of shrimp left to go and picked up his pace a little bit.

"No, we buy everything that we can fresh, and while I would prefer to buy locally, there is no outlet for shrimp around here." She came to stand next to the briny mass and picked up one he'd just finished. "Besides, there is no substitute for wild shrimp fresh out of the Gulf. This baby right here was swimming around only a few hours ago."

She bit into the shrimp, raw, and enjoyed the sudden pallor on Angel's face. He put his head down and moved even faster now.

Smiling in satisfaction as she turned away, Roxy chewed thoughtfully and considered swiping a few of those shrimp for Mac. He'd always loved shrimp cocktails, and these specimens were particularly tasty. He'd love to find that she was making one of his favorites.

Pleasing him was the last thing on her mind, she assured herself. She was just doing her job as his personal chef. If he liked the food, he'd eat more of it, and he'd feel better that much faster.

And then he wouldn't need her around anymore.

The idea suddenly didn't bring her any pleasure. Last night had been a wonderful hiatus, but she couldn't delude herself and be foolish enough to believe it would continue.

Mac had ignored her outburst and perched on a stool at the bar facing the workspace as she pulled together the simple dish. Vegetables, including onions, peppers, zucchini and summer squash, tomatoes and more, were each cooked slightly differently. Once they cooled, she chopped them and tossed then with cooked green lentils and a selection of fresh herbs. What made it special was the dressing, a combination of pineapple balsamic vinegar and the Arbequina olive oil she'd picked up at the store, Hawaiian red salt and fresh cracked pepper, and dried herbs.

He was curious about the lentils, about the sources for her produce, and about the small amount of grass-fed beef she was allowing him to have, the serving size so miniscule in his eyes that he called it a side dish. She'd lectured him on the over-portioning that was happening on so many restaurant menus until she noticed he was actually teasing her. Double entendres about sizes and portions kept them laughing after that.

Sipping wine and chatting about their respective days had seemed so easy, so much like old times. There was even an undercurrent of sexual energy that Roxy was sure came off her in waves. Mac couldn't possibly be having any such feelings, she was positive.

Mac had noticed her sudden silence and asked what was wrong.

"Nothing, really nothing at all. Just thinking about things I need to do at the restaurant tomorrow." Liar, liar, her heart chided.

"Yeah, I know what you mean. It's hard to stay in the moment when things are this crazy." He sipped his wine. "I'm not sure what's going to happen with the movie now. My numbers guy is heading back from vacation tomorrow, in wonderful ignorance about what happened today. Won't he be pleased to hear that we're in the middle of this production, right in the damn middle, and the leading man who was in so many scenes to date and so many more to come is unable to work?" Shaking his head, he leaned over and stole a handful of chopped vegetables.

"Hey, quit messing with my *mise!*" She waved her knife at him and he grinned, unafraid.

"Your what?"

"My *mise* – you know, *mise en place*, the area where a chef sets up food that's been prepared for – "

"– for a dish, I know. I'm not an empty-headed movie star, you know, all looks and no brains." He grinned wider, and she felt herself responding.

"Yeah, sure. You have standards," she put the word in air quotes, "and values, and honor."

She stilled at her last word, suddenly remembering a cold morning walking down a long San Francisco hill, dragging her suitcase as her tears rivaled the rain.

Damn him.

"I have at least one idiot around who fits that bill, though, and I should probably call the hospital and find out how he's doing." Mac got off the stool and rounded the island where Roxy stood, rooted to the spot with her knife clutched in her hand. He swiped another handful of veggies and gave her a quick kiss above her ear, then headed whistling out the door.

Whistling, suddenly so carefree and unconcerned that he was again turning her world upside down. Why couldn't he be raging at his actor or bashing his head against his laptop or yelling into the phone, doing something useful and leaving her alone? She had wanted him to relax. She didn't want reminders of the simple fun they used to have together.

The spot where he'd dropped that brief peck of a kiss still tingled.

"Delivery!" Roxy popped back to the present, realizing that she was staring at the half eaten shrimp in her hand. So much for getting a lot done today while she had the chance. Memories and daydreams, not to mention the hot nighttime visitations they created, were distracting her. She groaned and turned to the back door of the kitchen.

A huge array of roses, their neon yellow color bringing a burst of sunshine into the already bright room, filled the back door. Behind the bouquet, Tess was barely visible as she hefted the large vase on to the counter in front of Roxy.

"Aw, Tess, you really shouldn't have." Roxy looked at the flowers and then at her friend, now laughing in delight.

"I couldn't leave this one for Ralph to bring around. I had to see your face for myself when you open the card." If she clapped her hands and jumped up and down now, Roxy wouldn't have been surprised. Tess was beside herself with unhidden glee.

Staring at the display, her eyes pulled magnetically to the small white envelope nestled in the front. She didn't want to open it, afraid of what it might say. Moreover, she was afraid of what she might do when she read it, like break down and cry or dance around the kitchen where everyone could see her.

"Well? Aren't you in the least bit curious?" Tess was eyeing her strangely.

Roxy grabbed the card and her friend's arm and pulled her into the small office, hip checking the door shut behind them. She dropped into her chair, a hand bracing her now-pounding heart. She stared at the envelope in her hand.

"Come on, open it! I promise it's fine, he told me what he planned to write." Tess clapped a hand over her mouth.

Frowning, Roxy looked up. "He told you? God, how crass is that! A man buys flowers and then tells the florist what he plans to write in the card. So I know now that it's not in the least bit romantic." She sniffed, suddenly wondering why tears were threatening.

Looking anywhere but at the card meant her eyes locked on either Tess, who was still aghast, or out the window of the office to the counter where the explosive bouquet stood. It was now starting to draw attention from everyone else in the kitchen, and Alej went so far as to circle it twice as if he was looking for the card himself.

"Hell, they're yellow roses. The color means something, doesn't it? Isn't it something like hasta luego, goodbye babe, it's been real?" She shut her eyes at the prospect. Maybe he was pulling out of town now that the movie was jinxed.

Tess finally gulped in air and replied, "No, yellow doesn't mean that at all. Yellow roses mean joy, and promise of a new beginning, and remembrance." She stopped, and her eyes went wide. "Do you two have a thing going on? You brat, you've been holding out on us! Open the card!"

Roxy wasn't sure she'd ever seen Tess this excited. That's what being around big name celebrities did to people. It made them stupid.

"I thought you know what's in the card, that he told you what he was going to write." Roxy couldn't help teasing her.

"Well, he said he wanted to express his thanks for everything you're doing for him, and for remembering. What does that mean, exactly? Never mind, I can see you won't be telling me." Tess stared pointedly at the white card stock in Roxy's hand.

It sounded like he was saying goodbye again, though at least this time he was actually going to say it, not just pull a disappearing act in the dim light of dawn.

She hated the fact that her fingers trembled a little when she pulled the envelope open and extracted the small piece of paper.

'I hope that these remind you of something from long ago. Tonight, eight pm, my place. Dress up. And don't bring dinner.' The cursive M sprawled boldly across the bottom right corner.

*****

"How come you never told us this before?" DK passed the ice cream tub around to Serena, who took another scoop and passed it on to Tess. Gabby had sons-watching duty but promised to come over as soon as Rick got home. Marguerite was not picking up her cell. The girl tribe was circling the wagons around one of their own.

Roxy ran her spoon around the edge of the bowl, admiring the designs that the melting mix of pralines and cream were making in the mess she left behind. The mess she left behind, she thought, in more ways than one.

When Roxy's sudden weeping in her office became obvious, Tess jumped into girl tribe action. She'd summoned Alej to the office door and commanded him to take the staff and interns into the garden or the front of the restaurant immediately.

"But what's going on? Why is Roxy crying? Rox, you never cry. What's wrong?"

His alarm made him dive towards the desk, but Tess twisted him with surprising force and shoved him out again. "Now, Alejandro!"

As he shepherded everyone out, Tess kept the view in through the small window blocked with her body, and once the coast was clear, she grabbed Roxy's arm and pulled her out of the office, through the kitchen, and up the narrow back stairs. Once there, she'd slammed the door shut, turned the lock, and pulled out her cell to call the others.

"Wait, I can't just leave them like that. What will they think? I have to go back to work." She'd wailed and risen from the sofa where Tess dumped her.

"No, you are in no shape to do any such thing. Who knew that a few yellow roses were going to cause such an outbreak? Never in all my years, Roxy..." and she'd continued in that vein off and on until DK arrived, shooting up the front stairs and stopping just short of bowling into Roxy.

"I can't believe you're crying. You never cry! Well, you did shed a few tears at that big heart-render of a movie last year, but anyway..." She stopped and looked at Tess. "What happened?"

Roxy waved her arms at them as Tess prepared to launch into an explanation. "Wait, just wait, okay? I only want to tell this once, and I want to be the one to tell it. Who else is coming?"

Once Serena arrived, and once DK had made a raid on the freezer downstairs for comfort supplies, the three other women arrayed themselves around Roxy and waited. Since they all sat pencil straight and staring, Roxy knew that there was no way she was going to be able to dumb down the story and hope to get away with it. It was, it appeared, time to come clean.

"You never told us you had a love affair with Mac Smythe. I can't believe it. Someone that hot in your background and you didn't share? Shame on you!" Tess was trying to tease her into a better mood.

Serena on the other hand simply eyed her questioningly, seeming to know that they still hadn't heard the entire story. "It wasn't a love story at the end though, was it Rox?" Her question was gentle.

Sniffing again suddenly, Roxy put down the bowl and reached for the Kleenex box, grabbing a handful of tissues. "It probably never was a love story, at least to Mac. To me, yeah, it was." She sniffed again and blew her nose loudly. There were plenty of reasons why she didn't like to cry.

She looked around at her friends and sighed. "He was more like a comet streaking through my world. For him, it was brief and fleeting and probably meant very little. For me, it was," she faltered, "everything." A sob hiccupped out and she sniffed again.

"How did it end?" Serena's probes were gentle and the room was quiet, even the ice cream forgotten in the drama of the tale.

"We were getting ready to wander around the Mediterranean. Mac was done filming and he didn't have any commitments for a couple of months. The catering company didn't need me anymore since the movie gig wrapped up. I didn't have a new job lined up. We were going to go away, visit someplace that felt foreign and different, someplace where we didn't need to hide the fact that we were together."

DK reached over to squeeze her knee. "It's hard to hide something like that, isn't it, when his star was starting to rise already? And with you working for the catering company, well, your boss there wouldn't have liked it either if he found out."

Roxy gave a watery smile and nodded. Taking a deep breath to steady herself, she continued with the story.

"Mac got a page one morning, the day we were leaving. It was raining, not an unusual occurrence for San Francisco in the winter. He left me in bed in the hotel room and went out into the sitting area. The door was closed. The rain beat against the window. We hadn't gotten much sleep the night before. I dozed off again."

She stopped then, thinking back. Had he seemed more urgent that night, more demanding and more careful at the same time? It seemed, in memory, that there was a poignancy to his loving that night. Had he already decided to leave?

Of course he did. Otherwise, he wouldn't have had his go-fer ready to do his dirty work in the morning.

Sucking air in once more, she resumed the story. "This old woman came in, telling me to get out of bed and get out of the suite. I'd seen her around the sets a few times, and I assumed she was one of his go-fers. She told me in no uncertain terms then that she was sent, as she put it, to 'clean up his mistakes'. Those were her exact words." The memory made Roxy shiver.

"But why did you assume that Mac told her to do it?" Tess leaned forward in puzzlement.

Roxy sighed again. Yes, she probably would have waited for Mac, if it seemed that Mac was ever coming back.

"Yes, why didn't you wait until Mac came back in the room and have it out with him?" Serena's expression was puzzled.

Roxy shook her head. "No, I knew she was right. He wasn't coming back." She closed her eyes and again saw the room, heard the rain, felt the distain coming off the older woman. Keeping them closed, she finished, "Mac and I had laid our clothes out, what we were going to wear to travel, the night before. We were all packed, and our suitcases were standing side-by-side, ready to leave. We couldn't wait, or at least, I couldn't wait to start our new adventure together."

Roxy opened her eyes to stare sightlessly at the bookcases crammed with cookbooks on the far wall. These represented her accumulated riches over the intervening years. Inanimate objects. How sad.

Blinking to keep from starting the waterworks one more time, she looked at the concern on her friends' faces. To a woman, they felt her pain and were ready to support her, whatever that required.

Okay, so she had more than a bunch of cookbooks to show for the interim.

"He'd dressed in those clothes when he went to return the call from the page. His suitcase was next to mine when he left. And when I woke up, when that woman was yelling at me, it was gone. He left, just like she said. It nearly killed me."

The room was quiet and in the silence, Roxy could hear bustle and activity renewing in the kitchen downstairs. Alej would have things well in hand. She could relax, just this once, and let it all out.

"And now?" DK leaned forward, her eyes sympathetic. "How are you feeling about him now?"

Roxy held up a hand to stop the question, unwilling to answer that one since she hadn't admitted it to herself yet. If she said it out loud, there would be no avoiding it. The pain would slice her open once more.

"And the roses? Did he give you yellow roses before too?" Tess looked sorry that she'd ever brought the arrangement over.

Shaking her head sadly, Roxy gave a small smile. "Yes, he did. Had them delivered to the catering company kitchen the last day of shooting." She paused and felt new tears start. "Right before he left."

Chapter 24

He didn't know what the next few days would bring. He was scheduled to go fishing with Vince and Dane and their friend Rick tomorrow, leaving around six for a day on the water. Their picnic was courtesy of Roxy, who'd insisted on preparing it when he told her about the adventure three days ago.

The lunch was sitting in his fridge, next to the dinner he'd had flown in from Madeleine's favorite restaurant in San Francisco, Paush's. At least, it had been her favorite back then, and the guy was still an icon in the industry. He hadn't heard anything bad about the place, but come to think of it, he hadn't heard anything at all about it in quite some time.

It was too late to ponder the significance of this. She would be here in ten minutes. She was always on time. That was one of the predicable things about his Madeleine.

When had he started thinking of her as his again? This was dangerous, very dangerous. After all, she'd been polite and gracious when she called to thank him for the flowers, agreeing that she would be there tonight for dinner as he asked.

Hell, he hadn't asked, he'd demanded, and he knew how it sounded. But maybe she remembered that he'd given her yellow roses before, right before she left him as a matter of fact. Maybe she regretted that, and it produced that quiet tone in her voice.

Please remember me, remember us when things were good. His sip of wine did nothing to ease his nerves.

His dreams had become more realistic, more graphic, maddening to the point where it was hard for him to put his head on a pillow without both excitement and fear. He needed to act on them, to see if she was still the one woman in his life who could inspire him and sooth him and make him crazy with desire, all at once.

If it was real? Maybe, just maybe, he could convince her that they did belong together. And maybe she wouldn't run away this time.

And if it was all in his mind, maybe he could get her out of his system.

Yeah, right.

He wanted to think clearly. He needed to know in his heart of hearts that the reason he wanted to be around her all of the time was because they could have something together now. Not in the past, but now and into the future, and not because she seemed to be healing him.

That was the most amazing thing of all, he had come to realize. Aggravating or not, her distinctly limited diet and the Scotch sent down the drain seemed to be having a perversely good impact on him. The pain in his gut had disappeared, and he felt more energetic than he had in quite a while.

What was the old saying? You didn't know how bad it hurt until it stopped.

And if his dream-induced morning condition was any indication, he was feeling a whole lot heartier too. In fact, he was hoping that if he suddenly grabbed her in his arms tonight and dragged her up the stairs to his bedroom, she wouldn't decline the invitation. He wanted to prove to her that they could be together again, in all of the ways they used to be. And more.

Yes, it was going to be a terrific evening, he was sure of it. He would have Madeleine eating out of his hand and he could tell her how he felt. She'd agree that yes, she'd been feeling pulled back to him as well and the lights would fade to pinpoint on them locked around each other, cue the musical crescendo.

Frowning, he looked at his watch. It was a quarter after eight. Roxy was never late.

*****

It had taken a second tub of ice cream, a second bottle of wine, and a whole lot of discussion before Roxy was convinced that seeing Mac tonight was a good idea. Gabby arrived in time for round two and had helpfully added her opinion to the mix.

"You can't not go, Rox. What if this is your big chance to rekindle what the two of you had before, only better this time?"

Serena wore a different expression, a peculiar mix of concern and elation. "What if, and I'm just throwing this out there, what if you went to dinner, but told him how you really felt about everything that happened back then? I mean, talk it out with him and explain everything like you've done with us today. It could go either way, but it would be healing."

Roxy had been shaking her head before the last sentence was even completed. "How can I lay it all out there for him? What if this is just a goodbye dinner? He gave me yellow roses before, and then he left. I don't trust that whatever happens tonight, whatever he says, he won't be gone tomorrow before I can blink and turn around."

She set her melted mess of ice cream aside in favor of wine. Her friends continued to talk about the pros and cons, passing around the bottle when glasses got low. At some point, Alej sent Jeannine up the stairs from the kitchen to ask if they wanted dinner, or maybe a round of salads.

"Who needs salads when we have ice cream and wine?" DK asked, and Jeannine gave them a rare smile before disappearing down the back stairs again.

Roxy watched her leave thoughtfully. Her father dumps her, and this guy who supposedly cared about her and was the father of her child dumps her too. Men are scum. She would do well to remember that lesson herself.

She sat up straighter and set her shoulders back, smoothing her hair and gathering it up into a neat semi-bun. "I've decided what I'm going to do," she announced, and stood up to face them all from the center of the room.

"I'm going to go to dinner, and I'm going to listen to what he has to say. And then I'm going to tell him what I have to say. And that will be that." She wiped her hands of everything to match the figure of speech.

Her friends looked at each other and then back at her. "Ah, Roxy? What is it exactly you're going to say to him? I mean, do you have a script or something?" Serena frowned intently.

"A script? No, I'll just tell him the truth. That the past was the past and we've both moved on. We're different people now. We don't have anything for each other anymore, no attraction, and no spark. This is just business."

A script for a movie star, yeah, that had been funny in the moment, Roxy mused. But as she carefully smoothed her hair, hanging free now, and stood at his door nervously twitching the unusually dressy outfit, she considered again her friends' reactions.

"If he's trying to make things work between you, how will he take that?" Gabby's face had scrunched into worry.

"Are you sure you're not burning bridges, bridges you might want to cross later?" Tess was gathering bowls and stacking them in the dishwasher. She always needed to move around when she was disconcerted about something.

"This could backfire, you know. You could end up the bad guy in all of this." DK bit her lip after trying the rational approach.

"Roxy, honey, not all men are scum," Serena said reasonably. "I mean, look at the three wonderful men we've found already."

She had to concede that point. Dane and Rick were unique, though, the salt of the earth and trustworthy kind of men who you just knew were always going to do the right and honorable thing. Vince was close behind, though he still didn't have her completely convinced.

Mac, not so much.

So why was her heart running a race and her stomach doing back flips as she raised her hand to the door?

Chapter 25

He was getting ready to call her, to make sure she was still coming. Twenty-five minutes late was so unlike her, and she would have called him if she was that delayed, wouldn't she? He started to worry that maybe something happened between her place and town.

He'd seen enough of these roads to know how easy it would be to swerve off in a moment of lost concentration, ending up down a slope and out of sight of any passing vehicles. Or even just a sneeze would be enough to distract you, a twist of the wheel taking a car into the rushing rivers. And the wildlife – a deer running across the road…

His heart beat at a painful pace, the stress of not knowing what had happened making the hand holding his second glass of wine shake. He could call the restaurant and ask to speak with Alej. Or maybe he should call Vince or Dane to see if anyone else had heard from her. Someone must know why she wasn't here yet. He was probably overreacting, but it didn't hurt to be cautious at a time like this. He'd give her four more minutes.

Discarding the wine glass, his hand fisted around his cell phone. What if something bad had happened? He hadn't told her how he felt about her, how having her back in his life was lighting up places that he hadn't even known were dark. This wasn't old news from fifteen years ago. He could forgive her past abandonment. This was today, now, the present. And he wanted her all over again.

A knock on the door stopped him midstride in his nervous pacing of the hallway. Mac couldn't will his legs to cover the distance in anything that approached the speed he wanted. When he threw it open, his relief in seeing her on the stoop was so intense that it was like a physical blow. Following close on relief was a need to feel her in his arms that was more powerful than the force of a hurricane.

"Madeleine!" He bit out her name even as he grabbed her arms and pulled her forward, exhaling the breath he didn't know he'd been holding when his overactive imagination assumed the worst. Her purse dropped to the floor with a thud. The shock on her face at his greeting took only a moment to register. He would explain later. Now, he needed to feel her lips under his to know that he wasn't too late.

Turning her into the hallway, he kicked the door shut and backed her up until he pressed her into the wall. Her arms were trapped between them when he gathered her as close as he could and angled his lips. When she opened her mouth to say something, he dove in and tangled his tongue with hers.

God, how great it was to taste her again. In a hazy recess of his mind, he recognized that this was probably the wrong approach if he wanted to woo her back gently. But he was too damned glad she was here, not rolled over in a ditch someplace as he'd pictured. She was here and in his arms and that was all that mattered.

Slowly, he felt her resistance lessen. Her mouth was now moving under his, her tongue dancing in his mouth and tracing the outline of his lips. Tangling a hand in her hair seemed the right thing to do. Turning them so that he was now leaning against the wall and sliding the other down her back to pull her closer was the next logical step.

Her hands fluttered between them and Mac felt a moment of panic. She wanted to step away, wanted to put distance between them. He had to explain it to her.

Allowing her only enough space to free her arms, he started to tell her, "Madeleine, I was so worried about you. You see, you were –"

But he didn't get any further. As soon as her hands were free, she buried them in his hair scalp deep and pulled his face down again, pressing her body against his.

*****

Her innate good sense, the inner voice that kept her successful life on track, was repeating that this was a very bad idea. No good would come from passionate kisses wrapped around each other only a few feet inside his front door. She had things she'd planned to say, explanations to be made and demanded. Boundaries to be set.

To hell with good sense, her bad judgment snarled.

He tasted so damn good, better than she remembered, even from that brief kiss in what she'd come to think of as modern times. Better than he had fifteen years ago too. Maybe this, like fine wine, got better with age. That was a philosophical contemplation for some other time, a time when she could actually think.

Roxy angled to run her lips over his features, and he mumbled unintelligible things as his fingers combed through her hair. She didn't want to consider the consequences of what they were doing. The intervening years slipped away, and they were young and crazy and couldn't keep their hands off each other. For once, she didn't want to think at all.

Mac ground into her, his erection a shock pushing into her belly, and Roxy's breath picked up to another level of boiling that had her pressing back and writhing against him. His mouth when she reclaimed it tasted better than the finest treats that money could buy, rich and sinful and something she couldn't stop indulging in.

"I've missed you." His voice was rough and his words stilted as he ran his hands down her back to cup her buttocks and pull her closer, grinding against her through the clothing between them. His fingers trembled as he found the zipper on side of her dress and slowly lowered it down.

It was now time to make a decision, she thought hazily. Good sense reminded her that after fifteen years ago, this was not going to solve anything. They hadn't talked enough back then, and who knows if they'd even been on parallel paths.

Bad judgment said screw the consequences and concentrate on the taste of him, and on the fire building inside her that only he could satisfy.

"Come upstairs," he whispered hoarsely, his breath ragged in her ear. He held himself in place, shaking and waiting. Pulse racing, she shook her head to disagree.

"Here, now."

His surprise was evident as he pulled back and looked into her face. Uncertainty seemed to grip him.

Roxy was amazed that her hands didn't tremble as they moved to the buttons on his shirt. She concentrated on opening each one in turn, not looking into his eyes as she parted the fabric and set her hands on the hot skin below.

Mac lifted her chin and forced her to meet his gaze. His uncertainty had given way to concern and a more powerful emotion she didn't want to read. If he was going to disappear again, she wanted this and only this. Maybe her friends were right, and this would get him out of her system once and for all.

Good sense said that it didn't feel like this was going to get her anything but more hooked on him, but she wasn't listening anymore.

It was as if that skin to skin contact flipped a switch in him, because his hands suddenly became demanding, pulling her up higher against him so that he could rock in the vee of her legs. Instinct had her hooking a calf around his legs, gripping his shoulders tightly before wrapping his head in her arms and finding his mouth.

She heard a groan, then realized that she had made the pleading sound. Mac must have heard her too, because he moved away from the support of the wall and put a hard arm around her waist, trying to hold them as close together as possible as he made his way down the long hallway to the living room.

Walking her backwards, Mac stopped and unfused their mouths long enough to pull his shirt free of his slacks. She felt the sofa behind her knees. Roxy's hands went for his belt and zipper, and he swore colorfully as her fingers brushed the taut skin of his stomach. He pushed the straps of her dress off her shoulders and down her arms, skimming the sides of her breasts. Their sudden ache and heaviness sent another wave of heated desire racing through her veins.

The dress stopped at her hips, and he lingered there for a second before pushing it to the floor. His eyes got darker as he took in the lacy black bra and panties she'd selected to make her feel more feminine and in control tonight. She'd wanted to be firm and unyielding as she discussed things with him.

Look where it had gotten her so far.

"God, Madeleine, you are so beautiful." His voice was quietly reverent as it broke on his words, and his fingers feathered lightly as they traced the contours of lace at the edges of her bra. "Even more beautiful than before, if that's possible."

Under other circumstances, Roxy might have felt enough humor to laugh, realizing that her intensive scripting about how this was going to go was now scattered all over the floor. Now, she felt hot and lusty and aching for Mac.

The uncertainty was back in his gaze, the questions and the concerns. She could almost hear his wheels turning, examining what this would mean and weighing the consequences. But she was way ahead of him.

Sitting on the sofa and pulling him towards her, she ran fast hands down his hips, pooling his slacks at his feet. He cupped her cheek and searched her face. He must have found whatever he was looking for in her expression because he pushed her back and followed her down.

The heavy weight of him after all these years was a blessing. No other man had made her feel this anxious, this yearning, this powerful. She had tried to forget Mac and how they were together in the intervening years, but at the edge of every relationship she'd tried to forge, he'd been standing in the shadows.

Her urgency matched his, and when his fingers skimmed her throat and finally settled on the front clasp of her bra, she was writhing under him. Flicking it open, he leaned back for a moment.

"So perfect. I've never been able to forget. Like the finest tribute to all of womanhood." And his mouth closed around a nipple and tugged.

She almost levitated off the sofa, and her hands ranged down his back to cradle his butt and pull him closer. He backed away only long enough to pull down his briefs and push away her panties, tossing her lace over his shoulder into the darkness of the room.

Mac knelt between thighs and her legs came around his waist in unconscious memory of how they were together. A crinkle of sound let her know he'd found a condom someplace close by. Poised above her, his eyes seemed to glow that delicious dark chocolate color that always made her wild. "Madeleine, are you sure?"

She didn't want to think about it. She acted, pulling him into her and with one fast buck of her hips, impaling herself on him with so much force that they both cried out.

After that, it was hazy. The world reduced down to overwhelming sensations, the heat of skin on skin, the wandering mouths that nipped and sucked and marked tender flesh, the slap of their joined bodies as he drove deeper and she lifted to accept him.

Her orgasm was just a breath away, and the tension wound her so tight that she felt she would either explode with it or scream down the house. Mac linked a hand with hers and lifted away to watch her face, his own tender and strained as he ran a shaking finger over her lips. His pace matched hers, and as the clutch of orgasm ripped through them both, his eyes stayed open and on hers. She heard him whisper 'Madeleine' with wonder in his voice.

Chapter 26

So much for laying down some ground rules and clearing up the confusion of the past. So much for forgiveness and acceptance too. If he could have done it in his completely sated and drained state, Mac would have banged his head against any handy wall.

As it was, he half-turned on the narrow sofa and took Madeleine with him, hanging on to her tightly in his arms with a leg thrown over hers for good measure. His slacks were still caught on an ankle, the other leg turned inside out and trailing off his toes. He never did get his shirt off.

Madeleine, on the other hand, was completely naked and gorgeous, skin glowing and eyes closed as she rested a hand on his chest. The silk of her hair was caught under his head and all he had to do was turn slightly to inhale its herbal scent. The perfect pillow.

He didn't know what to say, though he thought he should say something. This hadn't been his intention. Well, scratch that. It hadn't been his conscious intention. At some level, maybe he'd hoped that after they cleared the air and indulged in that dinner and enjoyed some wine, she would agree to see if they still had any chemistry.

Any more chemistry, and the whole town would be one big explosion, he thought wryly. Their combustion was as strong and powerful as it had been years ago, and if anything, even more fierce.

He couldn't stop staring at her beautiful face. She shifted against him and a frown crossed her features. He ran a tentative hand down her body to caress her hip, and her eyes opened and stared into his. She bit her lip, and he wanted to take it in his own teeth and nibble. She shivered and untangled her hair from under him, pushing herself off his chest to sit perched on the edge of the sofa.

He should say something. He should do something. She could leave again, and panic rose so fast it choked him.

"Made-, I mean Roxy. You have to know that I didn't mean for this to happen. This wasn't what I intended when I invited you here tonight." He put a hand on her thigh to keep her close to him.

Her eyes closed again, and she leaned away from him, attempting to put her hair in order. Her head tilted back and she straightened, finally turning to gaze at him with a mix of emotions crossing her face. A small smile curved her lips and he released a breath. Maybe he was going to be forgiven.

Her voice was husky when she finally replied, "I know, Mac." And she traced the line of his lips as sadness settled on her features. Then she stood up and moved away from him, collecting her clothes.

*****

Well, that was an adult way of handling things.

Bad judgment taunted her with glee while good sense shook its head in disgust at her complete lack of sanity. The eyes that stared back at her in the bathroom mirror were accusatory and confused. What had she done? This wasn't what she wanted. Bad judgment whispered in her ear, 'or was it'?

Even the colorful kitchen curses of a long professional career were inadequate right now. She'd have to learn a few new ones, maybe in every language in the world, and then she might come close to the string she wanted to put together to reproach herself.

Fifteen plus years, and she acted like an irresponsible girl who had no sense and no idea what the big, bad world could be waiting to throw her way. She'd trusted Mac back then and ended up hurt and alone.

Now, she knew not to trust him, and still she ended up in his arms, with him tearing up a wide path directly to her heart. She was older and wiser and should have known better.

Good sense shivered and bad judgment smirked.

The make-up she'd carefully applied for tonight was either smudged or gone completely, so throwing cold water on her face to take the fear out of her wide eyes wouldn't make any difference at this point. In fact, it might help shock some sense into her. She couldn't stay in the bathroom forever.

She straightened the wrinkles in her dress and ran her fingers through the tangles in her hair. There was no doubt about it, she looked like she'd just been screwing around on a sofa.

And it felt so damn good. A hint of a smile reflected back in the mirror.

A knock came on the door. "Madeleine? I hope you're all right. I heated dinner and it's ready if you like."

Sex wasn't supposed to be on the menu tonight. How was she going to face him now? Could she return things to a coolly impersonal level? But they were way past that. Maybe she could ignore it. Maybe he would too.

"I'm coming, Mac." Bad judgment cackled at her choice of words. Good sense groaned.

She tugged open the door to find him leaning against the opposite wall with his hands in his pockets. His shirt was again buttoned but remained untucked. He looked mussed up and vague and entirely too sexy in the glowing aftermath of what they'd shared.

Pushing away from the wall, he put a hand out to her and she slipped hers inside it. He stared into her face as he raised her fingers, kissing each one individually and then turning over her palm, examining her kitchen scars and long-forgotten burn marks. She wanted to pull her hand away from his close scrutiny. He kissed her palm and tightened his grip, pulling her towards the dining room.

She caught the light of the candles first out of the corner of her eye, and when she took in the elegant table setting and myriad covered dishes, surprise and wonder at the care he'd taken swamped her. A single yellow rose, perfect in its simplicity, lay across one of the plates.

"I remember how much you like candlelight, and pretty place settings with all of the perfect forks and knives and spoons."

And yellow roses.

He smiled at her, an open expression that held none of the casual nonchalance she expected to find. It was almost as if they'd slipped back in time.

He made a show of pulling out her chair and flourishing the napkin before placing it in her lap. He kissed her cheek before walking to his own seat set close at an angle to hers. His knee brushed hers and she pulled away to give him room, only to find his hand on her thigh pulling her closer. Knee to knee, he poured some wine into each of their glasses and raised his in a toast.

"To old friends and new beginnings," he said, and when she clinked her glass to his, he took her free hand and squeezed it in a heart-stopping caress before letting it go.

This was like a fairy tale, and suddenly she had to shake herself to remember that yes, he was good at setting the stage for a performance. He'd left her all those years ago, and he hadn't yet explained it or apologized for it.

"I had dinner catered from Paush's in San Francisco. I remember how much you loved that place, so I hope it's still good." He moved serving dishes towards her. "I got all of your old favorites."

She went perfectly still. He had remembered all of her old favorites all right, a fettucini Alfredo and a wild mushroom ragout, a trio of salmon, a side of spring vegetables in a salad. Yes, he had remembered them all, and she bet that he had crème brulee for dessert too.

The restaurant itself had ceased being a favorite within a week of working there. But he didn't need to know that part.

They served themselves without speaking and began to take small bites of each selection. He frowned. Roxy did too.

"Is it me, or is it not quite as great as I remember it?" Mac looked up from a forkful of salmon.

Roxy thought maybe she was being hypercritical, her chef side instantly seeking perfection and finding the flaws instead. But Mac said it first.

"It's lacking a certain something." She flashed on Jeannine being kicked out of her father's kitchen and filed away this review to share with her apprentice later.

He was waiting, watching her closely as she picked at the food and moved it around her plate. A bare minimum made it into his mouth, and she was happy to see that he was trying to eat things she would have recommended for him.

He asked about the interns, and she shared that one of them was in fact Bart Paush's daughter. "And she came to work for you instead of him?" His curiosity was obvious, fork set aside now. One thing she recalled about him was his interest in the foibles of human nature.

"Yeah, and there's a story behind that." She frowned at the dishes on the table. "But maybe I should take some of the leftovers back for Jeannine to taste. She might want to know what's going on."

"Feel free. There's very little of this I can eat safely, I've realized. I'd rather feel better and miss out on this right now – not that it's a big miss in my opinion – than suffer." He plucked her hand off the table and kissed it quickly before placing it down and leaving his own covering it. "I have you to thank for that."

His smile was so broad and seemed so genuine that Roxy felt her eyes tearing up. Hell, for someone who didn't cry, she was doing a lot of tearing up these days.

"Dessert!" Mac leaped up and headed for the kitchen, the door swinging wildly as he shoved his way through.

"Do you want any help?" She called out, just in case.

"No, I can handle this myself. I may not be professionally trained, but a little thing like this? Piece of cake!"

She smiled and picked up her wine for a sip. He seemed more buoyant, more energetic and happier than she'd seen him since he arrived in Flynn's Crossing. It was just like he'd been...

And her thoughts snagged there. Just like he'd been fifteen years ago.

She refused to think about it now. He and the wolf pack had an early start for their fishing expedition in the morning, so she had every excuse to head out the door at a decent hour tonight. Her script for their discussion was meaningless anyway, and there was no point in pulling it out for a reading tonight.

"Ta-da!" Mac pushed open the door carrying two low plates. The scent of crisply burned sugar wafted in ahead of him and Roxy felt her mouth water. Crème brulee, just as she liked it.

Setting a plate in front of her with a flourish, he sank into his chair and folded his hands, setting his chin on them. He watched closely for her reaction.

"It's amaretto," he noted with a huge grin.

Roxy couldn't help herself. She grinned back and said, "Mac! You remembered!"

They stared at each other for a minute before her grin faded and his face became serious. He dropped his hands and grabbed one of hers, clasping it tightly. He continued to stare into her eyes.

"Madeleine, I remember," he paused for emphasis, "everything."

Chapter 27

"That was incredible, no doubt about it." Vince patted his stomach and leaned deeper into the shade of trees lining the river.

"What did you say it was again?" Dane looked at Mac, seated closest to the cooler holding their lunch.

"According to the lid, it's a spring risotto salad. It has no gluten, no dairy, and no nuts. Just basic good clean healthy food."

The three other men looked at him. Rick took up the thread of discussion. "I have to admit, it should be tasteless, but Roxy has a way with food unlike anyone else. Gabby cooks, and I cook, but we are always at a loss about mixing things up, or trying new combinations. We get our inspiration from Roxy's dishes."

"What is this, a new health food line she's going to introduce in the store?" Vince took another scoop.

Mac was sorry now that he'd done anything more than read out the title on the container. The less said about why they were eating this particular menu, the better.

"Don't know. I only know that when I said I wouldn't need lunch from my personal chef today, she insisted on packing us – all of us – this big old picnic for this little fishing trip."

When it looked like Vince was going to ask yet another follow-up question, Mac decided to redirect the conversation. "Back to the important stuff. I thought you said there were a lot of fish up here."

Dane chuckled. "Sometimes you find them, and sometimes you don't. One morning, this bank was crawling with fly fishers, all guys but this one woman..."

Mac closed his eyes and listened to Dane spin the story out. The men caught next to nothing, and the lone woman was pulling in trout after trout. No sooner did she release one and get her line back on the water, setting it in a graceful arc, than another fish would take a fly.

This would make a great vignette. Mac could see the snap of the line above the woman's head, the droplets showering down as it released the water it held. The taut thrown of the fly would be picture perfect, landing right in the middle of a sweet spot of stream lying just off the rushing current. And wham, a big fish would take the tied feathers and fuzz and leap out of the river to show off.

In his dream, the woman had long golden hair pulled into a loose ponytail down her back. She was smiling, a broad grin that covered her face ear to ear, with sunglasses hiding laughing eyes that he knew were a brilliant cornflower blue when she turned to share her triumph with him.

The reach of her arm up to cast the line allowed the material of her shirt to press against her breasts, the same ones he'd caressed for too short a time last night. The waders emphasized the round globes of her butt, and he ached to hold her to him again. Last night had awakened longings he'd forgotten he'd ever had.

Remember me, remember us, remember what we were to each other, he'd urged silently, when she didn't respond to his declaration with dessert. In fact, she'd looked shocked and distraught, so much so that he changed topics and instead told a long funny story about a well-known star and her spoiled bratty dog. It was his show-biz persona designed to put people at ease.

Finally coaxing a laugh out of her, he relaxed again. He tried a couple of other opening comments to lead them back to discussing 'us', but she had just as skillfully turned the subject away each time. Shortly after coffee, she'd pointed to the clock and made a big show of the late hour and his early morning fishing trip, gathering up her things so fast that when he blinked, she was already at the door.

"I had a wonderful time tonight, Mac." She stood half in and half out, keys in hand and a small nostalgic smile on her face. She reached up and placed a chaste kiss on his lips, then turned and got into the SUV without another word.

Stay, he'd wanted to say. Come back in, come upstairs, let us make love like we used to. Before, earlier, was just a daily rush, not the final cut of the movie. There's still a whole lot more to show you, other things I want you to remember too.

But he didn't say any of it. He sensed that he'd crossed some invisible but undeniable boundary, something he had rushed and shouldn't have. He wanted to make her realize that he could let go of the past if she was willing to meet him part way. Hell, he needed to make her understand.

A picnic, he should suggest they go on a picnic, he mused. She'd always loved picnics, getting away to enjoy nature and finding a secluded spot where they could nuzzle and sometimes a whole lot more. There must be plenty of places in the wilderness around here where they could get naked in the sunshine and feast on each other. Having just a taste of her wasn't enough, and he allowed himself to replay each move and sigh and heartbeat of last night as the sun baked his brain.

"…and Roxy cooked it for us that night, both browns. She did such a perfect job with them that I'm afraid to try it myself ever again. Big feisty salmon, yes, but tender delicate trout, no way." Dane's voice had the hypnotic quality of a natural storyteller.

"She cooked them for you? She never cooked any of my fish for me. Shit, what gives?" Vince sounded aggrieved.

"She probably hasn't forgiven you yet for all of your deep deception when you first came to town." Rick was laughing now.

"Hey Mac, can you believe that Roxy called me a snarky lifestyle writer when she found out who I was? Warned me off DK too. Of course, she probably never turned out a bad dish in her life, but really..."

Stuck in the sexy movie playing in his mind, Mac said the first thing that came into his head. "Oh, she can make a mistake now and then. I remember when she was wearing this really short top and low cut jeans once, enough skin showing to drive you crazy, and grilling this huge cut of beef..." And he stopped.

Opening his eyes, Mac found the men staring at him. Rick and Dane were curious, but Vince had a particular gleam in his eye.

"She made a mistake once? I want to hear this. Finally I'll have something to lord over her." Vince grinned devilishly. Then he stopped stock-still. "Wait, Roxy never grills in anything but chef's whites, even for casual stuff at home. Says it isn't safe." He frowned at Mac and leaned forward. "Just when and where did this steak grilling occur, exactly?"

This was an even bigger mistake, Mac realized. He'd been caught up in an imaginary world with Roxy at its center, a dream of having time to play, to enjoy life, to feel good, all with her. And his mind had flicked back to when she was starting out, when they both were, and she was still learning her craft.

He couldn't tell them about it, not without giving away the fact that they'd known each other way back when. And he couldn't make it sound like this was now, because then she'd never hear the end of it, and she didn't deserve that.

Dane and Rick joined Vince in a chorus of cajoling.

"Come to think of it, Roxy does act a little strange whenever Mac's name comes up in conversation. Remember when she was over at your house, Dane, and you were packing up your gear before our interview? She was definitely weirding out then, and Serena asked some rather pointed questions too."

Vince stopped and turned back to Mac. "Okay man, time to come clean. Just what the hell gives with you and Roxy anyway?"

*****

"To be sure, I asked Gabby and Alej to taste things today too, and they both said that the dishes weren't that great. Alej went so far as to say the food tasted like it was poor quality product to begin with. Gabby just thought it was yucky." Behind Roxy outside in the kitchen, Gabby made a sound that was distinctly similar to the gagging one of her boys might use.

Jeannine tasted each dish carefully, making notes on a small pad she always kept with her. Roxy watched her and wondered what was going through her mind.

The woman was now showing, no doubt about it. Alej had been hovering over her, making her sit down when the kitchen wasn't busy, and cajoling her to eat when she denied being hungry. The pooch of a belly made her chef's coat snug, the buttons tight and straining. She'd need the maternity version soon.

Finally snapping her notebook closed, the intern turned to Roxy. "Chef, I honestly don't know what's happening to Bart. My father has always been a stickler for perfection. There's no way he'd allow food like that to be sent out, and to a big Hollywood name no less. He'd make the meal himself, package it himself, and then he'd call the next day to ask about how things were."

She paused as if deciding if the question was appropriate, then shrugged and dove in. "Did he call Mr. Smythe to follow up, do you know?"

No, she didn't know. In fact, she'd hoped that Mac would have called her early after the wolf pack returned from their fishing expedition. But her cell had been silent.

"I don't know, no. But we'll see. Maybe Mac will have news about it." Roxy paused, hesitating to intrude. "Was this going on when you were still there?"

Jeannine started to shake her head negatively but stopped. A huge sigh escaped her and her lips compressed into a straight line. "I can't lie to you. Yes, it was going on before, though it wasn't this bad." She gestured to the dishes and glanced over at a silent Alej leaning against the far wall.

"I think my father might be failing in some way, his health I mean. I gently asked him to taste some of the dishes diners were complaining about. He'd either refuse and stomp off, or he'd yell that it was the best he'd ever produced and the customers simply had no taste. He'd rail on about how palates in the US were being dumbed down by fast food and then he'd start on poorly trained chefs and pretty soon, staff were walking out the door and never coming back." Sadness was evident in the shake of her head.

Roxy considered this news for a moment. "Maybe, just maybe, he realizes that he's slipping, and that's why he sent you away."

Jeannine looked up sharply. "Why the hell would he do that, when for decades he's been talking about nothing but what a legacy he was leaving for me, his chef daughter, to inherit? It doesn't make any sense." The woman shook her head again. "I thought he would want me around if for no other reason than to fix things."

It didn't make any logical sense to her either, not that Bart Paush didn't defy logic on many occasions, but Jeannine deserved an answer.

"Let me do some nosing around, okay Jeannine? I'm curious now too, probably just as curious as you."

The woman nodded, a hand unconsciously rubbing her bump of a belly as she frowned. Thanking Roxy, she turned back to the kitchen and headed to the back room to prepare the night's grilling options. Alej pushed away from the wall to follow her, never looking back.

Roxy stared after them for a moment, pondering a course of action. She still had quite a few friends in the Bay Area chefs' community, as did Alej. Between them, they might be able to get some semblance of a full story. Besides, it felt good to be out of her own drama and into someone else's.

And what was up with Alej anyway?

*****

"So how'd it go?" Gabby stirred a big pot of soup on the stove as Roxy stayed perched on her tall stool. "I mean other than the food."

Normally she liked it when her girlfriends came over and wanted to learn something new, but today, she would rather have had peace and quiet to process things.

What exactly had happened? She'd arrived late. Mac had overreacted to her being late and she acted on his overreaction. And they'd ended up naked on the couch, coming down off mind-blowing orgasms that luckily did not shake the house off its foundation, heading it down the hill on to Main Street.

At least her mind had been blown. By the expression on Mac's face, he wasn't in any better shape afterwards either.

The thought and care he'd put into dinner had been amazing. All of her favorites, and he'd then made choices for himself that showed he'd been paying attention to the lessons in healthy eating she'd been giving him over the past weeks. Holding her hand in the flickering candlelight, he'd been charming and attentive, even taking her fork and feeding her himself upon occasion. And when he'd dripped some sauce on her chin, his tender use of his thumb to wipe it away while staring into her eyes had her hungry for so much more.

She'd been frozen to her seat by the time dessert arrived, confused at the mixed messages she was receiving. He wanted her, or not? This was goodbye, or not? He hadn't said anything about the status of the movie, and even when location filming was going to be completed soon, what happened then?

All she knew for sure was that she'd never had a second to air the carefully designed talk she'd planned. She never knew what made him leave her all those years ago. And he still hadn't apologized for it.

Gabby poked at her arm with the handle of the big spoon, returning to her stirring when she had Roxy's attention. The big steamy kitchen and fragrant aromas of foods for dinner centered her.

"You aren't talking. That either means it went really badly, or it was truly amazing. So which is it?"

Roxy sighed and closed her eyes. "Can it be both, at the same time?"

Chapter 28

"I hate the fact that I have to leave right away. Why can't this wait until morning?" Mac slammed through the drawers of the dresser, searching for socks and other necessities to accompany the suits Martha was already hanging in a garment bag.

"I don't know, Mac. All I know is that the money people said to get you on a plane today, not tomorrow. They weren't even happy with you getting in tonight. I would have had you out of here earlier, but there was no way to reach you when you were fishing." Giving the suits a last satisfied shake, Martha turned to take the stacks of clothing Mac was yanking out and headed to the duffle suitcase.

"It won't be a long trip, either way. Either they'll give you the extra money you need and the time to get the film done, or they won't. At least Justin can go back to work soon, according to his doctors." When Mac would have thrown gym shoes on top of everything in the bag, she grabbed them with a slight tsk-tsk and carefully lifted the contents to place the shoes at the bottom.

He should be grateful she was willing to put up with his moods. After ten years of working for him, she did a good job of reading his thoughts and anticipating what he wanted, almost before he realized he needed something himself.

Of course, the one thing she wouldn't know is that he needed Madeleine right now, more than he needed anything or anyone else. He'd spent most of the day on the river with the guys distracted by memories of last night and of fifteen years ago. And it had gotten him in incredible trouble.

"What do you mean, you can't tell us?" Vince had towered over him, hands on hips, an expression of disbelief on his face.

"I can't tell you, that's all." Mac had tried to backpedal from his almost-confession of that time way back when, when Madeleine had failed to think through the implications of a sizzling grill and appropriate cooking attire.

"No problem," Rick countered, "we'll just ask Roxy ourselves."

That's what had Mac worried. They'd ask, and she'd either get embarrassed and yell, or she'd get mad and kill him. The latter was more likely.

"Look, guys, it's a complicated thing that's best left in the past." Shit, hopefully they wouldn't notice his slip of the tongue.

"Past? How much of a past can you have since you came to town, what, a month ago?" Dane leaned forward and stared at Mac intently.

Cursing his random memories and the drift of his mind that, while it was clearer than before, still got fuzzy sometimes, Mac turned to pick up his fly rod and head for the river.

"I'm going to get in a few more casts before we go, okay?"

No one responded behind him, but when he'd almost reached a distance where he was out of earshot, he heard Vince's pronouncement, "Shit, there's more to their relationship than he's letting on."

He cast in arcs over the water with an arm that was probably throwing the fly too hard, but his anger at himself was getting the better of him. He didn't want to betray Madeleine's trust in him, and he wasn't a guy who kissed and told. Plus, these men were her friends and had been around her a whole lot more than he had in recent times.

Without a sound, Dane suddenly waded in beside him and began fiddling with the fly on his own line. Finally satisfied with the knot attaching his hook, he cast in the opposite direction on the stream from Mac and stood by in silence.

Damn, he was going to have to say something. Dane wasn't asking, and Mac could hear the rise and fall of voices in the background as Rick evidently tried to talk Vince out of demanding to know the whole story.

"You know that we all keep secrets, right?" Dane's voice was quiet, almost as gentle as the gurgle of the water they stood in.

Mac sighed. This was a bigger secret than any these guys had ever seen, he was sure of it.

"Vince already told you about his big secret, about not telling anyone who he was or why he was here when he first arrived. Rick had secrets too, about his life before Flynn's Crossing and the challenges with his son Will. I kept some big ones from Serena for quite a while."

Cast, drift and reel in. The motion and tempo were soothing. And Mac was tired, physically beat by this much exertion in a day, and on top of last night too.

"What's your point, Dane?"

"My point is, we all know how to keep secrets. We've kept things to ourselves until the time is right to share it." He paused and Mac felt his stare. Finally, he looked over to find Dane watching him with sympathetic understanding.

"We'll keep yours too."

"Mac? Mac! The car is here to take you to the airport." Martha was standing in the bedroom door expectantly. He'd drifted away again, out of the here and now.

"I'm coming, Martha. I just need to call Roxy and tell her that I don't need dinner tonight. I'll tell her I'll be out of –
"

"Oh don't worry about that. I've taken care of it. I can let her know when you're going to return too, depending."

Heading down the stairs ahead of him, she directed the driver to the bags standing in the entry hall, leaning up against the same wall where Mac had pushed Roxy scant hours ago. When Mac stopped to stare at the spot, Martha gave him a little push towards the front door and handed him his briefcase.

"Your accountants put some briefing material together for you to review on the flight to LA. You'll have about an hour and a half of peace and quiet to design your strategy. I also took the liberty of packing you a sandwich and some snacks, some of your favorites."

God, this was like the mom in the old movies, sending you off to the school bus with your book bag and lunch box, and reminding you about your homework. Still, it might be just as well that Martha was handling Roxy. He wasn't sure what to say to her right now, other than to plead for her to give them a chance.

"Thanks Martha. I appreciate you staying on top of things. Tell Roxy she can call me whenever she wants, okay?"

Martha frowned as he turned from his seat in the car to say goodbye.

"Sure Mac, whatever you say."

Her voice sounded forced and her expression was even stranger, but Mac had only a second to realize it. Once he thought to study his assistant's face more closely, her expression was guarded and distant.

"Good luck, Mac. Don't worry, I'll take care of everything around here. I know you can convince them to do whatever you want them to do." She waved as she slammed the door shut.

What he wanted to do is find Madeleine and tell her that last night, while it wasn't planned, had been the best night of his life in a decade and a half.

Chapter 29

"I have to say, that guy Justin is a whole lot nicer now that he's been taken down a few notches." Alej sorted through receipts on Roxy's desk and handed her the neat stack. "I didn't expect him to be back on the set so fast, but I guess there's a reason for the show-biz sayings 'break a leg' and 'the show must go on'."

Roxy kept her eyes on the paperwork in front of her and glanced occasionally at the computer screen to hide her disappointment. Yes, the show did go on, and filming had begun again a scant two weeks after the actor's accident. They were working around Justin standing with hidden crutches or sitting while he delivered his lines.

She'd found out about Mac leaving for a few days from Barry. The assistant called to let her know that the big boss had to make an emergency trip to LA. The crew and actors had a week off while Justin began his recuperation. Then they'd see where everything stood.

After the passion and care he'd taken that night over dinner, she hoped he would call her himself, but her phones had been disappointingly quiet. If nothing else, she had hoped for a simple thank you call about the picnic, but he didn't bother with that either.

"The big boss said that one of us will tell you about restarting the cooking thing." Barry sounded distracted, tapping away on his end of the call.

"One of who, Barry? I need to know who to expect will call so that I'm sure to get the message right away."

Still sounding like he was doing three things at once, Barry replied, "Why, me or Martha I suppose. Martha told me Mac was leaving right after the fishing trip, and she told me to call you. It was all arranged before."

So now the go-fer of the go-fer was being told to call her. If she didn't feel so embarrassed about her own expectations, she'd get mad. And how far before? As in before that passionate last night?

She'd had a week to harden her heart against him, intent on being cool and distant when Mac returned and their evenings resumed. She could probably call him herself, but his cell number was private.

Besides, that would be making the first move, and the matching emotions of pain and pride wouldn't allow her to do that.

Damn the man for taking off without a single word to her. And after plastering the wall with her too. And the couch. And her heart during dinner.

Her pride came in handy when he changed their dining arrangements. Barry called with Martha's message. "He'll just eat with the crew, since they'll be shooting late each night and starting early in the morning."

No words from the big boss himself about rocking her world, or her rocking his.

Damn, she was letting Mac get to her, again. She was wiser and stronger than that by now, wasn't she? Maybe that one night had been a complete and total fluke. Or maybe he was sorry it had happened.

"Hey Roxy, do you have a minute?" Gabby, standing in the office door with her face scrunched in anxiety, brought her back to the present.

Roxy waved her in. "We're just doing the books, so you're welcome to join the party."

Silence and a lack of movement followed her invitation, so Roxy finally looked up to see Gabby staring at her pointedly, then glancing just as pointedly at the back of

Alej's head. "It's about that soup we were working on the other day. You know, last week?" And she stared hard at Roxy again.

Finally catching on that something important needed to be said in private, Roxy stood and headed towards the door. "Alej, can you keep slogging through that? The accountant wants it all tomorrow. Gabby and I are going to head upstairs for a few minutes."

"Of course, you know how much I love to run the numbers. It's my favorite thing, right after chopped off my fingers one by one with a dull cleaver." A groan followed them out through the kitchen.

Gabby grabbed Roxy's arm and urged her up the stairs at a quick clip, and when they reached the top, she checked behind them like she expected them to be followed before she shut the door quietly.

"What is going on, Gabby? Why are you turning into a suspense queen?"

Gabby paced the length of the living area and stopped in front of Roxy, pushing her back on the sofa. "I think you need to sit down when I tell you this."

"Tell me what? What's with the soup?"

Gabby paced back and forth one more time before grabbing a chair and seating herself directly in front of Roxy.

"You remember telling me about the big evening with Mac, the big seduction scene and then the fabulous dinner?" Gabby's fingers were knitting together in her lap, moving constantly.

"Yes, though I wouldn't call it a big seduction scene. More like a mutual bombardment of two asteroids blowing everything to smithereens in space. But yeah, I remember." An ugly thought occurred to Roxy. "Did you tell someone?"

Gabby gave her an affronted look and said, "Of course not! How long have we known each other?" And she glared at Roxy.

"Okay, okay, I know you wouldn't, so what's the big drama?"

"I didn't tell anyone." She paused. "But I think Mac did."

Roxy leaped up off the sofa so fast that Gabby almost upset backwards.

"He what?" Roxy was sure that the staff downstairs would probably hear her yell. Lowering her voice she added, "Why do you think he told anyone?"

Gabby's face was sympathetic. "Because Rick is asking me questions. Subtle, but specific questions." She heaved a sigh. "I keep telling him I don't know, have no idea what he's talking about, etc. But he keeps at it."

She added, "And honey, DK and Serena said the other guys are asking questions too."

*****

"God, that was a long day. But the dailies are looking good, even working around Justin's props." Mac rubbed his neck, trying to sooth away the stiffness.

Martha packed up the papers he'd strewn around the director's chair. "Yes, I think it's going well for you. It's a good thing that the moneymen were happy with the look of the film so far. Now you can make that final push to the end and head back home."

Home. Mac reflected on the word and wondered where that was. He'd been back in LA only five nights, spending them in his little mansion in the Hollywood Hills when he wasn't kissing ass to be allowed to continue on with this movie.

Funny, the mansion he'd owned for over a decade felt so empty.

The little house on the hill above Flynn's Crossing, on the other hand, was full of warm memories and funny stories and the hazy sense that it was where he belonged. And Roxy belonged there with him.

She hadn't tried to contact him since he'd been back. He was hoping she'd come along with the crew to serve meals, giving them a chance to talk under the cover of normal activities. But Martha had an explanation for that.

"I talked to Chef LaFollette myself and she said that the time she was spending preparing your food took her away from the rest of her business. And since the movie schedule is now running late, she needed to concentrate on other work. She said she would be happy to have one of her seasoned line cooks take over as personal chef."

He didn't care about the meals. He wanted to spend time with Roxy. Maybe he needed to take things into his own hands.

"Oh, and she said that you don't need to call her about this directly. I can relay your decision through Chef Alej."

What the hell? First, she was backing away from their agreement, and now she didn't even want him to call her. The line he'd crossed that night, taking her on the sofa without grace or gentleness, was more like a chasm. And it hurt to realize that he didn't know how to bridge it.

Chapter 30

He paced the dining room again, then drifted into the kitchen and opened the refrigerator to stare at the contents. Healthy foods, courtesy of Madeleine, and some not so good options, courtesy of Martha. Clearly, his assistant didn't understand his change in eating habits.

"Oh, these are your favorites, Mac. It won't hurt to have them. That chef is being overly cautious." Martha was the only one who knew that Roxy was making Mac special meals. He trusted her to keep his secret.

But the snacks Martha kept bringing him, much like the stuff she packed for him when he went to LA, were trouble. He'd picked at them, and when his stomach rebelled, he'd dumped them in the nearest trashcan.

Martha had taken it upon herself to restock more than just the fridge while he was gone. His favorite Scotch was back on the sideboard in the dining room. "Of course you can have this, Mac. I'm sure it won't hurt you."

He circled back to the dining room and looked out the window to Main Street. The late afternoon sun was hot and bright, and everyone was scurrying for the nearest shade they could find. The Saturday sidewalks were ripe with tourists instead. Hell, it was five o'clock somewhere, and he was ready for a drink.

The glasses that had been stored on the sideboard were missing, so he headed for the kitchen to find one for his Scotch. Damn, which cabinet again? Opening the first set of doors, he found seasonings and staples. In the next, dishes.

Finally, he opened a cupboard and found wine glasses. And standing next to them were some of the bottles of wine Madeleine had brought.

Hhmmm, wine or Scotch? A tough call, particularly since he was alone. Vignettes flashed through his mind. Madeleine telling him she'd poured his Scotch down the drain. Her, tasting that first bottle of wine she'd opened for him. Her lips curved on her wine glass that last night.

Opening a bottle of wine would remind him of her.

Hell, a glass of water reminded him of her.

Why hadn't she gotten in touch with him? She knew he was back. But not a peep. He'd thought about calling her, but he paused as he remembered Martha's explanation. She needed more time for her businesses.

Maybe she just needed time away from him.

Yes, he had monopolized her over the past few weeks, but she hadn't seemed to mind. She hadn't raised an issue about it even once.

Restless, he decided to wait on both Scotch and wine. The barest hint of an idea was forming and he was wondering if it was wise. Damn, he knew it probably wasn't, but he really wanted to see the woman.

*****

"We had a late addition to the reservations coming in at seven." Alej chopped grilled vegetables for a salsa side to one of tonight's specials and continued his explanation. "Daisy juggled some tables around and put them in the Sierra room."

Roxy frowned. Since the restaurant was an old coach lodge on a former wagon trail, the rooms were much more intimate than a modern building. She'd chosen to keep the original structure and the walls, opting instead for the cozy seating and warm feel each room had.

"Sierra? That seats sixteen easily, so it must be big. How many in the party?"

Alej frowned, putting down his knife and wiping his hands.

"That's just the thing, the guy said set a table for two. Just said that they needed a private room, preferable the most private one. And when Daisy tried to explain that she could accommodate them at a secluded table in general dining, he reiterated the need for absolute privacy." Alej shrugged at Roxy's puzzled look. "He's paying our conference rate for the room for the evening, plus whatever food they order, and offered a premium for the inconvenience. I say hurray, not that we aren't slamming busy already."

None of that made any sense. Why would anyone make a last minute reservation like that and pay so much for a full room? Alej said big deal, and it looked like it was. Marriage proposal maybe? More bizarre things had happened.

"And there's one more thing," Alej added, wiping the rim of the plate once he was satisfied with the placement of the salsa. "He said that he wants a chef's choice menu, and he'll pay accordingly, no ceiling on the price."

The chef's choice part wasn't that unusual. People did that all the time, deciding that having her pick their courses was more fun than being limited by a menu. But no price cap? And at the very last minute? If she stocked foie gras and truffles, this could get expensive, so the party seemed to trust her.

"Okay, two chef's choices it will be. I wonder who's on the receiving end of the big surprise in all of this."

Chapter 31

Mac put the roadster through its paces, inhaling the country air deeply. He was starting to realize why Madeleine loved it here. The two lane roads and picturesque views at almost every turn were inspiring.

The trouble was, he'd been in town all this time and other than the fishing trip, this was the first time he'd bothered to get off the set on his own and explore. Already he'd found two houses and a barn that might work better than what they had planned for a couple of scenes at the end of the film.

She'd been uninterested in the storyline of the movie. She hadn't even wanted a synopsis of the scenes.

"I can wait until it comes out," she'd insisted.

He wanted to present the completed movie to her like a gift, a tribute to their time together now and everything that they meant to each other way back when. And maybe everything that they could mean to each other in the future.

Passing a farm stand and acres of produce, Mac thought about his single foray into discussing a future.

"You know, if you were producing this kind of food in LA instead of here, you'd be making money so fast you'd be able to build a chain of Roxy's in all of the major world hot spots." What he hadn't added was that then, she'd be close by, close enough perhaps to consider moving in with him.

She'd laughed as she chopped vegetables, the colorful array on the board a testament to the richness of the area.

"Why would I move anywhere else? I have everything I want here. I have my own extensive garden, I can buy whatever else I need from local growers, and I source much of my protein locally as well. You'd be amazed what you can find within two hundred miles."

She'd gone on to extol the virtues of locavore foods and using fresh farm to table ingredients whenever possible. She hadn't looked up, or she would have noticed the disappointment on his face. Everything she wanted was here, which effectively left him off the only A-list he wanted badly to be on.

This was where she belonged. What did that mean for the feelings that were growing so quickly inside him?

He pushed it aside as he pulled up to the famed restaurant. Mac had heard that almost everyone who first arrived at Roxy's was surprised, and now he understood why. The building must date back over a hundred years, a long low two story set back from the road. Gardens wrapped around the building, and they were verdant and aromatic, mixing flowers and vegetables and fruit trees with what looked like careless abandon. He suspected, though, that each plant was in its place to serve a specific purpose. Madeleine wouldn't have it any other way.

The front door, up five steps and leading in from a spacious front porch, opened into a central interior hallway. There was no sign of the vast empty space that usually greeted guests at an upscale eatery in LA. Instead, open doorways led off the old style hall.

The young hostess wore a nameplate that identified her as Daisy, the same young lady who had taken his reservation a couple of hours ago. When he walked in, she looked up with a broad smile already in place, and froze in that position with her eyes widening.

"Ah, Mr. Smythe. What a pleasant surprise. Welcome to Roxy's. We're so happy you're joining us tonight." As she fumbled the computer keys and quickly scanned the discreet screen hidden from public view, he knew she was in a panic. Her eyes darted from spot to spot. He rarely gave his real name when making a reservation, and he could only assume that she was trying to juggle space for him on a busy Saturday night.

"Daisy, thanks so much. I have a reservation. We talked a couple of hours ago. I used the name Barry Ditka."

She flushed and smiled in relief, visibly relaxing and settling her shoulders back into her previous welcoming posture. "Oh I'm so glad, Mr. Smythe! I was afraid we weren't going to be able to accommodate you for a couple of hours otherwise."

Checking her screen again, she picked up two menus and a wine list, looking into the empty space behind him. "Party of two, right? Would you like to wait in our bar or perhaps have a drink on the veranda or wander the gardens while you wait for your guest?"

Mac smiled and declined, saying he'd rather wait at his table. Daisy led the way down the hall and turned right into a room with a real fireplace dominating one wall.

It was large, but it didn't feel cavernous, even with a small table set in the center with only two places. The other furniture had been pushed back against the open walls, and vases of flowers and fanciful statutes distracted the eye from any appearance of temporary storage. The fireplace was filled with more vases and a mildly fragrant flower, peonies he thought, tumbled out of the grate in place of a blaze. Windows overlooked a busy patio full of patrons, and gardens stretched in the distance beyond it.

It was charming, disarmingly so, and so at odds with what he'd expected from an internationally known chef that he smiled broadly in delight. Daisy was waiting tableside, allowing him to make up his mind on the chair he preferred. Both afforded views of the outside gardens.

Picking the seat that also offered the best view of the doorway, he took the wine list first, and as he opened it up to peruse the selections, Daisy hovered and finally asked, "And who will be joining you tonight, Mr. Smythe? I'll make sure that they are shown to your table immediately when they arrive."

"No need, Daisy. My dinner companion is already here."

The girl frowned in confusion, opened her mouth to ask him more, and then closed it and backed towards the door with a forced smile. She spun around at the last minute and headed down the hallway in the opposite direction from the front door.

Madeleine trains them well. He felt a surge of pride at everything she had accomplished. Here, in her element, he began to realize that she'd made the transition to Roxy with style and grace.

He recognized many of the wineries noted on the wine list from the selections she brought to his house. Even better, some of the favorites he'd enjoyed were available by the glass, so he could pick and choose. He planned on making this a long and leisurely evening, and he hoped he could cajole his guest into join him in a glass or two throughout the adventure.

Chapter 32

"A gentler hand with the sauce, Ticia, there you go. You want the flavors of the salad to rule the dish, not the dressing." Roxy nodded her approval and the intern smiled. She was showing more confidence these days, even making suggestions on the appetizers and salads that exhibited a thoughtful understanding of the goodness in fresh and tasty ingredients.

The main hallway door burst open, a definite violation of policy in Roxy's book, and she turned to see who needed to be reminded about the sedate and calm presence they all worked towards. Daisy came flying through and stopped just inside with arms outstretched as if blocking a demon out of the kitchen.

"He's here." She was panting in her excitement, and it was hard to tell if she was thrilled or mortified.

"Who's here, Daisy?" Roxy frowned at her. This wasn't the girl's usual laidback attitude.

"The guy who wanted the whole private dining room." Her eyes were wide and darted from person to person. The whole kitchen ground to a halt to watch the show.

Roxy waited for her to elaborate, then lost patience and asked, "And? Does he have two heads? Is he naked? What's the big deal?" Alej came to stand next to Roxy, mirroring her posture of hands on hips.

Daisy shook her head as if to clear it, and started over. "The reservation was for Barry Ditka, but it's not him. Or at least, it's a name he must use when he makes reservations, but it's not his real name."

Roxy looked at Alej, who shrugged. Then she looked back at Daisy, walking slowly towards the girl. "Daisy, you're not making any sense. Is there something we need to know?"

The girl looked impatient now, and Roxy almost expected her to stamp her foot in frustration. "No, I mean yes. Barry Ditka is really the actor, Mac Smythe." As a dreamy expression crossed her face, she added, "And he's as great looking in person as he is on the screen."

The sudden silence in the kitchen was only broken by the sounds of food bubbling or sizzling. Ticia had a ladle mid-air over a salad, Jeannine was frowning at the grill, tongs hovering, and Bob, who had popped his head out of the corner where he was assembling desserts, promptly disappeared as fast as a turtle pulling back into his shell. Angel and the rest of the staff broke their frozen positions to return to their stations and tasks with sudden studied attention.

No one said a thing. Roxy herself wasn't sure what to say. Mac showing up here with a last minute reservation probably shouldn't feel weird, but he'd been here for weeks and had never set foot in the restaurant. An ugly thought crossed her mind as she remembered that the dinner reservation was for two people.

"Daisy, who is his guest?" Roxy pitched her voice low to avoid sharing the question with the whole kitchen. If he was with a woman, she didn't want to see who it was, kind of like not wanting to look at an accident on the freeway. But she was afraid she'd be tempted to peak anyway.

"Well that's what's so weird, Chef. He didn't have anyone with him, and he said that the person he was going to dine with is already here."

*****

Mac sipped the Viognier and enjoyed people watching out the window. The patio was full, and at every table, patrons were smiling and enjoying their dishes. He'd noticed looks of rapture cross faces at a first or second taste. And more than a few sat back with hands on full bellies, laughing and groaning as they made more selections from a dessert cart.

He looked around the room, wondering how many of the tables in here were scheduled to be used tonight, and decided that based on what he could see, they probably all were. It amazed him that they'd squeezed him in as a nobody name and honored his request despite the circumstances.

"Sir, would you like to wait a little longer for your guest before we bring out an appetizer for you? Chef has prepared something that she feels will be a favorite of yours." The man was discreet, moving in and out of the room on quiet feet without a hint of hurry. His care in pouring the wine directly from the bottle, label towards his patron, indicated that this was the way they served wines by the glass all the time. Classy.

"No, I'll be happy to start. The aromas have my mouth watering." Mac gave him a friendly smile and then put out a hand to halt the waiter's retreat.

"One more thing, Steven. Could you please ask Chef LaFollette to come see me before that first course?"

Training aside, Steven showed only minor surprise at the request. Mac had asked for the chef's choice dinner, so it wouldn't be too unusual for the guest to talk with the chef at the beginning of such a meal.

As he twirled the deep golden wine in his stemware and waited, Mac picked up on the subtle music playing from speakers hidden in the room. It sounded New Age and gentle, like the burble of a small waterfall in the background. It fit the calming blue of the walls and the greenery surrounding the room, designed to relax the guest and invite them to linger.

He wasn't necessarily feeling relaxed yet himself though. He waited on edge to see what she would do with his summons. Still at a loss about why she hadn't tried to reach him, he hoped that this approach would give them time to talk. And he could ask why she was avoiding him.

Mac felt Madeleine first rather than heard her. A warm rush settled in his neck and ran down his spine, and if he'd had any thoughts of immediately moving from his seat, it would have been impossible. It was silent in the room except for the faint music, a lilting songstress now singing in a tone too low to be understood.

He picked out her faint reflection mirrored in the window, but for whatever reason, she hadn't moved from the doorway. Setting his napkin aside with deliberate care, he unfolded his legs and stood slowly, waiting until he was completely upright before turning towards the door.

She was framed by the darkness beyond, her chef's coat standing out so white against that backdrop that it appeared to shimmer. Her blonde mane was pulled back in a chignon, and her face was neutral and composed.

Damn her for turning him inside out and standing there unruffled. She wasn't the award-winning actor in the room – he was.

"Chef, thank you for joining me." He held out a hand to her, palm up and waiting. She frowned slightly and ignored it, moving to stand instead behind the chair set at an angle to his and resting her hands lightly on the back.

"Director, thank you for joining us at Roxy's tonight. I know you'll enjoy an excellent meal."

Game playing, he thought. He didn't want to resort to that, but she seemed to be unchallenged by his presence. "Won't you sit down, Madeleine? I've looked forward to your company for dinner. Ever since I got back into town over a week ago in fact."

Her frown deepened and she shook her head negatively. "I have a kitchen to run and many guests to serve. But I'm sure that you'll be pleased with my selections for you."

At a stalemate, Mac stood beside his chair and waited for her to indicate what she planned to do. She appeared to be ready to wait him out no matter how long it took.

Finally, she broke the silence. "Mac, I have to get back to the kitchen. Is there something specific you need from me?" She was already walking towards the doorway.

He pulled his chair out to turn it and face her, and sat down with every intention of holding her there as long as he could. She waited in the door now, her impatience evident in the slight tap if her toe and the cross of her arms.

"I can't stop thinking about it." He watched her from under hooded eyes, hoping for a reaction. He wasn't disappointed when her fidgeting increased.

"About what?" She bit her lip, then made an effort to resume her previous composed expression, leaning against the doorjamb in a pose that passed for relaxation if someone didn't look too closely.

He made his voice velvety soft and replied, "Those kisses, the first time a few weeks ago, and that last night we were together before I had to leave for LA. Those kisses, and so much more."

She stayed where she was, but he could see her sudden arousal in the press of her breasts against her chef's whites and the slight pant in her breathing. Her blue eyes darkened and became wider. Good, he was getting to her just as her mere presence rocked him in every cell.

A small smile played across her lips. She straightened and stalked towards him with measured steps, finally leaning over to put her hands on the arms of his chair and effectively trap him. He inhaled sharply, drinking in the subtle scent of her, as fresh and luscious as the meals she prepared.

Pulling closer, she stared him right in the eyes, and whispered, "I always was a great kisser."

His heart thudded painfully and he felt himself get hard as he drowned in her eyes. But before he could act, grab her and lay her across his lap as he took one of those famous kisses from her, she stood up and turned, smoothing her jacket as she walked, and spun at the last minute in the doorway.

"Please enjoy your dinner," she said as she disappeared into the darkness.

Chapter 33

"What do you mean he wants you to join him?" Alej's tone was a fierce whisper, probably overkill since they had the door closed to the small office off the kitchen. The view outside the window showed nothing strange. All of the chefs were working away at their duties and no one, absolutely no one, looked up.

"He wants me to join him in eating the food that I've selected for him. To be his guest for the evening, so to speak." Toying with her pen only proved how rattled this made her, since she boggled it more than once in the process.

Still, it had been highly satisfying to see the shocked and aroused expression on Mac's face when she'd leaned in to him with her bold statement. She'd been close enough to see his pupils dilate to pitch black. He didn't need to know those kisses had only been that great when she was with him.

"Are you going to do it?" Alej was suddenly still, and while his voice remained quiet, he was searching her face much too closely for her comfort.

"No, of course not!" She threw the pen down and rose out of the chair abruptly. "I don't have the time, and I don't have the inclination. After all, it's not like what happened –" She froze.

Alej leaned back and looked up at her. "What happened? Did something happen? When did something happen?" His sharp questions weren't going to be satisfied with a brush-off, Roxy realized.

"Way back when, years ago." Sinking back into her chair, Roxy examined the bulletin board on the wall beside her desk with desperate interest.

"Years ago? He's only been in town for a couple of months." He broke off with a frown, before demanding, "Is he the one?"

She shifted to move papers around on her desk.

"Roxy, was he the man you were running away from in San Francisco?"

When she continued to stare at the desktop, Alej sighed. Sympathy coated his words. "You know that you're stronger now. You're a different woman."

She nodded, unwilling to trust her voice.

"What happened, Roxy? You aren't falling for him again after everything that happened before, are you? I know you're spending a lot of time with him, but..." Alej shrugged his shoulders and waited.

"Damnit no, I am so not falling for him again, really, I'm not." She rarely swore out loud, but she opened her mouth to spew out a good long string to keep Alej quiet. Then she fell silent, her mouth agape, thinking about the night of passion and the dinner of caring that Mac had treated her to before his LA trip. Gulping, she added instead, "I'm just, ah, enjoying his company right now."

Her chef snorted and rose out of the chair, uncharacteristic seriousness on his features. Turning to stare at the kitchen and the workers moving about their tasks, he finally responded.

"Be careful, Rox. Be very, very careful."

*****

Mac thoroughly enjoyed the first course, a delicate soup made with fresh heirloom tomatoes and garlic that was smooth and airy. The single slice of avocado on top enhanced the flavors. He sipped the last of his white wine and thought that the evening would be damn perfect if Madeleine would take a seat next to him.

But would she? Or would she see this as the ultimate challenge, leaving him here on his own for however long he took to eat?

Dusk was falling outside, and flickering torches and lamps glowed on the patio, giving everything a festive party light. Some of the tables had turned, and a very few were standing vacant, waiting for their next round of guests. Mac suspected the restaurant would be going strong for a while yet.

Steven stood in the doorway, bearing a tray with small plates on it. The sampler of appetizers made his mouth water, and Mac pulled the wine list towards him to choose another glass.

"Ah, Mr. Smythe, if you wouldn't mind, Chef would like to make the wine selections for you." He paused, looking a little confused with what he was supposed to say next. "She says that she knows what you like."

Mac smiled and eased back in his chair. It would be better, much better, if she was sitting here with him. But since she was making all of these choices for him, he was on her mind no matter what. That thought gave him a small sense of victory.

Setting the tray down out of view, Steven left the room again, returning only moments later with a bottle of rose wine that he set about opening with practiced ease.

"And how did you like that soup, sir? The vegetables all come from our own gardens, except for the avocado of course. But I would bet you can get homegrown avocados where you're from, right sir?"

Mac had no idea where any avocados he ate in LA came from. He never thought about the source of his food, eating with occasional appreciation and more often mindlessness. It was only here, under Roxy's tutelage, that he was beginning to think he'd been missing out on many things for a long time.

Steven moved to a sideboard and selected a wine glass, polishing it with a brief swipe to make sure it was completely dust-free before setting it on the table. Then he placed both cork and glass next to Mac's hand and poured a short taste for approval.

Swirling and appreciating the warm vibrant color, Mac took a sniff and a sip and pronounced it excellent. In fact, the strawberry tart finish had him reaching for the bottle to examine the label more closely, digging his reading glasses out of his pocket for the very fine print.

He missed the waiter's movement behind him, only looking up when the man placed two serving plates in the center of the table. Each bore a different style of appetizer, and each looked fresh and wholesome and completely mouth-watering. Steven came back with two more servers of different varieties. And on his final trip, he placed a small plate in front of Mac and another at the empty space next to him, along with a wine glass.

Cocking his eyebrow at the young man over the top of his glasses, Mac noted that the waiter wasn't looking at him. Instead, he was standing, wine bottle in hand, and facing attentively towards the door.

As if on cue, Madeleine breezed into the room at a studied pace, looked over the table, and nodded her approval to Steven. She didn't meet Mac's gaze as she dropped gracefully into the adjacent chair, and he slowly lowered his reading glasses and played with the temple, working himself up to a helicopter whirl of plastic as she slowly sipped the wine Steven poured and nodded affirmatively once again.

The waiter made himself scarce, and she sat back, looking out the window to the darkening patio and the dimmer view of the garden. The music had now changed to a passionate male voice singing something about loss and remembrance.

Got ya beat, buddy, Mac thought as he appraised her across the table. They seemed to spend a lot of time waiting for the other to blink first, and the idea made him smile. In some ways, this was much more fun than they'd had when they were young and impetuous and unable to keep their hands off each other.

Sipping slowly, Madeleine leaned forward and finally turned to him, her gaze steady and uncompromising, giving nothing away about her thoughts. Mac found himself leaning forward as well, his body craving a closer connection to hers even now. They stared at one another as the song suddenly ended.

She took another sip of wine, and placed the glass carefully on the table in a precise position. Wetting her lips with the tip of her tongue, she frowned at his sudden intake of breath.

He was as randy as a high school kid on the promise of getting to advance to another base. Mac chided himself on his complete and total lack of control. Roxy's mouth opened in a small oh of understanding, and he thought he heard her breath quicken as well. It was hard to tell over the increased beats of his own racing heart.

Finally, she leaned back and said, "So, Mac, where were we?"

Chapter 34

"Really, he said that to you? What did he think, you were going to let him in the kitchen so that he could make his mother's special red sauce?" Mac laughed at the punch line of Roxy's story about a well-known screenwriter who had paid a visit to her restaurant, then insisted that he could make better marinara sauce than hers and challenged her to a throw down on the spot.

"Yeah, well I agreed that his mother's sauce, being as she is Italian, was probably as authentic as they come, but I wasn't claiming to make her red sauce." She grinned, relaxing back in her chair with a deep bowl of red wine in one hand and the other casually set on the arm of her chair, her fingers a hair's breath away from Mac's.

God, how she wanted to touch him. She longed to trace the contours of tendons and sparse hairs on the backs of his hands, then turn over his palms and continue her exploration of his fingers. And eventually, she'd lace her fingers with his and hold on tight, just as she used to do so long ago.

The kitchen had run itself for the rest of the evening. Alej came in only once, and that was to check on how they were enjoying the dishes she'd mapped out before she'd boldly decided to take Mac up on his challenge. Because it was a challenge to see if she could stay in the same room with him without jumping his bones. She needed to get him out of her system, once and for all.

He took the need to fight her craving out of her hands by linking his fingers with hers. He still toyed with the reading glasses with the other occasionally, an appropriate prop for him. He'd put them away once, only taking them out again to read the label on yet another wine selection.

Roxy shivered, thinking that it would be best to get the focus off her and on to him, if she was going to avoid turning into a melted puddle at his feet. He was so easy to talk to, and he made it simple to bask in the glow of his appreciation.

"But Mac, it isn't like you've been sitting idle. How many movies was it last year, three? And you directed one of those as well, right? And how many awards were you nominated for, and how many did you win? I've lost track."

He chuckled, dipping his head in an aw-shucks movement. His smile was a different story, though, and she sensed that her notice of what he had been doing was something that pleased him greatly.

Putting down the glasses to take a sip of his wine, he focused on swirling the maroon liquid in its bowl for a time. "My successes and my too-frequent near-misses or failures have been chronicled widely in the Hollywood press. In fact, with every new release, the media feels compelled to take out and examine each failure in excruciating detail. 'Will he be able to pull this one off, or will it be another...' and then they fill in the name of a big flop of mine. They expect me to fail."

He paused and looked directly into her eyes. "That's why it has been so important to me to feel better again. I couldn't have gone on for much longer hiding my weaknesses, and thanks to you, I don't think that will be a problem anymore."

Her toes curled, she was sure of it. The warmth in his eyes made her stomach turn to molten marshmallow, the kind that melted on your tongue after you've scorched it in a hot flame.

"But your story is much more interesting and not written to death about. And I want to know all about it, every little detail. Now you have all of this success, the restaurant and store, the catering, a worldwide following." He paused and his face grew serious. "I'm so proud of you.

But tell me," he added, leaning forward to prop his chin in a hand, "how did Madeleine become Roxy?"

Restless despite his praise, Roxy fidgeted in her chair and looked away from his intent stare. He was sincerely proud, she could see that. But his eyes were dark and probing as he questioned her. Did he want to hear about the years of struggles, when all she could see when she closed her eyes at night was his face? That required a level of trust they no longer had.

"You're right, I've been able to do a lot. It took hard work, as it still does. I have a great staff, wonderful friends, and a community that supports us. I'm in exactly the right place in my life, exactly where I'm supposed to be."

He waited, continuing to examine her face. She felt a trace of a blush creep up her cheeks. He seemed determined to wait her out.

Deciding that honesty was the easiest, she met his direct gaze with a stare of her own. "When we went our separate ways in San Francisco, I went to work as a kitchen grunt. In Paush's as a matter of fact. The year plus I spent there was a lesson in perseverance. But that's where I met Alej."

His expression sharpened on the name. If she didn't believe differently, she'd say he was jealous.

"Where did the nickname Roxy come from?"

She smiled at the memory. "Alej was into British rock bands at the time. He liked to play music from the band Roxy while we prepped proteins. One day, he started calling me Roxy. And since Chef Bart liked to sneer 'Madeleine' at every turn, I found I liked Roxy a whole lot better."

She didn't share that the other voice, his voice, running through her brain as it chanted her birth name like a caress, made it impossible for her to heal. Roxy was born out of self-defense, her new identity a shield against her past.

It was his turn to fidget now, and he looked away, staring outside to the patio where the number of patrons had dwindled to a handful at this late hour. The lighting inside their dining room was low as well, and the music had been turned up a couple of ticks so that they could now hear the words. 'The Best is Yet to Come' crooned Frank Sinatra.

He dropped her hand abruptly and stood up, walking to the window and leaning against its frame on one hand, the other sitting at his hip and giving her a great view of his backside in snug tailored slacks. The views had improved in so many ways over the past few weeks, and with a flush, she remembered how his butt felt under her hands, firm and muscled once again.

If she took him to bed, could she ever get him out of her system? He was in almost every waking moment again, in unexpected surges of memories so strong, she forgot what she was saying in mid-sentence. She suspected – no, she knew – that setting him out of her mind would be so much harder now than it had been the last time, and back then it had taken her years to adjust.

"You live here now, upstairs, right?"

She nodded, then realized he couldn't see her. "Yes, it's convenient, and there's plenty of space." She paused, then added, "I'm close to work, which I love, and the space suits me."

Looking away from him, captivated for the moment by the view on the patio, she swirled the Malbec remaining in her glass and wondered if she had the courage. Could she enjoy him one last time and let him go?

Still standing facing away from her, he said into the quiet, "Have you ever thought that if we hadn't fallen apart way back when, neither one of us would be where we are today, at pinnacles in our chosen professions?"

She gulped. Yes, she had thought about it often since she'd first heard that he would be directing this movie, the one she had already contracted to support with her catering. But he didn't know what it had cost her in the beginning, the first years in particular. Would they have stayed together if he hadn't sent her away?

*****

He'd thought about the twists and turns of his life often over the years, and always below the surface, there were thoughts of Madeleine and their time together. What if she hadn't left? Would he have moved up the Hollywood ladder faster, with her providing an emotional rudder for his existence? The crazy years, the ones where he was drinking too much and partying too hard and working too lazily would have been replaced by... what?

Still, he was so proud of everything she'd achieved, and it sounded like it had taken every bit of her time over the years to accomplish it. Yes, he was proud of her successes, but the disappointment lingered. What would the years have been like if they'd been together? Would they have kids now? Would he be writing and directing all the time, instead of spending half of his time still acting to maintain his street cred? Would 'Roxy' even exist, or would she still be Madeleine?

He only knew for certain that he needed to connect with her on a deeper level, taking them both to a place where she could see how much she meant to him, more today than ever before. Then they could decide if they had a future. What that future would hold, he wasn't sure, but he needed to try.

She still hadn't explained why she'd walked out on him. Mac wanted more than anything to be part of Roxy's life today, to understand how Madeleine turned into Roxy and let the past go so completely without a word or a trace. A brief simmer of discomfort moved through him, resentment that she could leave behind everything they'd had together so easily bubbling to the surface once more.

He cleared his throat, watching her ghostly reflection in the mirroring of the darkened window. Dessert was yet to come, but he was impatient. The kitchen could store it. Maybe they would want it later.

Staying where he was and watching her image closely in the glass to read her emotions, he said, "Show me your home, Madeleine. Show me where you're living out your dreams. I need to see you there."

Chapter 35

Alej had frowned at her request to package up the dessert selections so that they could take them upstairs. The plates were set in containers well sealed with cling wrap, and she'd waved off her chef's words when he tried to reason with her.

"Are you sure this is a good idea?" No, she wasn't sure, but she stared at him sternly until he'd shrugged and sighed, giving her a pat on the back. "I'll be around when you need me."

Selecting a dessert wine to compliment the last course, she'd taken off her chef's coat and left it in the laundry bin off the kitchen. Rejoining Mac in the dining room, she nodded towards the plates and wordlessly he picked them up. Then she turned the lights lower and led the way up the front stairs.

It was too dark to see up here unless you knew the layout, so she stopped when he was safely on the landing. As she turned towards the light switch, Mac lunged in with unerring precision and kissed her with a passion that left her shaking. Impatience radiated from him and lit the same feelings in her.

Hand still outstretched for the lights, she almost boggled the wine. His juggling of the plates was just shy of a disaster.

She giggled against his mouth, realizing how silly this was. They were two grown adults, experienced in the world, and in many ways, they were more clumsy and awkward than they had been years ago. The idea made her laugh until tears started down her face.

Mac frowned at her in the still-dim light. "What? What's so funny? Why are you crying?"

She waved at him with the bottle, unable to explain. He frowned at her, finally locating a table for the plates he held. Depositing them with a clatter, he rescued the wine bottle from her fingers before it crashed to the floor.

"I think you've lost it." He grabbed her as she bent over, holding her belly and crowing away, and dragged her up against his body.

She stilled instantly, shocked by his hard arousal. Gulping to steady herself, she reached out and hit the light switch, flooding the room with warm glows from wall sconces. His gaze pinned her with both humor and passion, a heady combination when what she wanted to do most was drag him off to her bedroom. When his lips locked on hers, she forgot why she thought any of this was funny.

His mouth nipped from her lips to her jaw before tracing the tip of his tongue to the pulse pounding on the side of her neck. Lingering there, he waited a few beats, then set her apart from him and adjusted his slacks. She glanced down and away, amazed again that she could have this effect on him.

Of course, her nipples were straining and a pool of heat had settled between her legs. Oh yeah, he wasn't the only one affected.

Taking a deep breath, Mac glanced around the room, walking slowly to the bookcases that held her collection of vintage and modern cookbooks. He pulled out one and paged through it, replaced it and tried another. Then he moved around the room, examining the photos she had used to decorate her space. There was Seattle, Portland, Flynn's Crossing, and oh yes, San Francisco.

Her heart throbbed and she could hear her own blood swirl through cavities too narrow to contain it. It was painful to watch him in her space. She would never be able to look at it in the same way. Turning again, he walked towards the open kitchen and ran a hand over the counter space as he stopped in front of her industrial stove. It was overkill for a home, but she loved it anyway. The hand he ran over its shiny chrome made her shake. It felt like a caress on her skin.

"It's you," his voice almost a whisper. "It is all so very much you." He finally met her gaze again, the passion in his eyes replaced by torture. "But why, Madeleine? Tell me why?"

Why? Why what? Why had she built her life as she had? Because she thought she was going to build a life with him, but when that didn't happen, when he left her, she had to build one for herself. And she'd done a damn good job of it too.

Her emotions were shifting so quickly she was struggling to stay sane. She shrugged as a simmer of irritation radiated through her and held his eyes. "Because I had to, that's why. After everything that happened, I needed to move on."

He paced towards her then, the hammering of his shoes on the wood floor telling her how annoyed this made him. The temperature of his mood shifted from seductive to incensed, and she could feel the sharp change.

He had no right to be angry. If anyone did, it was her.

"Was moving on that easy for you?" His hands were gripping her upper arms, shaking her with the intensity of his words, even as he held her still. He pushed his face mere inches from hers and ground out, "Was it so damned simple?"

Roxy's anger rose a few notches until she was boiling with it. "Simple? Simple?" She heard the scream in her voice even if she didn't raise it. Years in the kitchen had taught her the value of a low-pitched rant. "It was never fucking simple!"

Her body was vibrating with unspent rage, held in check too long against the one target now in front of her. The warm welling passion that lit her up a few minutes ago was gone. Her heady laughter had drained away completely. Wrenching out of his hands, she stalked to the bedroom and slammed the door, cursing the lack of a lock to keep him out. He crashed it open a scant second later and loomed in the doorway, as agitated as she was in an equally enraged stance.

A few weeks ago, his chest had seemed hollow and concave, a shadow of his former self. His shoulders, once so strong that she swore she could walk across their muscles, had sagged. And the eyes that had enjoyed the light of life had been haunted.

Not anymore.

"What the hell does this mean, Roxy? It was you –"

"No, it was you!" She shook a finger in his face. "You started all of this with your careless attitude."

A predatory gaze darkened his features further, and Roxy knew at once that she'd gone too far.

"Well I guess if I started it, I'd better finish it," he ground out, and he yanked her into his arms so fast it felt like whiplash.

She'd once seen a grease fire take off on a commercial range in a Portland restaurant. It only took a nanosecond for it to flash from spark to full ignition, and an instant more to engulf the wall and hood before automatic sprinklers kicked in. This, she thought, was moving so much faster.

Mac held her arms at her elbows in a painful grip and lifted her until only her toes were left to balance her weight on the floor. His eyes burning into hers, he took her lips in a bruising kiss leaving her with no doubt that the fire had in fact passed the point of easy containment.

*****

Mac sensed the change in her, felt her bones melt under his hands and her body go pliant, wilting into him. She accepted the onslaught of his mouth on hers without opposition. Her hands, trapped by his vice grip on her elbows, fluttered and went still.

He felt his own anger drain away, the heady suction of it leaving his body in the dark room. In its place, a buzz not unlike the shiver that came with the first sip of Scotch or fine wine shook him. He felt his own muscles weaken in response.

He needed to put an end to this rollercoaster of emotions, though he wasn't sure how he could do it. One minute, Madeleine delighted him, and the next, she tore his guts to pieces and left them bleeding on the floor. He wanted her more than he ever remembered wanting any woman in his life. Hell, he wanted her more than anything, period.

His hands shook as he loosened his grip and she swayed to the side, catching herself at the last moment even as he reached for her again. Her eyes blinked open and stared, shock registering first, replaced slowly by resolution. A hint of sadness danced across her features and she turned away from him.

"Madeleine, I don't know what to say. I don't understand what happens. It's like we burn each other up."

He wanted to make this right, but he didn't have a clue what right would look like. In fact, he sensed that anything he did now would probably be wrong, and going on gut instinct, he reached out and wrapped his arms around her, pulling her back against him until he could rock her in his arms. He put a soft kiss on her head and inhaled the herbal scent of her hair, transported to some pine-encircled meadow with tall waving grasses and damp mosses.

It was that scene set in his mind, warm sunshine on soft skin and her long blonde hair wrapped around him that spurred him to move. Keeping his arms around her, he turned and seated them both on the bed. She nestled into his shoulder, her arms coming around him even as he caressed her back with slow hands.

Trapped in his vision of her sunlit and smiling at him, his hands found the bottom of her shirt and his fingers played with the bare skin hidden by it. Roxy didn't lift her head, but in her sudden stillness, he knew she felt the difference. He wondered if she would push his away once again.

Putting a finger under her chin to raise it, he kissed her still-closed eyes, and he felt a shudder move through her. He teased her lips with his own until she sighed and parted, her tongue darting out to meet his and her arms tightening around his neck.

Mac realized he could sit like this and explore her mouth alone for hours, though the temptation of peeling away the layers between them and pressing skin to skin was strong. Stronger, though, was the wonder of having this successful and powerful woman wrapping herself around him every bit at tightly as he held her. He shivered at how completely she moved him.

She broke the kiss and leaned away from him, his hands still on her back so that he could snatch her quickly if she made a move for the door. Instead though, she traced his features with her capable fingers, covering his lips last. Finally, she looked into his eyes.

"Mac, are you sure?"

*****

The meadowlark knew when the sky was lightening. It sang for her every summer morning in the tree outside her bedroom window. Four notes down the scale, a pause, and two tones up. What it didn't know was that it was Sunday, and Roxy didn't have to get up early today.

The tropical scent of the old mimosa's blooms greeted her next. She felt like she was coming up from deep in a wonderful dream, and the fragrance was somehow part of the mystery and happiness she couldn't yet identify. Her limbs felt heavy, any effort to lift them meeting weighty resistance. It was like she was being held, and held tightly.

That sensation got her opening her eyes fast, and she registered the heavy arm around her waist, a hand resting protectively on her breast. A long hairy leg was thrown over her own to pin her to him, and at her back, his heart beat its reassuring rhythm even as he snored lightly in her ear.

Mac. Mac in her bed. Mac and her in every conceivable position throughout the night, with barely any sleep in between.

God, what had she done?

In the mirror against the far wall, she could see their reflection in the early dawn light. His face was relaxed, and he looked as young as he had when they'd first met. The lines and circles of too many years in between were hidden by the shadows.

And her? Her eyes were wide and frightened, and she knew why.

There was no way she was going to forget this past night, not if she lived to be over a hundred.

He'd smiled when she'd asked her question last night. He never said he was sure. He showed her.

He undressed her slowly, taking time for deliberate, sensual kisses and lips that traced the skin exposed. Scars were examined closely and touched with tenderness.

Fingers rubbed tense muscles, easing into erotic massages meant to please.

The need to touch him, to consume him, became overwhelming, and her hands were eager when they reached for his shirt, for his belt, for the zipper on his slacks. Years fell away, and even the lines and shadows added with long years of hard living didn't alter his appeal. He was still the only man who ever made her feel treasured and complete.

When he entered her the first time, they'd both smiled widely and the race was on. She laughed as she rolled him once, then he crowed his triumph when he got her underneath him again. She cried uncle first, but then she got to cry out again and again, and shaking with spent passion, he finally conceded that maybe she had him beat on that round.

She woke in the wee hours of the morning, wondering why, when it was still so perfect between them, they had fallen apart years ago. Why had he left her then? What had that woman said, she was there to clean up his mistakes? Did a mistake feel like this?

Waking him with fingers caressing the long length of him, she stared down at his handsome face, all traces of his pain wiped away. His eyes were dark and intent on hers in the single small light they left on. The crinkle of the condom foil had him grinning. She rose over him, taking him into her in one fast decent that had them both crying out. Their hands and eyes locked, they'd moved slowly until they quivered and exploded together and fell into a panting heap, arms pulled tight, communicating their shared amazement without saying a word.

And not long ago, she'd felt his mouth traveling down her body, giving each cell along the way pleasure. When she'd returned the favor, his hands had locked in her hair and he'd mumbled her name, 'Madeleine', until she could have wept with the power of it.

What the hell was she going to do? Even now, she felt hard throbbing nestled against her bottom, and she almost laughed out loud thinking about his statement sometime during the night.

"It's been years since I've pulled an all-nighter like this. I didn't think I had it in me anymore, even for one round. You and your magic menus, you've cured me." Then he'd grabbed her and silenced any words she thought to share with deep disturbing kisses.

Her last thought before losing her mind was that she was damn glad she knew how to cook.

At some point in her new morning ponderings, her eyes drifted shut. She realized that Mac was no longer snoring behind her, and she opened her eyes to find him staring solemnly at her in the rosy light of early sunshine on the shades.

Then he rolled her over to face him, and his face lit with that killer smile.

Chapter 36

Dessert was even better as breakfast. Even better when eaten in minimal clothing sitting across from a beautiful woman you'd made love with all night long. Mac smiled at the idea, even as he stroked his foot against Madeleine's bare leg next to his at the kitchen island.

"I might have to think about offering some version of this for a breakfast croissant or something," she said, and he couldn't help himself, her intense expression was so damned cute that he had to lean over and bite her neck.

"Hey! Ow, you monster! I can't believe you can even move after last night."

Oh yeah, he could move all right. Right now, he wanted to move closer to Madeleine, take her in his arms, and tell her that whatever had happened between them in the past, this was time for a new beginning. Clean slate, no hard feelings, no excuses. Just them, together, moving forward.

He picked up his fork instead, loaded with whatever this creamy concoction was, and fed it to her. "What will you call it? Sexy Sunrise?" He ducked when she'd tried to swat him, but she was smiling with her mouth full of last night's dessert and some had gotten on the side of her lips. He leaned forward to lick it off, and he felt a shot of adrenalin-laced desire spear through him and settle in his towel-wrapped lap.

God, what she did to him. It wasn't only her body, though he'd appreciated the fact that the years had been very kind to her, much kinder than they'd been to him. It wasn't only her savvy success and what she'd built for herself.

Most of all, it was the caring that she let few people see. Roxy probably didn't even see it herself, the times when she set aside her own needs or desires to help someone else. It was in the way she mentored her staff, herding them along like little birds until they were ready to fly the nest. Then if they huddled, afraid to fly, she'd give them a good swift kick, and later on, each one would thank her for it.

Back years ago, there was a hint of the woman she would become at the edges. The confidence, the belief that she could do incredible things, the power that came with that success, all came later, and he'd love to listen to every story she had about the intervening years.

The one thing he still wanted to know, though, was why she'd left him. She'd told him then that she loved him, and he'd made the same pledge to her. They were going to have long weeks to explore each other and their feelings and figure out where life took them next.

But he'd returned to his hotel suite in San Francisco, still puzzled by the brief exchange with his agent, to find her gone.

Martha had been sitting primly in the living room of the suite, hands folded in her lap and lips pursed. Mac hadn't questioned her presence, other than to say she should leave and return in a few hours to take them to the airport. Then he'd gone into the bedroom.

No Madeleine in his bed, not in the shower, and not in the suite. And her suitcase and all of her things were gone.

"What do you mean, she left?" He'd raged at Martha, pacing the width of the room until he stopped threateningly in front of the older woman.

"I don't know, Mac, I just don't know. She asked me, last night at the wrap party, to please make sure you were out of the suite for a while early today. She almost begged me, in tears, poor girl. So I paged you and said that your agent needed to talk with you, and I called him and said you wanted to talk to him before you left." Martha looked distressed.

"You lured me out of the room so that she could leave, is that it?" He wanted to throttle her.

"Well, Mac, she'd always seemed, I don't know, a little flighty, you know? Like maybe the movie business was over her head and too much for her. So I guess she needed to leave." She rose, and began straightening the room, settling things in place that he'd upended in his pacing.

"Did she leave anything, a note, a message?" He couldn't understand how Madeleine could leave like that, one minute telling him she loved him, and the next, gone. Poof.

Martha shook her head sadly.

He pulled away from the recollection. It did him no good to dwell in the past. If she'd disappeared before, she might do it again.

No, wait, that was asinine. She had businesses to run, a wide circle of tight friendships, commitments. Even if she ran away from him, she couldn't leave all of this behind too.

Madeleine was staring at him with concern on her face. "Mac, what is it?"

He opened his mouth to ask her. It was on the tip of his tongue. He wanted to know, to understand, so that the past would quit haunting him and he could concentrate on their future.

Her cell phone rang, followed in quick succession by a landline sitting on the corner of the kitchen counter. One line, then two ringing and lighting up the face. Roxy looked between the three rings and frowned.

"What the hell?" She picked up the cordless receiver on the landline and punched a key. "Yes?"

Listening, the frown rapidly turned to worry, followed quickly by a distancing determination. "Okay, alert the rest of the crew. If you can't find them, leave messages and assign someone to keep trying them. I'll be in the kitchen in five."

She slammed the phone down, and immediately, the second landline and the cell became quiet as well.

"What's wrong?" He stood to move towards her, ready to offer whatever support and comfort he could.

"Cal Fire called. There's a blaze, a big one, about twenty-five miles from here up in the canyon. They need us to move."

He frowned at her. "Move? Twenty-five miles is a long distance away. Why do you have to evacuate?"

She looked at him then as if he'd grown a second head. Two heartbeats later, she shook her head. "Not evacuate. Move in. We're catering for the firefighters, and it looks like it's going to be a long one."

Chapter 37

"We can take the interns, and that leaves the regulars to do the work, which they can manage without us, or we take some of them off their regular stations and leave the interns, which means one of us needs to stay." Alej was standing in jeans and a t-shirt, arms crossed and more imposing than he would be in his regular chef's whites. A steady stream of staff was flowing into the kitchen by now.

Roxy stared around at the sleepy faces. Either they were scheduled to work later today, and they were dressed for work, or they were called in from a day off and were in civvies. Most carried expressions of mixed excitement. Something out of the ordinary did a lot for people's energy levels.

"We take the interns with us, along with two of the store kitchen staff. We can handle the rig with that." She looked back at the staff and interns, picking out two of her most senior people. "You'll be running the restaurant, Patrick, and Sarah, the store kitchen. Any problems, work them out. And if you really can't solve 'em, call me on the cell. I hope we'll have reception, but if not, I'll make arrangements to use a Cal Fire radio and get you a set here as well."

She turned to the mixed faces of her interns. Angel was almost popping out of his sneakers in agitation, though he didn't seem to be jazzed by the prospect of the field trip.

"Ah, Chef? Maybe I should stay here, ya know? I can do the work of at least three people, after all, and that would free up more of the others to help you..."

"Angel, for once, just once, please do as I ask without a discussion, okay?" She glared at him, and he skipped from foot to foot with more anxiety. His face was pale under his usual dark complexion, but he nodded.

Roxy let her gaze travel over the rest of the interns, waiting for other comments. With her shoulders thrown back, Ticia was working on a show of bravado, and Bob stood in an at-ease parade stance, emotions hidden except for the gleam in his eyes. Jeannine, pleasantly plump in what appeared to be the first maternity ware she'd found, was silent and serious.

She frowned at Jeannine. In the rush, she'd forgotten about the baby, the one who was growing by perceptible degrees each day and probably wouldn't benefit from the smoke.

"Jeannine, you'll stay here and work the restaurant. With you on the grill, Patrick will have strong support."

The woman flashed a frown, opening her mouth to argue, then realized her hands were resting on her own belly. Her jaw clamped shut on a quick nod of understanding. Roxy let go an inward sigh, realizing that she didn't want to have to argue about this too. Tagging three other chefs to join the fire crew, she dismissed the rest with a wave.

"Get some gear together, people. Jeans, boots if you have them. Jackets, because it will get cold at night. We'll be cooking around the clock and in shifts, so you have to be ready for whatever conditions we find up there. Meet us back here in an hour."

The chorus of 'yes Chef' pleased her.

She turned to head up the stairs to load her own gear, and ran straight into Mac standing behind her. He steadied her and smiled.

"You are one great director, you know that?" He swooped in to give her a kiss, and she started, afraid that someone would see. "It's incredible sexy," he added.

She spun again, in time to see Alej give her a studied and almost imperceptible nod and Bob and Ticia exchange questioning glances before they ducked out the kitchen's back door. Great, something else to deal with now on top of the fire duty.

It was time to set some boundaries. Their night together had settled nothing, only adding more fuel to the fire between them. She would call this a recipe for disaster. He was leaving. She had a job to do. And her life was here.

"Mac, not now, please?" She took the stairs two at a time, trying to plan what they would need to augment the catering truck's stores while simultaneously creating a packing list for her clothes.

He followed her step for step up the stairs and when she would have continued to the bedroom, he grabbed her arm and pulled her around to face him.

"Madeleine, I get it. You have work to do. But you have to know that last night, this morning, well, it meant everything to me." His eyes were pleading, confusing her when she could least afford it.

She shook off his hand and stepped back a pace. "You don't understand. I have to pack. I have to go. I have a fire kitchen to run and I don't know how long I'll be gone."

She swallowed thickly, suddenly aware that it could be at least a couple of weeks until she returned.

The movie was due to wrap on location in two weeks, maybe less. She coughed to mask her sudden gasp of realization. Two weeks, and he'd be gone again.

Mac was frowning on her, standing hands on hips in his dress slacks and shirt left untucked, filling the gap at the top of the stairs. It was an incredibly tempting pose, all suave and worldly he-man out to save the day. "So?"

She pulled her hair into a ponytail and began the quick ritual of tying that into a bun to mask her frustration as she backed into the bedroom. "I won't be here. I won't be available to be your personal chef. And the catering truck won't be here either."

Knowledge dawned on his face, and she breathed a sigh of relief that the contractual obligations, at least, he got.

"No problem. We'll find another way to get the crew fed, though it won't be as good as Roxy's." He grinned at her. "And it won't be the chef part of the personal that I'll be missing most."

God, why was he so damn desirable just when she needed to make a quick exit? Of course, then he'd be making his own quick exit too.

Turning, she pulled out sweatshirts and jeans, dumping them on the rumpled bed. She only paused a moment when the combined scents of their overheated bodies throughout the night came to her in a wave.

"You'll be careful?" He'd come to stand right behind her, folding and stacking the clothes she threw on the covers. When she yanked a duffle out from under the bed, he gently placed the neat piles inside.

She snorted. "Of course I'll be safe. There hasn't been a crew base overrun in, god, I don't know how many years. We're not on the front line. This is where the crews come to rest, not fight the fires."

He didn't respond, and she swiveled around to find him staring at her with an unreadable expression on his face. It made her stop in her hasty pillorying of her dresser drawers for socks and underwear.

Mac stepped forward and without a word, folded her into his arms, clothes and all. He put his chin on her head and rocked her gently back and forth. They stood that way for minutes, and Roxy felt the tandem itch of time standing still in his arms, and passing too quickly for her.

Finally, he pulled back and stared into her face again. Gently, oh so gently, he feathered a kiss across her lips.

"Be safe out there, Madeleine. Be very, very safe."

*****

He watched with the others in Sunday's early smoke-smudged sunlight as the catering rig and assorted other vehicles convoyed out of the restaurant's parking lot, led by a California Highway Patrol's escort with lights flashing. Another cop brought up the rear, and quickly, they all accelerated and were out of sight.

"Mr. Smythe? Would you like some breakfast to go? Chef said to tell you it's on the house." Patrick stood next to him and waited for his response.

On the house. Only a couple of hours ago, they were wrapped in each other's warmth, holding on tightly to the wonder of being together. At least he'd been holding on tightly. He'd never had a chance to ask Roxy what she thought.

He admired her commanding presence with her crews. She never raised her voice, never yelled, and yet everyone moved in double time, eager to please her. People stacked boxes in the catering truck's cold case, paper products went into other vehicles, and everyone was checked to make sure they had their knives and other assorted personal chef gear.

Doing his part on the line to move food and goods, Mac had a moment next to Roxy to ask, "Everyone's responsible for their own cooking gear?"

The look she gave him let him know what a dumb question that was. "A chef's knives are an extension of his or her body. I would no more pillage one of Alej's knives to use than he would one of mine. They're… personal."

He filed that away for future reference, so that he wouldn't accidentally pick one of hers up one day and engage the wrath of god, or in this case, Chef Roxy.

While she was inspecting the interns to make sure they had everything they would need, he'd found himself standing next to Alej. The man was paying no attention to him, intent instead on an examination of his own scuffed boots.

"Hey, Chef Alej?" Mac waited for Alej to respond to his query, and the man slowly lifted his eyes to meet Mac's gaze.

It shocked him to see how much anger and disappointment was in the stare. Malevolence in his movements, Alej stood straighter and crossed his arms in a gesture of defiance.

"Yes, Mr. Smythe?"

Mac wanted to lighten the mood. He never understood why, when the rest of the catering crew had warmed up to him, Alej never had. But that didn't matter now.

"Watch out for her, okay?"

Alej frowned at him, then they both turned to look at Roxy at the same time.

"Chef Roxy can take care of herself. She learned that a long time ago." Alej's gaze sharpened to a knife's point as he stared back at Mac. "She had to."

There was something more in Alej's piercing stare and heavy frown. He regarded Mac the same way he would something unsavory on the bottom of his heavy hiking boots, unclean and spoiled and definitely not good enough for Roxy's kitchen.

"I know she can. I am awed by everything she's done. Who would have thought that little Madeleine would grow up to be such an amazing woman?"

Mac returned to staring at her, her profile lit by the low sun and haze of smoke. The fire was now noticeable, with the early morning breeze off the mountains carrying the heavy stench of burning wood down the canyon and towards Flynn's Crossing. The air would be uncomfortable to breathe and the sky would be pink with haze, Mac knew.

He remembered the last big fires in LA, how the heavy ash had rained down a dozen miles away and the plume of smoke carried for a hundred miles. Everyone in Flynn's Crossing would be aware of the fire and edgy with the knowledge that some of their own people were fighting it.

"You never did give her enough credit, you know?" Alej's words surprised him, and he turned to find the man examining him with intense anger.

Mac was confused. Before this location shoot, he'd never met Alej. He didn't understand the animosity that the man carried for him.

"I don't know what you mean." Mac moved towards Roxy, and Alej stopped him with a hand on his arm.

"She has a job to do, man. Let her do it. You've messed with her head enough for now."

Mac looked pointedly at the hand restraining him and back up at Alej, but the man wasn't budging.

"You know nothing about how awesome she is, nothing at all. You just see the results. You don't know what it cost her after you split."

Mac frowned at him. "I know she had to work hard after we split up, but it was her own choice. It was what she wanted."

Alej dropped his hand and laughed loud enough to earn him a hard stare from Roxy herself standing thirty feet away. It was a highly unpleasant sound, one that smacked of rancor and old hurts. He gave a final harsh guffaw before shaking his head at Mac. The disgust on his face was clear.

"It was what you wanted, man, when you wanted. Roxy didn't get any say in the matter. Let's just say it took her a very long time to pick up the pieces."

With that, Alej turned to walk away, but Mac caught his shoulder and spun him around.

"What do you mean, she didn't get any say?" Alej shook him off and stepped back again.

"Don't you have to leave again, Mac? And this time, don't send anyone else to do your dirty work for you."

He shook his head, bewildered as he re-ran the conversation with Alej over in his head. He'd never gotten any further explanation of what the man meant because Roxy called for them to load up and hit the road.

Mac didn't want her leaving like this, with things unsaid between them. But she hadn't left him any time for words. She walked up to him and gave him an unguarded stare for a brief instant, pain and sadness on her features. Then she pulled his head down and found his lips with hers for a brutal kiss. At the end, it turned tender and gentle.

Before he could react, she stepped back, her face filled with regret.

"Goodbye, Mac," she whispered so quietly he could barely hear it.

She had turned before he could even get any words out, and she never looked back. Climbing into the rig, his last view of her was her blonde hair pulled in a ponytail through the back of her ball cap, an arm waving to her team out the window.

"Ah, Mr. Smythe? How about that breakfast now?"

Chapter 38

"I appreciate anything the downtown business association can do for us, Ms. Willowspring, Mr. Wolford."

Mac had taken on the responsibility of meeting with possible food suppliers in town. Barry and Martha volunteered to find other sources for catering, but it made him feel closer to Roxy if he did it himself.

Martha had been particularly unenthusiastic about it. "Really, Mac, you don't have the time to be working on this. You have the movie to finish. Let me handle the food issue. I'm sure I can find us another option, one better than Roxy's offered anyway."

He would puzzle over that remark later. Right now, he had Barry running around checking the lighting on the location sites they had planned to use around the area. The smoke from the fire continued to blow in their direction, and the sky and sun were not cooperating from a filming perspective.

And he kept Martha more than busy clearing schedules and extending crew contracts. After two extensions already, conflicts with other scheduled engagements were making holding on to people a dicey proposition.

Yeah, the name of the film definitely needed to be 'jinxed'.

The man across the table, the owner of a shop specializing in olive oils and the like, added, "Mr. Smythe, as the head of the business association, I can tell you that the merchants would love to work with you. We'll do the best we can. It might not be Roxy's catering quality, but it will definitely be good."

"Please, call me Mac. I can't tell you how much I appreciate you helping us out."

The woman sat back, her elegant features and the slice of white in her otherwise raven hair adding to the regal bearing. She examined him directly. "Call me Tess. This is Chase. If we're going to be working together, we don't need to stand on ceremony. And a good friend of Roxy's is a friend of mine."

This made Mac pause. Everywhere he went in town, he was treated to the same speculative glances. In some cases, it was more like a critical inspection. Sometimes he measured up, and in other cases, he had a feeling he did not.

"You understand, the association's first priority is supporting the fire crews." Tess looked up at him closely. "That means Roxy gets first dibs on everything, and I mean everything around here."

Mac nodded. He wanted her to have whatever she needed. He wanted her to be safe.

Most of all, he wanted the damn fire out so that she could return and they could settle things.

"I agree. I'm not sure what's going to happen with the movie right now anyway." He glanced out the window of the flower shop, and Tess and Chase turned to stare out as well. The hazy red of the sky meant the smoke hadn't blown in any other direction, and people were coughing as they walked down Main Street.

Turning back, he said, "I may have to move the movie somewhere the smoke isn't an issue for shooting."

"That would be a shame, Mac. We've appreciated the opportunity to show off our little town in your film. It brings in business, much more than just your crew and all that you spend here locally. People come looking for the locations of a Mac Smythe movie." Tess grinned.

Mac had never considered the ramifications of this. He knew movies drew followings – just think of what happened in New Zealand after the Rings series or in the Pacific northwest after the Twilight craze. But a little town like this, with no clear identification on any set?

Chase was smiling at him too. "Yeah, we'll get a lot of fans craving the experience of standing in the same location as you do in a scene, or looking at the street from the same vantage point you used. That's what happens after a town becomes known in one of your movies."

Curious now, Mac stared at the man. "And you know this why?"

Chase's smile became nostalgic. "My wife Marci was a huge fan of yours. Saw every one of your movies multiple times, the good ones and the awful ones. She subscribed to your fan newsletter too."

Hearing this from a good-looking guy about the same age as him made Mac uncomfortable. How would it feel to have your wife lusting after another man, however unattainable that guy would be? He was surprised he hadn't been waylaid by this Marci in the past few weeks.

Staring at his hands as if he didn't know why they were there, Chase continued. "There are tours after your movies. Fans can sign up to visit the locations of a picture, experience some of the same ambiance of the film's theme, that kind of stuff. Marci was always pointing them out to me. She really wanted to go to that one you did in Rome, what was the name of that one?"

"'Night in Navona'." He remembered that film clearly. The sights of Rome were breathtaking, as amazing as he'd anticipated. He and Madeleine had planned to visit, and she'd found travel brochures of places she wanted to see and marked them on a map.

She'd left the map behind, along with the brochures and travel guides that they'd planned to use for their adventures. He'd found them thrown in the bathroom trash the day she left him in San Francisco. But the scenes they'd set lived on in his mind for years, and when he was shooting that film, sometimes he thought he saw Madeleine waiting on the edge of a crowd in a square, or balanced on the rim of a splashing fountain, urging him to hurry and finish so that they could go exploring.

Chase was tapping his fingers on the table, staring unseeing out the window. Taking off his glasses, he rubbed the bridge of his nose with eyes closed, then set the glasses back and stared again.

Mac cleared his throat. "Would Marci like an autograph?"

The sorrow on Chase's face was stunning, a shock to the system, like an explosion that left behind only darkness. Then he blanked the expression carefully and turned back to face Mac, looking as old as wisdom itself.

"Marci died a year ago, cancer. She never really stood a chance, but she fought it anyway. I guess I owe you thanks, since watching your movies helped her through the pain of the last few weeks." He watched Mac carefully, considering.

Standing finally, his face was solemn. "Let me give you a word of advice, one I was given long ago and didn't take. I was too busy, too important and too concerned with my own career. When you love someone, never let a day go by without letting them feel it, because you never know how much time you have."

Mac couldn't tear his gaze away from the raw pain in the man's eyes. And the message was even clearer. Treasure every day.

Chase turned abruptly and went to the shop's door, pausing with his hand on the knob only long enough to say, "Call you later, Tess," in a muffled voice before the door snapped shut behind him.

The intent gaze from Tess was speculative. He detected a little sympathy and even more curiosity. She sat silent and watchful, waiting for him to pick up where he'd left off before Chase's revelations.

"Roxy's told me a lot about you, and about the girl tribe. I'm glad that she has close friends like you to support her." Mac licked his lips, realizing suddenly that his throat was dry, parched in fact. That sense of being judged and found lacking was again in her eyes.

"We're lucky to have Roxy. She brings a reality check to our little group, reminding us that fairy tales don't always come true." The woman halted her words and raised a hand when Mac would have talked over her comments. "I don't judge, not you, not her, and not the situation. I've heard that you try to be honorable man, Mac. Do Roxy a favor, and act that way when it's time for you to leave her again."

Chapter 39

"Man, I love this stuff! Who knew?" Bob flipped eggs into the air from the first pan, landing them squarely in the center even as he moved to repeat the performance with the second pan. And the third and the fourth. He was grinning from ear to ear.

It was catchy, his excitement about finding a passion in the cooking arena other than desserts. It made Roxy smile as she watched him. He was thriving in this fast-paced uncomfortable environment.

Yeah, who knew?

She rubbed the back of her hand across her scratchy eyes and tried to ignore the tired ache of her back. They slept in shifts in bedrolls on the ground, next to the wildland firefighters and smoke jumpers and support staff. They were part of the crew, and after the past week plus, they looked just as exhausted and grimy and grim.

The fire would abate, dying back when the winds relented, only to pop up in a new direction when the breezes shifted. Rumbles of thunder trembled up and down the mountains, and unfortunately, they only offered dry lightening to spark new fires rather than the rains that could turn things in human favor. The shows were spectacular, and to a man and woman on the lines, everyone talked with reverence about seeing the skies come alive long after sundown, brighter than sunlight in daytime.

"They're doing well, eh boss?" Alej came up to stand beside her, intent on the movements of their workers on the line. Ticia was laughing – outright laughing, mind you – and teasing a fireman into taking some fruit to go with the pile of bacon and eggs on his plate. "It's healthy, now, and you want to stay big and strong, don't you? My, look at those muscles!"

Whatever the man said in response only made Ticia laugh harder and turn to tease the next man. Roxy had noticed that the men and women all seemed to appreciate the singular caring attention she dished out as easily as she did the sides for their plates.

Ticia too – who knew?

This environment wasn't stressing them out. Instead, Ticia and Bob were blooming under conditions that would have made the most experienced chef think twice about their chosen profession.

Angel was another story. After his verbal gibes and teasing met with silence from the crews he was serving, he'd become surly and mute. The gibes had been poorly timed and less than respectful. His badass attitude from the streets wasn't sitting as well here.

"Has Angel told you what's bothering him?" She turned to examine Alej's smoke-tinged face. Out here, they all looked like they were sporting dark ashen tans. Fallout from the fire was unavoidable.

Alej stared back at her in disbelief. "Why would he tell me? I'm just the guy who was with him when he was at his most vulnerable on the way to the hospital. It's not the kind of thing that inspires confidences. Besides, we wolves don't 'do' feelings." He grinned are her, wolf-like, his white teeth in stark contrast to the dingy color of his skin.

"Wolves? Since when are you, or Angel for that matter, wolves?" In the midst of the craziness, this was a fun little distraction.

"Since the night the film folks did their performance for the town and you called the guys the wolf pack. It's kind of stuck. Vince liked it so much he's thinking of having t-shirts made up. Dane's looking back through his photos to find a picture they can use, and Mac's thinking about creating some kind of movie tagline to tie into it. In fact, Rick said – "

Roxy held up her hand. "How do you know all of this? Are you and the guys on the phone all the time, like gossiping high school girls?" A little sniping felt good, easing the pressure around her heart and the band of pain in her neck.

"Jeannine told me. I've been..." He bit off whatever was going to come next, accurately reading the expression on Roxy's face that this was not the right response.

Hell, he was still at it. She'd warned him, more than once now, to stay away from Jeannine, even if she was more like a short-term hire and less like an intern every day. Damn it all, why was he acting like he was joined at the hip with the woman? And a pregnant woman at that.

"Are you talking to Jeannine?" She crossed her arms and set her feet apart in her tough chef stance. She was feeling less than forgiving at the moment.

"Yes Chef. I've been talking to Jeannine. You see..." He snapped his teeth shut with an audible click when she started shaking her head.

"Alej, what's happening back at the restaurant and the store? That's all that I want to know. And I'll warn you again. The situation with Jeannine is problematic on so many different levels that I don't even know where to start." Roxy felt the ache of another stabbing headache begin behind her eyeballs, radiating up to her scalp and down to her steel-knotted neck.

Looking like he might explode with words, Alej opened his mouth again. "Look, Rox, there are some things we need to discuss. I've been checking..."

She tuned him out as she heard a warning shout from behind them. The large turnout off a logging road where they were parked had an edge that dropped off precariously. Below, the fall was about two hundred feet before the land shelved out again.

In this early morning's weird orange light, a lone man stood at the edge of the drop-off. Squinting, Roxy could make out Angel's short form. He'd come off the night shift with Alej less than an hour before and should have been crashed out in his sleeping bag. Instead, he faced in the direction of the fire, a constant hum of a glow on the close horizon, and he gestured threateningly in its direction.

"Alej, is that...?" Before she had a chance to finish the question or move into action, the tall form of a firefighter – even from this distance, it was obvious it was a woman – jogged up to him and put a protective hand on his shoulder. She bent her head to talk to him. Angel gestured again, more wildly this time. The firefighter put her other hand on his opposite shoulder and forced him back to the camp.

Roxy let go of a breath she wasn't even aware she was holding. Next to her, she heard Alej blow out air too.

"Okay, danger averted. Angel has something personal against this fire. Not sure what's happening, but I'll see what I can learn. Anyway, Roxy, the wolf pack has a caravan coming up the mountain later today. They're bringing us supplies, along with a load of stuff the fire crews requested."

She snorted. Funny how a random comment turned into a new pet name. She was happy her best friends had found their true loves, even if it was never going to be in the cards for her.

"The wolf pack is riding to the rescue, huh? This I have to see." She punched Alej in the arm for emphasis.

His face fell serious again. "Rox, we have to talk. You and I have been together for a long time and..."

His next words were bitten off in the loud claxon notifying everyone that there was a new emergency. Firefighters scooped food into their mouths as they ran, and Bob and Ticia lofted energy bars at them as they scrambled. Roxy noted the concern on both of their faces as their breakfast guests ran in the direction of danger.

Angel stood alone to the side, arms crossed and face sullen as he watching the racing firefighters, before turning back to the bunk area and his bedroll.

*****

"Your crew, they do good work."

Roxy recognized the tall woman as the firefighter who had turned Angel back to safety.

"Thanks. We appreciate your kind words. It's good for them to see others put in hard work, much more dangerous work too."

The chuckle of response made Roxy realize that perhaps she could have phrased that differently. She would have turned red if she had the energy.

"I'm sorry. I should thank you for sending my intern back to the camp. I'm not sure what he has against this fire. It's become something personal to him."

The woman nodded as she selected an energy bar from the pile and munched, turned towards the distant glow of the fire herself.

"I've seen it happen time and time again. It gets personal for no reason other than you're scared, or you feel defeated, or you remember another fire and another time when it beat you. You want to win. Has your friend been in a fire before?"

Thinking back to everything Angel had shared – and since he loved to talk, he'd shared a lot – nothing simmered to the surface. She shook her head.

"What did he say to you, if you don't mind my asking? And I'm sorry, I'm Roxy. I'm in charge of the cooking crew." She put out her hand, remembering to lighten her grip. Too many years in the kitchen and some people came away shaking their hand to return circulation once she latched on.

"I'm Yank. I'm from Idaho, pulled in for this fire. Not that we don't have a ton going on up in my neck of the woods, but I've been out for two months on disability and they sent me here when I got back on."

For once, Roxy found she didn't need to lessen her grip with another woman.

"Yank? That sounds like a nickname with a story behind it. Why didn't you head out with the others?"

Roxy thought the woman fit her profession. The conditions made it hard to call her hair anything other than smoky blonde. And when she lifted her sunglasses and looked full on, her eyes were as gray as the ash that fell around them.

"There are reasons. Reasons and issues. But back to your friend." The woman held her body still, too still, given the direction of their discussion. It was like she was holding herself in.

The brush-off of personal questions was intriguing. Not that Roxy was prone to be nosy, but there was sadness and lingering deep pain that hung around the woman more densely than aromas from a grill.

"I don't know why he's acting like he is. Usually, Angel is full of fun and camaraderie – almost too much in fact." Roxy chuckled, and Yank joined in after a couple of beats.

"Yeah, I remember the first couple of days. He was all spitfire and mouthiness, if you don't mind me saying so. But he's gone quiet." Yank hesitated and looked back to the fire. "If he was a firefighter, we'd be real worried."

Roxy looked back at the bunk area, trying to pick out Angel's form among the few sleeping bags that were filled. Almost everyone had run into action at the sound of the claxon.

"Listen, thanks again for turning him around. I'll keep an extra sharp eye on him. In the mean time, is there anything I can get you? The line is on a break, but I'd be happy to prepare something for you."

"How about some grilled foie gras with a cherry reduction, toast points, a wonderful arugula salad, and maybe some fine Prosecco?"

Roxy blinked twice, hard, before bursting into the first real laugh she'd had in days.

Chapter 40

He wanted her to be happy he'd joined the convoy. It had been almost two weeks, and he found himself aching in a desperate way that he didn't want to consider just to hold her again, however briefly.

"Ah, boss-man? You're sure it's okay for us to be here too, right?"

Barry sat in the passenger seat of the rented truck with his hands clutched between his knees, and looked around the fire camp with eyes as round as dinner plates. His gaze moved quickly over the catering rig, the shower and laundry truck, and the lines of bedrolls. Most of all, though, he stared in unconcealed horror at the line of fire up at the crest of the mountain in front of them.

Mac couldn't have even begun to stage a set as brutal as this. On the drive up the hill, the sky had darkened to unnatural dusk with a curtain of black smoke between the sun and the road. Originally, they'd all tuned into a radio frequency Rick had set up so that the convoy of supply trucks could stay in contact. The initial chatter had been lively and full of over-testosteroned male energy. But as they'd drawn closer to the fire line, silence fell when they fully realized what the firefighters were up against.

The highway through to Lake Tahoe was closed until the fire was under control. Sheriff's deputies checked their clearance, and after conversations with the fire boss who sanctioned their trip, they were allowed to continue with a deputy escorting them, lights flashing. The yellow and blue strobes seemed to be overkill until they realized that the smoke made landmarks and road edges otherwise difficult to pick out. Soon, each truck drove in a slow procession with its emergency blinkers keeping a steady rhythm.

She would be happy to see him, right? Mac certainly hoped that was the case, and the sudden attack of nerves had him putting his foot down a little too hard on the brakes. The deputy directing them gave him a sympathetic look, evidently thinking the shocking sight of the fire's fury was making him edgy.

"Boss-man?" Barry took off his spectacles and wiped streaming tears from his eyes, as a sudden gust of cinders rained over the trucks and smoke blew in their open windows.

"Yeah, Barry, it's fine for us to be here. I'd rather be doing something to help out here than sitting back and waiting for the smoke to clear enough to shoot those final scenes. Right, man?"

Barry coughed twice, put his glasses back on, and looked at Mac. "Sure, Mr. Smythe, sure."

Mac sighed. This was the guy who would take Martha's place someday. And after years, they were still on this odd professional standing. "Barry, do you think that you could finally bring yourself to call me Mac?"

"Sure, Mr. – I mean, Mac." Barry turned his red eyes to scan the site again. "I don't see Chef anywhere, do you?"

Why was Barry ogling Roxy anyway? Maybe he wasn't ready to be promoted – ever. His sudden attack of possessiveness was something else he didn't want to think about.

Mac was already making his own survey of the area. His eyes moved fast over the various support vehicles and emergency personnel. Further on, sleeping bags lay in tight rows, a few sporting bumps indicating occupation. Finally, he picked out the catering rig and its line of tables full of trays to the right of the more private areas of the camp.

And standing in front of it all, in the center of the maelstrom, was his Roxy. Her hair was pulled back and up and a scarf that had probably been white at some point was wound across her forehead, pirate style. She still wore chef's whites, though the color was now more of a dingy gray. In fact, everything in the camp seemed to be colored with that same pallid hue.

His heart kicked up its pace until he could hear his blood racing through his veins. The ride had been tense and harrowing, but the reception at this end could be even more threatening.

"I'll check on what we're supposed to do next, okay Mr. – I mean Mac. Okay?"

Barry jumped out the door before Mac had a chance to respond. That was fine by him. He'd rather have a moment to lean on the steering wheel in relief and drink in the wonderful sight of Roxy across the clearing.

Her exhaustion was obvious in the tight set of her shoulders and the hand that was rubbing her lower back. She probably wasn't aware she was doing it. Her frowning face was turned in the general direction of the sleeping bags, settling into a small smile when it hit the retreating back of a tall firefighter.

The spur of jealous made him sit up straight. Had she found someone else already?

His eyes zeroed in on the retreating back with a fresh surge of jealous anger, and when the tall figure turned, he was relieved to see that the firefighter was undoubtedly a woman. The shit-wave of ease this brought him almost made him giddy.

THUMP! Thump-THUMP!

The pounding against the metal door of the truck reverberated worse than any rock concert drumming he'd ever heard. Vince's grim face appeared in the truck's side window.

"Hey man, time to get moving and unload. Fire boss says we have to be off the mountain before fourteen-hundred, so two p.m. to us civilians."

Mac scrambled for the door handle, intent on getting to Roxy first and damn the consequences. They could unload in short order – no problem. Hell, it only took them a couple of hours to fill the truck in the first place. That gave him a precious sixty minutes to hold on to the woman who was now staring in the direction of the convoy.

Roxy's gaze flickered over each truck in turn, as drivers and passengers dropped to the ground. Mac hesitated, letting everyone else walk the expanse to where she stood before he fell in behind.

One by one, the men approached her with spirited greetings. Each member of the wolf pack got a hard hug. Even Barry got a handshake before she pulled him into her, which seemed to make him unmistakably overjoyed even viewed from a distance. He watched her scan from face to face, looking more disappointed with each new arrival.

He was the last one in the slow shuffling line. His heart was beating too fast. It was the conditions and the stress and the excitement, he was sure of it.

Shit, he was lying to himself again. It had nothing to do with the conditions.

It had everything, all of it, to do with holding his Roxy.

*****

Her heart got a little heavier with each clean face in front of her. Sure, she was glad to see the guys. The wolf pack. Be careful what you say…

"Hey Vince. What's the news?" And she surprised herself by standing on her tiptoes and hugging him hard.

He coughed and frowned at her. "You feelin' okay?"

She knew it was out of character for her to grab and hold on, particularly when it came to snarky Vince. It had taken her a long time to come to trust him, even after he'd committed to DK with a big ring on her finger.

Today, he looked like a wonderful old friend, and she was damned glad to see him.

She frowned at the smoke billowing from the fire line when her eyes watered. She coughed as well and set her face in a scowl before turning back to him.

"So, snarky, did you bring us anything good?"

To his credit, he didn't snipe back at her and instead put a steadying hand on her shoulder, a hand she didn't even know she needed.

"Rick and I, Steve and Deke, we've got the stuff for the fire crews, parts and supplies they needed. Dane and Dave are loaded up with bulk items – don't want to discuss that stuff with you." He winked, and she immediately felt better.

"And Mac and Barry, they have the food."

Crap. The clench in her stomach wasn't something she could avoid. Mac, here.

She couldn't catch her hand before it slapped over her hair and ran with disgust down the ragged ponytail, grimy despite the camp showers, and at a distinct disadvantage.

"Roxy, relax. You look fine. Believe me, you could be sporting a third eye and snakes in dreadlocks seething on your head and Mac would only be too delighted to see you."

She blinked, then turned surprised eyes to Mr. Snark.

"Yeah, Roxy, I notice things too. And you have nothing to worry about. Of course, you could work on the welcoming committee aspect of your greeting." He paused, looking her up and down. "And lose the scowl on your face."

She stuck her tongue out at him. He burst out laughing and pulled her into a quick hug.

"Go get him, tiger. He needs you as much as you need him."

She blinked rapidly as she pulled back. His behavior was so un-snarky that she was at a loss about how to process it.

Chapter 41

"Hello Roxy."

The rumbling gruffness of his voice was a divine symphony. She'd forgotten how much the low timbre could make her insides churn with pleasure. She'd wanted to forget, and yet here he was, standing in front of her as if unsure how the next scene was supposed to be played.

"Hi Mac." She cleared her throat to make her voice strong and secure. "I, ah, didn't expect to see you running with the wolf pack."

He smiled at that, rocking back on his heels as he stared at her. His hands were shoved deep in the front pockets of his jeans, which only drew attention to an area of his anatomy that she couldn't afford to think about right now. She made an effort to focus in on his face. She must be more tired than she thought.

Finally putting his arms out to her, he added, "Don't I rate a greeting like the rest of the guys got?"

An eyebrow raised with his question was hidden under the hair falling in his face. His eyes were already red and watery from the smoke. The intensity of his gaze on her face made her squirm, remembering how filthy she was compared to his clean t-shirt.

Her feet had grown roots into the rock. Unsure of what she wanted to do, act nonchalant about seeing him again or throw herself into his arms, she stood still and indecisive. She watched some of the light fade from his eyes as he waited too.

"I, ah, hope you're okay with Barry and me helping out with the convoy. With the amount of smoke drifting downhill, we can't shoot the final scenes. They're all outdoors. And moving them indoors would change the dynamics of the plot too much. You see…"

His voice trailed off and he looked at his boots, so new that the leather wasn't yet scuffed. She was happy he was babbling, because it saved her from trying to find her tongue.

Pulling in a big sigh, Mac met her gaze again. "Anyway, you don't care about that right now. We've got a truckload of food and supplies for you. The merchants in town donated some of it. When the vendors for your restaurant and store found out what you and your staff were doing out here, they kicked in even more, a lot of it for free. And everything else is," his voice faltered as if he was trying to decide what to say, "covered."

It did her heart good to realize that so many people were chipping in. And it was too good to see Mac, her traitorous heart and trembling body reminded her. Then his last words sunk in.

"Covered? Covered how?" Roxy felt her spine straighten. She didn't want to end up owing someone new as a result of this work.

"I paid for it." His serious expression registered even as his words slammed into her brain.

She wasn't sure whether to be shocked or thrilled.

"Mac, you didn't need to…"

His hand was already up to stop her. "I wanted to. Seeing the hard work that the firefighters are doing, and the difficult job it must be to keep them fed while staying upbeat yourselves, it was the least I could do."

*****

He wished he could decipher the look on her face. Thoughts raced across it so fast that even a speed-reader would have a hard time following the story. She still hadn't made a single move towards him. He tried to tuck the disappointment he felt about that into a back pocket to ignore.

"Mac, I – thank you."

He smiled, and he hoped that some of the tears in her eyes were from her feelings about his gesture rather than the fresh billow of smoke that passed over them.

Finally, she moved forward. It was a slow motion scene, the kind that he shot focusing in closer and closer on the faces of the actors as they neared each other. Arms rose, oh so slowly. He opened his embrace to her and she tucked into him.

God, she felt so good wrapped in his arms. Her head was under his chin, and he put a kiss on the pirate scarf and wisps of escaping blonde silk. A shudder went through them, though he honestly couldn't tell if it came from her or from him.

How long they stood like that, locked on to each other, he wasn't sure. He didn't care. He figured he had about fifty-two minutes left that didn't involve unloading the truck, and he was going to make the most of it.

Dipping her back slightly over his arm and putting fingers under her chin to raise her face to his, he looked into blue eyes wide with wonder. And maybe desire. Shit, he hoped it was desire because right now, he wouldn't be adverse to using one of those bedrolls for something other than sleeping.

"Madeleine, I've missed you."

Her eyes got wider and she opened her lips to say something. He couldn't control his need any longer, and he dropped his mouth to hers, swallowing her gasp.

Her taste was as exotic as ever, layered now with the flavor of smoke. Pushing his tongue deeper into her mouth, Mac felt a surge of powerful joy when her tongue mated with his. Roxy wasn't fighting him, and in fact, she melted against him and her arms moved up to circle his neck tightly.

Pressing her more snuggly against him, he knew he couldn't hide the hard desire throbbing through him. His arousal wedged into her belly, and it took every ounce of his resolve not to tear their clothes off, lift her until her legs encircled his waist, and drive into her wet heat. Her heart was beating as hard as his. There was no way she was immune to him, even if she hesitated to welcome him with open arms.

She pulled back, her eyes glazed over as she watched him, confused. He didn't want to let her go, not yet. Hell, probably not ever.

Pushing against his arms, she stepped back again, and the chill left behind in the heat of the day slapped some sense into him. They were in the middle of a fire camp, for god's sake.

She pushed a hand into her hair, dislodging the scarf and partially undoing the ponytail. Or maybe he'd done that when he curled his hands into her scalp.

"Mac, I'm..." She stopped and looked towards the ridge at the line of fire and dark black smoke. Giving her chef's coat a hard tug, she turned back to him.

The sadness in her eyes knifed him in the gut. The heated throb in his groin missed a few beats and started to retreat. Her expression was more chilling than ice water.

She started again. "We can't..."

A shriek of fear followed by a long scream cut over whatever she was going to tell him next.

Chapter 42

The blood-chilling echo snapped her out of the reverie she'd fallen into in Mac's arms. As much as she'd wanted to stay there, she knew she couldn't. This on-again, off-again affair they found themselves in was driving her nuts. But she'd have only herself to blame if she let her feelings rule. Worse yet, if she let him know about those feelings...

Shouts and stampeding feet towards the edge of the flat campsite drew her attention. Beside her out of the corner of her eye, she saw Mac give a small shake of his head before he too looked in the direction where everyone was running. Near the front of the crowd was the firefighter, Yank, along with Alej who was gesturing wildly.

"He went over the edge! Damnit, I told him to stay away from it, but he wasn't making any sense!"

Even as Roxy started to move forward, she felt Mac's hand at her elbow.

"We're not done yet, Roxy, not by a long shot." His voice was a harsh whisper, though how she could have heard any undertone in the noise and commotion she wasn't sure.

Alej was distraught, and she saw Yank put a comforting hand on his shoulder and another on his arm to restrain him as other firefighters and emergency personnel were peering over the cliff's drop-off. When he caught sight of Roxy coming towards him, Alej started yelling again.

"The idiot! He never listens, never does what he's told. Always wants to do things his way. I tried to stop him, Rox, I really did."

She found herself starting to jog towards him. When she was close enough to make out the full anguish on his dark features, his fright communicated itself to her.

"Alej, what happened?"

He gaped at her, opening and shutting his mouth a couple of times before sucking in air. That made him cough, and he bent double as the racking sounds continued. Yank kept her hand on his back and turned to answer.

"Your cook, Angel. He was on the edge again, just like he was before. He was yelling at the fire, saying something in Spanish. I'm not sure what it all meant, other than I got 'loco' and some curse words a couple of times. He was shaking his fist at the fire."

More people ran past them now, some with ropes and pulling on hard hats, others anchoring the ends of the lines to truck bumpers and hitches. Four men clipped on rappelling harnesses, snapped into place on the lines, and began lowering themselves out of sight over the edge.

Roxy's stomach started to roll as the possibilities began to occur to her. Mac, huffing behind her, put hands on her shoulders and pressed his hard body against her back. Her rock, her support.

Yank turned from watching the men disappear to continue. "Alej yelled for him to come back away from the edge. We were both moving forward to him. I wanted to pull him back and talk to him. Maybe we could have calmed him down."

Alej straightened, his face full of distress. "I wanted him to move back, come over and discuss whatever was bothering him. But he just kept yelling at the fire. And I can tell you what he was saying. It was something like, 'You won't win this time, bastard, even if I have to put you out myself. Never again. Never again. You won't win.'"

They were all silent as they watched the crews communicating by radio with the men dangling over the cliff. The brush was thick and thorny but not very strong, and over the sounds of emergency work, they could tell that branches were breaking as they continued downward.

"Did he fall over the edge, or did he jump?"

Roxy turned to look at Mac, surprised at his question.

"Why would he jump, Mac? That's just crazy." She felt compelled to defend Angel, even if he'd done something stupid.

Mac looked between them. "After the destructive fires in southern California the past couple of years, some people went a little crazy. You'd see them on the news with each new blaze. It's like they developed a personal vendetta against any flames. The firefighters were pulling them back behind the lines every time."

Yank was shaking her head in agreement. "He's right. Usually, it's people who were impacted by the fire in a major way, like they lost a house or a business. I know he said he was from LA. Did Angel or his family lose anything in one of the wildfires, or maybe even an urban one?"

Roxy looked at Alej, and they both shrugged. It wasn't something that Angel would brag about in his usual rants. Mac's hands tightened to massage her shoulders.

"It isn't your fault, Roxy." His voice was gently consoling, even as his hands were strong and soothing.

"No wonder he didn't want to come to the fire camp. But he never said why." She fell silent, listening to the squawk of radios and watching the activities of the rescue underway.

*****

Two hours later, the litter came into view over the edge, and everyone, rescue workers and support personnel, broke into applause. No one said a critical word about what brought them to that point, the fall of someone who probably shouldn't have been on the mountain in the first place.

"You don't always know what people will do, Roxy." Dane was standing next to her with the rest of the wolf pack, their unloading completed while the rescue had been in progress. Mac kept an arm around her shoulders, unyielding each time she'd tried to push him away until she just stopped trying.

"I saw it many times in war zones and in emergencies of all kinds. Some people step up and get things done, even when they're terrified. Others fall apart. You never know." He patted her arm consolingly and turned to walk towards the convoy. They were getting pressure from the fire boss to move down the mountain while conditions allowed it.

"I'm not leaving." Mac's words were quiet in her ear.

Now was not the time for him to get all cavalier and try to rescue her. Anger rose like bile after a bad meal and she decided to allow it. It gave her something to do with the torrent of emotions racing through her.

"Listen, Mac, I have a job to do and I don't need to be distracted, okay?" She shoved at his arm again, but like before, he didn't let go. She huffed out a heavy gust of frustration.

Alej was one of the first to get to the stretcher hoisted to safety with Angel strapped on tightly. The gurney was already in place, and on the count, the rescue workers moved Angel up and on to it.

Yank had been relaying information over the past hours as they learned Angel had fallen about sixty feet, caught finally on a larger pine tree growing from a ledge. He had broken bones, lacerations and probably a concussion, and he was out cold when the rescuers got to him. The breaking branches of bushes down the side of the mountain slowed his fall and lessened his injuries, but blows to his head and possible internal injuries made life flighting him out a necessity.

Roxy moved forward, and only when Mac saw that she was heading towards the gurney did he let go. When his arm dropped away, she caught her breath at the lonely emptiness of its absence. She stood up straighter and moved forward, unwilling to let the unhappiness in her heart win out.

Angel was talking, which was a good sign. When was he not talking? She almost grinned.

"Angel, they're going to take excellent care of you, okay?" She bent down to look into his bruised and bloodied face. His pupils were dilated with shock and pain but he attempted to smile at her.

"Sorry Chef. I screwed up. But my angel, my guardian angel, he took care of me. I saw him."

He looked loopy and she let the remark go by. They'd already given him some painkillers for the ride in the litter. The life flight medical personnel were pushing her aside.

"Don't worry, Angel. Everything will be okay."

Alej ran up to her side as the gurney was shifted towards the waiting helicopter, rotors already turning.

"I'm going with him, make sure he gets everything he needs, and notify his family."

She turned to look at her number two and shook her head. "This is getting to be a regular thing. Pretty soon, you'll need to get certified in emergency training and I'll need to find another operations person to run the business."

He frowned at her attempt at a joke. "Listen, Rox, when this is over, we have to talk. I need you to know some things."

His words puzzled her, but before she could ask him what he meant, he was running to the helicopter. His wave was brief as he turned his attention to Angel and the medics.

Chapter 43

"Boss-man, I mean Mac, are you sure this is a good idea?"

Barry held the strings of the apron in front of him as if he wasn't sure how to tie a bow. The long drape covered his jeans, leaving his t-shirt at the mercy of whatever he got himself into. The rapid blinking of his eyes behind his glasses was another indicator that he was less than comfortable in the kitchen line.

"Come on Barry, it will be an adventure. Haven't you ever dished up food before? How hard can it be?"

Mac hoped like hell that they could keep up, but he didn't want to share that with his personal assistant. In fact, if Roxy found out they had stayed behind and trying to help out…

"What the hell do you think you're doing?"

Busted. He pulled up his most convincing grin and turned to face Roxy's expression of disbelief.

"We're helping out, of course. Look, you're down two sets of hands. While we can't cook, we can at least help serve. What's it going to hurt?"

Evidently his most convincing grin wasn't working today, or at least not on her. The cooking staffers were all watching the interchange with mixed expressions. Some were amused, some were frowning, and the African American woman had her mouth agape in a large O.

They stared at each other for a full minute, neither one of them willing to back down. In the distance, Mac noted that truck engines were revving up as the convoy headed back down the hill, minus one vehicle.

Slowly, Roxy shook her head, not saying no, exactly. At least that's what Mac chose to assume. He turned away so that she wouldn't see his smile, and snapped on a pair of latex gloves with the flourish a surgeon might use. As he flexed his fingers over the trays of food, he took a chance and glanced back. With a hand covering her eyes and her head still shaking slowly from side to side, Roxy huffed out a loud breath.

"Fine, fine, just damn fine. Go ahead. But no lagging. And you!" She pointed at Barry, who looked like he wished he'd gone over the cliff too. "Don't you know how to tie on an apron?"

Mac couldn't hide a full-fledged smile as she stomped over to the young man, grabbed the ends of the apron strings, and yanked them snug around his middle. She yanked hard again as she made a neat bow. Barry looked like his circulation had been cut off.

"Everyone back to work. This delay isn't getting anyone fed." She waved her hands at the team and people scattered to their stations, heads down. More than a few were smiling though.

As Mac watched surreptitiously, he saw a brief grin cross Roxy's features as well. He picked up the large serving spoon and made a big show of stirring the meat and vegetables in the serving tray.

"You don't have to do this, you know."

He felt the heat of her body before she spoke, so when she did, he avoided jumping at her sudden appearance at his side.

"I know I don't have to do it. Barry, he'll do it because I told him to. Don't worry, I'll watch him and make sure none of his mistakes are life-threatening."

His attempt at humor missed its mark. She put a hand to the back of her neck and rubbed hard, looking towards the edge of the cliff where Angel had made his untimely disappearance.

"Crap, I don't know what's happening this summer. First, I end up with four interns instead of three. Two of the four are trouble for very different reasons, and I'm just waiting for the other two to do — something. And then there's you and the movie and this crazy arrangement we have." She shook her head again, the hand transferring to ease her lower back.

He set down the ladle carefully as if it was made of fine breakable glass. Her words cut at him.

"Is that all we have? An arrangement?" He grimaced when he heard the tone of disappointment in his own voice.

She stayed facing half away from him, the hand still massaging the base of her spine. It was a spot, Mac knew from experience, where her skin was especially soft and the nerve endings would fire at the merest feather of a touch. It also probably ached like torture, given that she'd been on her feet for most of the last two weeks.

He set aside the pain her casual statement caused him and the torrid need to run his tongue over that gentle curve where her hand now rested. Now wasn't the time for either emotion.

Keeping his tone offhand, he added, "Never mind. You're busy. It can wait until things are back to something that looks more like normal. Though neither one of us has had much normal these last few weeks."

She barked out a sound that he decided to take for a laugh.

"You're right about that, Mac. Since I learned that you were directing this movie, my life has been pretty much as fucked up as it could possibly be."

The carving knife at the next station couldn't have cut as deeply or as quick. He sucked in smoky air as renewed pain shredded his heart.

*****

Walking away, she heard his sharp gasp and realized that she was probably being cruel. Better to do this now, though, than fall victim to his abrupt departure later. Maybe if she pushed him away, he'd get the message and leave her alone. She didn't need a repeat of San Francisco. As it was, it would take her a long time to get herself back on even footing again, back to a point where the highs of his current presence and the losses of his soon-to-be absence didn't boil over everything she'd worked so carefully to balance over the last fifteen years.

"You must be wiped out. I can see it on your face."

She turned around in shock to find him standing next to her, putting his hand at the base of her spine and rubbing with his knuckles. The pressure was just right, easing the soreness that standing in rugged conditions and bending at unusual angles had caused.

"Mac, you don't have to." Still, she couldn't help but moan when his other hand started massaging the tightness in her neck.

"That's what – friends – are for."

His deliberate pause wasn't lost on her. If he thought of them as friends, so be it. She knew that it could never be that simple. There were consequences to their relationship, at least on her side. As hard a shell as she tried to construct around her heart, it still beat too strongly when he was around. That shell had already cracked into tiny pieces.

She didn't respond to his comment, and he seemed to be content with that, continuing the massaging, both hands in tempo, until she began to feel some of the knots untangle and the physical aches ease.

The ache in her heart would always be a different story.

Rather than let her mind linger on how his lips would taste right now, if she would only turn halfway, she stepped forward and out of his grasp.

"Ah, thanks. That helped. You should probably go now. You and Barry can catch up with the convoy."

When he didn't respond, she was forced to look up to find him staring at her with a mixture of desire and hurt in his eyes. He wasn't doing anything to mask it, and Roxy didn't think anyone, including Mac, could be a good enough actor to fake his rapid breathing or the unmistakable bulge under the long apron. But that was just sex, right?

She turned back to stare at the fire on the top of the mountain. "You know, I'm thinking that perhaps this catering rig is jinxed. What with the interns and the movie and everything. And Angel, though I believe he brings that on himself."

The surprising chuckle behind her warmed her. His heat reached out to her even as he took the steps necessary to close the distance between them.

"Did I tell you? I've changed the name of the movie. Now, it's going to be called 'Jinxed'."

Chapter 44

"So you see, his grandmother gave him the nickname Angel. Seems he was always getting into scrapes as a kid, and his grandmother was convinced that he must have a guardian angel looking after him. Ergo, Angel."

Alej sat in his customary chair across the small kitchen office. The restaurant was abnormally quiet. To give everyone a break after their hard work on the fire line and in covering for both the dining patrons and the store, Roxy had closed Roxy's restaurant for a week.

"Did he simply fall, furious as he was with the fire, or did he jump?" She wanted to know, in part because she needed to decide if Angel was going to be invited back once he completed his long recovery process.

Alej hesitated. "He won't say. I learned from his mother that he's been particularly angry with any fire since one came up a canyon near LA and reduced a restaurant he was working at to cinders. Evidently, he thought he would take over the place one day. The people, they took the insurance money and moved to Seattle. Angel took it all personally, I guess." He shrugged his shoulders.

Roxy considered this. There were always fires around here. It was part of living in a dry mountain region where the rains were absent for a continuous string of months each year. Angel had a long rehabilitation to undergo. He'd broken one leg in multiple places, and he had another bad break in his right arm. The reality was that he was going to have to work hard for a couple of years before he could even consider cooking again.

"He doesn't plan on coming back, no matter what." Alej's quiet statement made her look up quickly. "He also says that maybe he's not cut out for being a chef anymore. Even when he's feeling better."

Her friend stood and stared out the window to the quiet kitchen, arms crossed on his chest and a frown on his face.

"That's probably a good decision, don't you think? Besides, we had planned on using only three interns this summer anyway, so having four has been, well, gravy."

Roxy knew that some part of Alej still smarted from her harsher words about adding a fourth intern without her approval early in the season. They'd never talked about it, though she'd gone out of her way more than once to mention how well Jeannine had worked out and what a great team Alej had built from the group.

He must be as exhausted as she was. And yet he'd asked that they meet and talk before he took his time off to rest.

She pushed back her chair, the squeak of old rollers loud in the otherwise silent space. When she moved to stand next to him, he put an arm around her shoulders and pulled her against his side.

His voice, once he started talking, was hoarse and rough.

"You and me, we've built quite an empire here, haven't we? I mean, who knew when I taught you how to skin a salmon, what with your unexplained tears and big shocked eyes, that we'd get to this."

She was having a very bad feeling. Call it her sixth sense, but intuition was screaming that whatever Alej was planning to discuss with her, the 'some things' he'd intimated as he flew off to the hospital with Angel, she wasn't going to like.

Instead of trying to block it or change the flavor of the conversation, she stayed silent as he gave her shoulders one more squeeze before turning her to him.

"Roxy, there's no easy way to say this. I'm leaving. I'm going at the end of the movie shoot, once you don't need to be running the catering rig along with the restaurant and store. Patrick's ready to move up – more than capable – and it's time."

Her gut dropped as she stared at him. Regret washed over his features. He pushed her into his vacated chair and knelt in front of her, taking her hands.

What did he think she would do now, faint? She pushed away the hands and got up, circling the desk rapidly and seating herself before she fell into the chair.

"Alej, why now? Has something happened? Is it something I said? Because if that's it..." She let the words hang between them.

"No, no, nothing like that. I've been, I don't know, restless recently. Wanting to try some new things. You, you're content here in the mountains. You have the girl tribe, and you pour everything you have into the business." He paused as if he wanted to comment on that, but wisely decided to leave it be.

"Me, I want a family of my own. I know that you swore off that. I still think you should give love a chance again, but who am I to say. My point is, I'm not like you."

"What are you planning to do?" Proud that her voice wobbled only a little, she tried an encouraging smile.

Alej's face lit up with happiness. "I'm going back to San Francisco, back to Paush's. Me – and Jeannine."

Now she couldn't help it. She gaped at him.

"You and Jeannine? As in together?"

He had the grace to look sheepish. "I know you warned me about getting too close to her, but hell, I couldn't help myself. We don't know where this is going to take us, but we want to try it out." Dropping into his seat again and leaning forward eagerly, he continued. "Bart has agreed to step back from the restaurant. Seems her father has been having some 'senior moments', enough to realize that he needed to see a doctor. He has an early stage of Alzheimer's, which explains all of his weirdness and the fall-off in quality from his kitchen. He's signed the whole thing over to Jeannine. We're going to run it together."

Chapter 45

The chasm that Alej's upcoming departure would leave in her life was becoming apparent. Her business was secure, but she was losing daily contact with one of her best friends and a trusted business partner. On top of Mac's imminent departure, her nerves were burnt to a crisp. Roxy chopped the vegetables slowly, much more slowly than her norm.

When Alej learned that Mac and Barry had jumped in to offer assistance after Angel's accident, his questions had been pointed and stark. She denied feeling anything other than friendly relief that they provided back up for a few days in the fire camp.

The girl tribe had been more insistent. More and more, the women had been asking her odd questions about her personal chef gig and what they termed her 'relationship' with the man. Here she denied letting Mac get to her even as she admitted that he was looking better and better each day.

To Mac himself, she'd been cordial but distant, unwilling to let her feelings show. He wouldn't have the satisfaction of knowing how deeply his departure would cut her, not this time. In the end, long days in the fire camp meant both of them were too exhausted to do much more than exchange superficial words.

What was that saying? Something about a tangled web and lies.

"Roxy? You are up there, right? You're truck's out front, and we're all coming up, so you'd better not be doing anything indecent." Gabby's voice rang out loud and clear, followed shortly by the stampede of multiple feet climbing the front stairs.

"See, I told you she'd be cooking. That's what she does to relax. Even when she's exhausted." Gabby crossed the room to give Roxy a quick hug and halted in surprise when Roxy grabbed her and hugged hard right back.

"Hey, what's this? Are you okay?" Tess grabbed her next. A heavily emotional greeting on Roxy's part was so unusual, it could be compared to a sighting of Big Foot in the Sierras. As she moved from woman to woman, she realized that she had just amped up their concern.

Serena and DK followed, with Marguerite bringing up the rear.

"*Cherie*, what is wrong? And why are you chopping so many vegetables? You could feed an army with these." Marguerite waved a hand at the tubs of carrots, celery and onions that covered the island in her personal kitchen.

Serena was reaching for wine glasses, even as DK was unloading a couple of bottles and some snacks.

"You've been out of touch for a while now. The restaurant's been closed for four whole days, so you've had plenty of time to rest. You haven't returned any of our calls and they haven't even seen you in the store. We decided it was time for an intervention." DK punctuated her last sentence with the satisfying pop of the wine's cork.

"Salty crunchy snacks. Great wine. Boxes of tissue." Serena pulled out three with a flourish. "And all of us."

Three boxes of tissue? That was probably overkill, but Roxy was suddenly glad that they'd decided she'd been by herself long enough.

"Listen, thanks for coming over. Really. You don't know what it means to me to have great friends like you." And she turned back to her chopping, the only way she knew to keep her tears from falling.

"Ow! Damn!" She dropped the knife, staring at the cut on the end of her left thumb in disbelief.

"Whoa, Rox, you cut yourself. You never cut yourself. You're always so in control, even when you're not." DK turned to the others, and as one, they gathered in closer and pulled Roxy away from the cutting board.

That was it. She couldn't hold it all in any longer. The tears began a slow glide down her face.

The sudden shocked silence erupted into noise and activity around her, gentle comforting hugs along with hurried rattles and exclamations from the kitchen. Her friends directed and guided until they were all seated in the living room. A few paper towels had stopped the bleeding on her thumb – the kind of cut she'd had a hundred times in her career – and the gauze Serena was using to wrap it was more than what was necessary.

She let herself be coddled, though. It made them feel better.

Hell, it made her feel better.

"So what's happened? This is all so unlike you. You're always the rock, even when you don't need to be, you know?" Serena's words were delivered in a soft croon.

Roxy stared at a framed photo of the Sierras on the far wall, taken not too far from where the fire had occurred. It had taken the firefighters three full weeks to get it under control. Full containment without risk of another flare-up would take longer, but at least the number of crews was reduced. They hadn't needed the catering rig anymore on this fire, unless things turned ugly again.

She hadn't spread Alej's news yet. It was clear he'd prepared for his departure. He had an agreement ready for her to review, buying him out of his share of the business. The terms were very reasonable and nothing she couldn't handle. She'd only asked that she be allowed to delay the word to the public for a few days to consider what kind of a spin she wanted to put on it.

She sniffed into a wad of tissue and looked from friend to friend. "Alej's leaving."

Voices collided around her as they all started talking at once. She let it continue until they quieted by themselves.

"Is something wrong? I thought that the two of you were very close business partners, *non*?" Marguerite's questions were echoed by the nodding heads of the others.

"No, nothing's wrong, at least not here. There's a woman involved, one of our interns. Well, she wasn't on the schedule to be an intern, but..."

And she told the long and involved story, from landing at Paush's herself years ago and Alej's tutoring, spanning the years up to Jeannine's arrival and their sampling of a dinner from the restaurant as it was now.

She left out the part about Mac, lust in the hallway, and the candlelight presentation of that self-same dinner, at least for now.

"It appears that Alej has found a new partner in Jeannine, who is expecting her child around the holidays. He's delighted, even if it's another man's baby. She's got stars in her eyes. I truly do wish them well." She took a restorative sip of wine and sighed.

"But what are you going to do? He's been your right hand for so long now." Tess's eyebrows met in a deep frown.

Roxy smiled. "I'm lucky. I have many talented people working in my enterprises. This gives everyone a chance to move up. In fact, I'm going to invite two of the interns to stay – Ticia and Bob."

Serena nodded her approval, then turned thoughtful. "And Angel?"

"He's already gone. You heard about the accident at the fire camp. He's got months or longer of rehab ahead of him. I talked to him in the hospital before they transferred him to southern California, close to his family. He knows it will be a long time before he can cook again, and he says he's thinking about a different profession all together." She cracked a smile as she remembered his parting words. "In fact, he's thinking about becoming an actor now."

The women all chuckled at that, commenting on the movie bug biting everyone this season.

"Yeah, Vince is thinking about trying his hand at writing a screenplay," DK added.

Gabby seconded that idea and the group continued its light banter until they realized that Roxy wasn't participating. Tess grew serious first, watching Roxy carefully. "So how did it go with you and Mac? The guys told us he and his assistant stayed behind to help on the catering line."

"Dane mentioned that it looked a little tense between the two of you," Serena added.

It was probably time to come clean. She had been carrying around the memories, and soon she'd be weighted down by a whole new set when the movie pulled out of town. Mac would be leaving her once again, and despite the years in between and being stronger and more confident herself, it still hurt like hell.

"When you got here, I was thinking about that old saying, though I can't remember all of it. Something about tangled webs and lies?" She stared into the depths of the wine.

"'Oh what a tangled web we weave when first we practice to deceive.' Sir Walter Scott, early 1800's," Gabby supplied helpfully. When everyone including Roxy stared at her, she got defensive. "What? I was an English major in college for heaven's sake!"

Turning back to Roxy, she picked up their discussion. "Did Mac do something to deceive you? Did he lie to you? What is he, married? Secretly gay? Or in love with another woman?"

Roxy couldn't help it – she burst out laughing. "Gabby, only you would find some twists on this to turn it into one of the romance novels you write!"

Her friend blushed and opened her mouth to protest, thought the better of it, and took some pretzels and crunched instead, smiling.

"Okay, something's going on. You have to tell us, Rox. Now we're all in suspense," Tess urged.

Roxy lifted her eyes to the Sierras photo once again, willing it to bring her some peace as she came clean about the rest of her story. Even while she wanted to tell them, she knew what their reaction would be. Mac was still in town, scheduled to film the last two major outdoor scenes over the next two days. He probably wouldn't have any interactions with the girl tribe.

Still, she was protective of him. He would come off as the villain in their eyes, and truth be told, the present dilemma was as much her fault as his. She could have refused to be his personal chef, refused to put herself in daily contact with him.

And the sex part? That was clearly consensual. The feelings that she still had for him, the love that had survived the intervening years even when it wasn't returned, that was all on her.

Mea culpa.

"It was Mac. It's always been Mac. And it's Mac again."

This time the noise exploded as all five women burst out with questions. Roxy let it runs its course, knowing that at some point, they'd each run out of steam and wait for her to say whatever came next. She grabbed a handful of pretzels and gulped them, crunching with some satisfaction as her friends came to her fierce defense.

It took three whole minutes for them to get to the end of their rage on her behalf – she knew for sure since she timed it. It was very comforting in an odd way. Once they all fell silent, Roxy looked around them, pausing on each dear face.

"It's not his fault, at least not this time."

"But - !" Gabby started to argue, halting as soon as Roxy raised a palm.

"Years ago, yes, that was all on him. He left me, and he didn't even have the guts to do it face to face. He sent a flunky to do it. But now? Now it's different." She stood up to pace, the movement helping her sort out her feelings.

"I could have turned away multiple times over the last few weeks. Hell, I could have made myself scarce and never had anything to do with the movie catering. I could have insisted that Alej handle it all. But I guess a part of me, some part I didn't want to admit to, wanted to see Mac, to see if the feelings were still as strong."

"Have you been carrying a torch for him all these years?" Serena's question wasn't a surprise. In her heart of hearts Roxy knew she that all of the men she'd tried to date in between had fallen short when compared to Mac. It was easier to say all men were scum than explain why she felt that way.

"Ah, yeah, I guess I have. No one else ever moved me or fascinated me the way Mac did, the way he still does. Stupid, isn't it?" She flopped back to her place on the couch.

"No, Roxy, it isn't stupid in the least. When you meet someone who lights up your heart, everyone else is consigned to the shadows." Marguerite's expression carried the same deep understanding as her words.

"I probably will kick myself for bringing this up, but I have to. Rox, are you in love with him?" DK bit a thumbnail before shoving the offending hand into her pocket.

Roxy sighed. The soup just got thicker the longer it simmered.

"Yes, I love him. I never stopped, but I hid it from myself because what was the point? He forgot about me, and I had to move on with my life." She felt the tears threaten to start again.

"And how does he feel now?" Serena passed the box of tissue in preparation.

"It's a fling to him, I'm sure. He keeps hanging around me, and I know it's just the sex. Why else would he want to stick so close by?" She gave up trying to hold back the waterworks and let a few tears slide down her face, grabbing a stack of napkins along with the tissues just in case.

Tess cleared her throat. "Roxy, I couldn't figure it out before, but now maybe it makes sense. Mac's been very worried about you these past weeks. In fact, he was pestering me three or four times a day to hear about how things were going. When the convoy was being organized, no one could keep him from joining the trip. His eyes lit up with the prospect of it and he was as excited as a little boy. They made him sign a special waiver, protecting the county and the fire service in case something happened to him. They didn't want to be responsible."

She leaned forward to make her point. "His assistant, that woman Martha, had a fit. She didn't want him going, said he was putting himself in danger for no good reason. And do you know what he replied?"

Roxy shook her head, suddenly fascinated by the story.

"He said that you were up there, and that was the very important reason he needed to go, to see you and be with you. He signed that waiver so fast the fire chief didn't even have time to blink." She paused again as if measuring her words carefully. "So you see, maybe it isn't just a fling to him after all."

*****

After the girl tribe was finally convinced that Roxy had sniffed the last of her tears dry, they left, albeit with admonitions to call if she needed anything. She'd taken a long hot bath, a luxury she rarely allowed herself the time for. Her friends' parting words echoed in her mind.

"If you love him, you owe it to yourself to tell him. No matter how he responds, you'll know for sure and maybe, just maybe, you can move on in your love life, either way." Serena, ever the counselor, was intent on helping her find closure.

"Look, Vince and I didn't exactly have an orthodox beginning to our relationship, but we ended up in a great place. Who knows what some honesty will bring you? Not saying what was on my mind nearly cost me the future with the man I love. Don't make the same mistake I did." DK had hugged Roxy hard before she descended the front steps.

"And besides," added the ever-romantic Gabby, "what if you say the words, and then he says them right back? Have you ever considered that this might be a strong possibility?" Tess was agreeing with a vigorous shake of her head.

Marguerite was last, looking older than her years and undeniably sad. "You need to know, my friend, that the end result might not be what you hope for, but never knowing? That would be a true tragedy." Her wise eyes stared intently until she arched an eyebrow, gave Roxy a fast hug, and took up the rear of the procession down the stairs.

The water had long since become tepid, and even repeated additions of a hot stream from the tap no longer warmed things up enough to make them comfortable. She couldn't hide here any longer. The restaurant would reopen in two days, which meant tomorrow was the last quiet day she would have. The day after, the staff would be back, and with their return, announcements would be made, a flurry of changes would begin to take place, and her life would take yet another unexpected turn.

Tomorrow, she would spend some time going over her garden's offerings and vendor supplies and menu ideas. Everything would be ready for her staff to come back to work.

And then, in the quiet of the afternoon, she would visit the set and see if she could talk with Mac. It would be on his turf, but she could ready herself and have it be on her terms. She needed to have things out, once and for all.

Chapter 46

The hum of the commercial kitchen was comforting. She spread her lists of orders out on a worktable and drafted the menus for the coming week. There would be specials crafted from the daily surprises that she loved to receive from her suppliers. Those would be turned into additions for her guests.

Roxy realized with a pang that Alej would soon no longer be there to argue with over those menus. It had become part of their regular routine, the give and take of two chefs ruminating on how best to use the bounty of ingredients the area provided. She would have to encourage Patrick, who was going to receive the promotion he so richly deserved, to be willing to bicker with her.

The back door opened, not an unusual occurrence at this hour of the day, as vendors started arriving with produce and proteins for delivery. It was so common, in fact, that she didn't even turn her head to see who entered. The soft click of the door shutting blocked out the noise of vehicles on the road outside.

"Just a second, okay? I need to make myself one last note…"

There was no response. That was odd. She started to frown as she scribbled and dropped the pen, intent on turning around to bark out at whoever had come in that it was a good idea to announce themselves.

And met Mac's eyes, intense and unreadable across the space of the room.

*****

He would shock her, showing up here. She would never expect it. He was betting on that.

"Madeleine, how are you? Did you have a chance to rest after the last couple of weeks?"

His voice was lower than normal. In fact, he had to force himself to a volume loud enough to carry across the room. All of the emotions he was feeling tied him in knots, making it hard to breathe, much less talk.

It was that, or shout at her as the feelings overwhelmed him. There didn't seem to be any middle ground for him where she was concerned.

Her hair was loose for a change, a curtain of gold falling around her shoulders and swaying as she shook her head slowly. Her eyes were no longer saucers, the blue settling into the familiar cornflower that always held him enthralled. Her mouth changed from a surprised circle to a single grim line.

"I'm fine Mac, thanks for asking. And it's Roxy, remember?"

She turned back to her papers, making a big show of stacking everything, pounding the edges on the counter until they lined up, and placing the pile in a file folder at her elbow. Pulling her hair back, she stood up straighter and folded her hands on the table. Finally, she looked back up at him.

"Did you need something? Because I thought I made it clear when we were up on the mountain that our arrangement," she put the word in air quotes, "was over. Aren't you filming the last scene tomorrow?"

Damn her, she was acting like none of this mattered. The last two months, the intimacies they'd shared, and the times he could see the echo of the love they'd had before in her eyes. Like the fact that he had to leave this weekend made no difference to her at all.

He ground his teeth together in frustration. He wanted to tell her how he felt, letting her know that he loved her, whatever the consequences.

"I believe we still have things to say to each other." He took two paces into the room as he said it.

She frowned more deeply now, with unmistakable hurt in her eyes. "Say what kinds of things?"

He found it impossible to open his mouth, his feet stuck to the tile floor and his hands opening and closing pointlessly at his sides. She continued to stare at him, and as time passed, her expression held more and more disappointment.

And hurt. The hurt was getting stronger.

Breathing in to avoid passing out, he said the first thing that popped into his head. "I was wondering if you'd like to come visit me for a while, in LA. Maybe a long while. You know, so that you could be with me."

It sounded lame, coming out like an invitation to visit instead of a commitment to be at her side for the rest of her life.

Why was it so hard for him to say the words? He'd said them thousands of times to leading ladies on so many sets, he'd forgotten most of the their names as well as the movies. Hell, he'd even said it to a dog in one film.

But when it counted, when it was most important, he couldn't say them to the one woman he'd always wanted to shout them to, Madeleine.

Three little words, eight letters in total.

He coughed, throat dry and aching. It wasn't the remembered smoke from the fire. The one time when it wouldn't be an act, he couldn't bring himself to drop the barriers he'd erected years ago when she left him on that rainy San Francisco morning.

What if she didn't return the sentiment? The risk was too great.

She stared at him across the expanse of the sparkling commercial kitchen. Only the hum of refrigerators and freezers broke the silence. Her eyes were narrowing, the cornflower blue reminding him of deep water on a summer day.

Moving forward and rounding the prep tables between them took too long. By the time he was in front of her, the tears in her eyes turned them into shimmering pools. He saw the effort she made to pull them back, her shoulders rising and her spine straightening as he looked down at her.

He knew she would knife herself in the hand before she let him see her cry.

*****

She had to know, so she had to ask him.

"Why do you want me to be with you?"

He hesitated, then smiled his best movie star smile and ran a single finger down her cheek.

"Because I want to show you off. Because I want to take care of you, and give you everything you need and everything you want. Because I want to pleasure you in every way possible, and when I'm done, I want to start all over again."

She stepped back one pace, two paces. It hurt, more than the worst burn or deepest slice of a knife. Because what he wanted wasn't enough.

Confusion filled his face and he lifted a foot to step towards her, but her raised hand stopped him midstride.

"You should go, Mac." Silently, she added, go, before my heart cracks open and I serve it to you on a well-decorated platter.

"Why?" The wattage of the smile dimmed. He still didn't get it.

"Because it isn't enough!"

As the echo of her shout stopped bouncing off each polished steel surface and resonating in every pot and pan hanging on its rack, she turned her back to him, selecting a knife at random from the rack and pulling a tray of mixed vegetables towards her.

And she chopped.

The clock on the wall didn't seem to make any progress, and he didn't say a word. He was still there. She could feel his presence, the energy she would recognize with every nerve in her body until the day she died. Finally, it became too much.

"Why the hell are you still here?" She was surprised she could control the yell of her voice so that the sound in the kitchen only reverberated once.

"I want to invite you to the final day of shooting. We've been keeping the ending a secret, and I'd like you to see it." When she didn't turn around and didn't reply, he added, "I think you'll find a lot of meaning in it."

When she still bit her tongue, a harsh sigh sounded behind her. His voice was low when he said, "It's my way of saying thank you for everything you've done for me, Madeleine."

She couldn't bring herself to respond. He wasn't able to call her by the name she'd chosen for herself when she was alone. And he was willing to bring her to Hollywood, treat her like a possession and show her off, but he wasn't able to say the three words she needed.

Of course, she couldn't bring herself to say them either. The hurt from years ago, telling him so often how much she loved him and hearing him say the words in return only to have him spurn her, was too scary.

Her precision with the julienne cuts on each and every vegetable took time. She was intent on the resulting matchsticks, and them alone. Concentration made it easier for her to control the wild beating of her heart as it broke again.

Only when the brightly colored array was lined up like neat ranks of soldiers in identical formations on the scarred board did she turn around.

She was alone again. He was gone.

And only then did she allow herself one lousy tear.

Chapter 47

The thwunk of the darts as they hit the board mixed with three different sports networks playing on the TVs and the dense clatter of semi-full glasses being set to rest on tables. It was a guys' kind of place, the sounds identical to those heard in bars around the world when men got together in a place where they could feel at home.

Mac's dart missed the bull's-eye. In fact, he narrowly hit the board at all, the dart hanging precariously close to the edge of the outer circle. Male laughter erupted behind him.

"Man, you're really lousy at this, aren't you?" Vince came to rescue the remaining darts as Mac stepped back, his chance to score any points and avoid buying the next round of beers now eliminated.

"Yeah, I pretty much suck at it. I don't know why I've never been able to get the knack of the throw exactly right."

He moved back to the tall table where the others hunkered on stools. Rick and Deke, a rancher from the southern part of the county, were having an energetic discussion about water rights. Mac had a hard time focusing on the rapid exchange about seepage rates, flow calculations, and something call evapotranspor-something. Seems you needed an engineering degree to participate in that one.

"Next round's on me, guys." He slapped money on the table and signaled the waitress, an older woman who balanced a full tray of pints over her head as she moved through the tight confines of the packed bar with skill that spoke of her decades of experience. She lifted a chin in Mac's direction in acknowledgment.

"You lost again? Man, you are truly hopeless. What guy can't learn how to throw a dart?" Steve shook his head in disbelief, even as he enthusiastically finished the last of his ale.

"What can I say? This isn't something they taught us in acting school. If I had to throw darts in a role I was playing, they'd need to bring in a dart-toss stunt double."

The men laughed at Mac's self-deprecation, even as Vince whooped about a full-on bull's eye on the board.

"Read 'em and weep, boys. I am the continuing champion and reigning supreme dart player." Vince pointed to the chalk scoreboard in victory.

Everyone slapped him on the back and agreed that he did indeed reign supreme at this, even if he wasn't that good at almost everything else. Vince looked offended and started to swear at the group of them as they burst into laughter again.

Glancing around at the animal heads mounted in the darker reaches of the tall stone room, Mac drained his own bock beer and considered how life had taken him in a completely new direction. First, finding Madeleine again, only now she was Roxy and she had built a very successful life without him. And once he was feeling better, she seemed to care even less about whatever would happen to him in the future.

Then he found a group of guys he'd come to think of as friends, even close friends in fact.

He would miss this, Mac realized with renewed sadness, leaning on the table as the cacophony of noise eddied around him. The unsteadiness ranging through him had nothing to do with the one beer he'd finished, and he fought the urge to roll his shoulders and duck his head in deeper than any turtle could.

Over the past two months, the camaraderie of the wolf pack, as dubbed by Roxy, had grown tight. Dane,

Vince and Rick had already formed a solid friendship based on the girl tribe women in their lives. After that first interview when he was newly arrived on the movie set, they'd welcomed him with solid backslaps and raucous conversation. Steve and Dave, both county workers, had become part of the group through Rick. Deke was a cousin and good buddy of Dave, and he'd joined them off and on as they met here at Mallory's or enjoyed the various fishing streams in the area.

He didn't have a tight circle of guy friends in southern California, men he could trust to watch his back and come to his defense when needed. He had to pay for that kind of protection. The concept was depressing.

Being a loner in the movie industry was often the safest path to take. Get selected for a role over someone else and have the film become a blockbuster, and pretty soon, the guy you thought of as a buddy was suddenly busy stabbing you in the back on every media feed and social networking site. Trust and friendship were hard to come by and even harder to maintain.

The waitress appeared at his shoulder with a tray of refills. "One more round, boys? You celebratin' somethin' or what?" She picked up empties and thudded full glasses on the table, all the while keeping that tray high in the air.

Yeah, everyone had their skill, and she made the balance of that tray seem like a true art form.

"Our buddy here's leaving us, heading back to the hot lights and high times in Hollywood." Vince slapped Mac on the back as he picked up his beer. "We won't miss your ugly mug much, but I for one will miss your lack of skill at darts." And he took a loud and appreciative gulp of his beer.

Rick and Deke dropped their intense discussion to tune back in to the others. "But you're going to coming back some time soon, right Mac? I mean, you can't avoid it, can you?" Rick looked like the answer was a given.

"Yeah, how long before you can break away, do you think?" Steve's question seemed to be on every man's mind as they turned to stare at him.

Mac felt the churning of his gut, a feeling not unlike when he was sick, except this had nothing to do with anything he'd eaten. "Ah, don't know exactly. There are a lot of steps in post-production for the movie, and then we'll begin the media circuit once we have the final release date, and…"

"But you'll have time off during all that. Com'on, you're the director for shit's sake. You can get away. She'll expect it." Vince took another sip of beer, but this time his serious gaze stayed on Mac's face and he didn't blink away.

Playing dumb might be the best strategy. "Who'll expect it?" He posed the question and raised his glass, intent on making his expression as neutral and uninterested as possible. He was, after all, an actor.

Deke snorted. "Hell, man, I don't even know you that well and even I could see the sparks coming off the two of you. You lit up like the casinos in Tahoe when you saw her at the fire camp. I thought you were going to jump out of the truck while it was still in gear, you were so eager to get to her."

The general laughter and nudging elbows meant that no matter what he said now to the contrary, no one was going to believe him. He'd worn his feelings for Roxy on his face and everyone knew how deep a hole he'd dug himself into. Everyone, it appears, except Roxy.

"You've got it wrong, guys, seriously. That was just concern for a friend, that's all. Roxy became a good friend while she was my personal chef, and I was worried about her." He tried for another casual sip of beer in the silence that followed his comment.

"Don't feed us a line of bullshit, okay Mac? We care about Roxy, care a lot about her as a matter of fact. She works hard not to need anyone, and there isn't a guy here who wouldn't jump to help her without even being asked." Vince had slammed his glass back on the table so hard, amber ale was pooling around its base and surrounding tables had stopped to listen in on their conversation. The sports feeds boomed suddenly in the second silence in as many minutes.

Dane cleared his throat and looked up, the frown on his features making the scar on his face stand out white and fierce. "Are you saying that you don't feel anything for Roxy now, not like you did all those years ago?"

He'd tried to forget about letting out the fact that he and Madeleine had a relationship years ago, lulled that day in the warmth and camaraderie of fishing. Once the ribbing had died down, the guys had been intent on finding out, as discreetly as possible, Roxy's side of the story. Sworn to secrecy that they used repeatedly to lord over Mac, they'd been plying their women with subtle questions about Roxy's past in San Francisco. At least they thought they had been discreet.

Mac thought they were probably handling things like loose locomotives heading downhill fast, but there was little he could do to stop them. He just kept insisting that there was nothing going on now but friendship.

No one believed him.

"Listen, I've got an early start tomorrow and the wrap party tomorrow night, so I'm going to head out. This should cover it. Take it easy." He dropped a stack of bills on the table and slapped Vince on the back, raising a hand to the others in salute before pushing through the crowd towards the door.

The cooler night air was a relief. It hadn't been stuffy in Mallory's, exactly, but the tension of the turn in conversation had ratcheted up the volume and the heat, at least for him.

"Mac, hold up."

Dane and Vince exited the bar and walked towards him, intent on their mission. He had a bad feeling they were going to try to convince him the there was a future with Roxy, but he knew differently.

He waited, intending to let them start their arguments so that he could counter as quickly as possible and leave. The thought of leaving in a matter of a couple of days, leaving Roxy here and flying to a place he was supposed to call home, weighed on him. They didn't need to remind him of how painful it was going to be.

Dane and Vince glanced at each other, and Vince waved a hand as if to invite Dane to go first before they both turned back forward.

"Look, Mac, we know how hard it can be to walk away. And how it's even harder to stay. Commitment hasn't come easy, not for any of us."

Vince chimed in, "Yeah, and Dane was the first, so you can only imagine the walls he had to scale to win Serena."

Dane gave him a hard look before turning back to Mac. "I wanted to walk away, I really did. I was convinced that I was better off alone and that the world was better off if I never participated in it past what was absolutely necessary. Serena wore me down, pure and simple."

Seeing them together today, Mac couldn't dream that they'd been anything other than joined at the hip since they'd first met. Evidently, the real story was much more intriguing.

"It's not the same, okay? I know what you found is special, I can see that. Hell, the whole world can see it." A sudden wave of harsh envy hit him. Serena had wanted to fight for Dane. DK stuck by Vince. The comparison to what was happening between he and Roxy was almost funny.

He let out a laugh, the cruel tone self-directed as he shook his head. "It's not like that, man, not at all. Roxy could care less if I lived or died at this point. It's not like she's tripping over herself to even see me, right?"

Dane was already shaking his head. "That's part of the point though. Roxy isn't like Serena or DK. Roxy is convinced, and she'll tell anyone who asks her, that men are scum when it comes to relationships. Present company excluded, except for Vince."

The comment earned Dane a punch in the arm from Vince and a short chuckle from Mac.

"My point is, I don't think she ever got over you all those years ago. Don't you see, Mac? Why else would she swear off relationships? She's still hurting from what you did to her all those years ago."

They didn't get it. "What do you mean, what I did to her? I loved her. I wanted to build a life with her. We were going to go to Europe and travel the world until my next role. I wanted her next to me, always. And she left me."

The anger and hurt at the memory of her walking away that rainy morning was suddenly fresh and green, as monstrous and painful as when he had returned to the hotel room to find Martha sitting there, shaking her head and delivering the bad news.

"Ah, that's not what we hear." Vince looked like he'd swallowed broken glass rather than his beer, but he squared his shoulders and continued.

"We've been doing some digging. Quizzing the womenfolk, not that they give much away because they're banded together tighter than a squad of commandos, but Alej could shed some light. And man, unless she was involved with some other actor fifteen years ago in San Francisco during the rainy season, you got it wrong."

Chapter 48

"I know you'll join me in wishing Alej and Jeannine the best of luck in their future at Paush's. If anyone can turn things around there, it's these two."

Loud applause and catcalls, along with all nature of snide comments and good-natured cursing, rang out in the kitchen as the key cooking staff from the store and the front of house and kitchen staff from Roxy's restaurant congratulated the outgoing chefs. They would leave at the end of the service week. Everyone who had been offered a chance to step up had been excited about their opportunity, even the interns.

Ticia was overwhelmed to be offered an entry-level job in the restaurant, the bottom rung of the kitchen ladder. Once she'd dried her tears and quieted down from her repeated thanks, Roxy had a chance to get a word in edgewise.

"I know you'll do fine, Ticia. You have the right sense about the food, an instinct about how things go together. You just need to trust that, okay?"

"Yes Chef, absolutely. I've learned so much from you and the others, and I'll just keep learning and listening, I promise."

Roxy smiled. Self-confidence was still something she needed to work on, her smooth banter with the firefighters aside.

"Feel free to argue with me once in a while too, okay? I'm not perfect. Patrick and the others aren't either, and we've all been where you are, starting out. If you see something that you think could be done differently, making a meal better, say so. I promise, my bite doesn't leave a scar."

Ticia looked startled for a second before her smile gleamed from ear to ear.

"Yes Chef. I promise to talk back every once in a while." And she giggled.

Roxy had to grin right back. This one was a true diamond in the rough, and with some polish, she was going to be amazing.

Deciding to use Bob's dessert talents between the restaurant and store, Roxy had proposed he work with the current pastry chef to hone and expand his skills. She was a little surprised when he countered her offer with one of his own.

"You see, Chef, I didn't know."

She was confused, and looked questioningly at the tall man sitting across the desk.

"Breakfast, Chef. I didn't know I would be good at that. I learned that I loved that, up on the fire line. I have an idea, if you want to hear it."

Intrigued, she waved him on.

"I could work at the store in the mornings, making breakfast on demand for the customers. You know, kind of like a breakfast bar. They'd come to the breakfast bar, order their meal, and while I'm making it, they could go order their coffee. By the time they get back, it's done and bagged."

The precarious position on the edge of the chair meant that he might be slipping off to the floor any second, but Roxy could only appreciate his enthusiasm.

"That's an interesting idea, Bob. We have ready-to-go breakfast meals, but they aren't hot. We have the café area where people can eat if they want to. I'd like to think about it. But I have to ask you – what about desserts?"

His Oriental face split into a wide smile, lighting up his features in a way nothing else could. "Oh, I still want to do those too. I figure I can do breakfast from six in the morning until maybe ten, and then switch over to desserts for the rest of the day."

She was impressed that he seemed to have thought the plan out. When he pulled out a spreadsheet and handed it across the desk, outlining costs, units of production, and marketing concepts, her own grin rivaled his.

"Okay, Bob, let me look through this and get back to you. I like the idea, and I love your initiative."

It was only ten in the morning, and she already felt like she'd run a marathon through the kitchen and garden and back, a hundred times. The emotions of the day only made things worse.

She was truly happy for Alej, since he seemed so overjoyed himself. The light of love shined out of his eyes every time he looked at Jeannine, and the woman's gaze mirrored it. They deserved to be happy.

She thought back to Mac's visit. There, the chances weren't good. In fact, they were nonexistent.

Today was the day, shooting the final scene. It would be followed by the wrap party, which Roxy's would be catering tonight, and then tomorrow, Mac would leave. And she would be getting on with her life again.

It hurt. But she was strong. She would put it behind her once more.

The phone interrupted her misery, the caller ID showing DK's name. A welcomed respite from feeling sorry for herself.

"Hey, DK, how are you?"

"Roxy, I think it's more important for me to be asking how you are. And why aren't you on the movie set?"

Roxy frowned into the phone. "Why should I be?" She hadn't told any of her friends about Mac's insistent invitation.

The impatient grunt at the other end of the line was accompanied by a rattle of keys. "Come on, Mac invited you. He told Vince, and Vince told me. And Mac really wants you there. When are you leaving?"

Fidgeting in the chair in embarrassment that her private business with Mac was now a topic of discussion among her friends and their guys, Roxy put a firm note in her voice. "I'm not going. There's no reason to."

"Mac asked you. He wants you to see the ending. Come on, none of us know what the ending will be. Even the crew doesn't. And the cast has been sworn to secrecy. Aren't you even a little bit curious?" Her last question was delivered on a slight pant.

Roxy frowned at the phone again. "I can wait until it comes out. Besides, I have work to do." Though how she would concentrate on it, she wasn't sure.

The roar of a truck engine sounded through the receiver. "I'm picking you up, and I'm not taking no for an answer. I'll be there in ten, so be ready."

Opening her mouth to protest again, Roxy wasn't given the chance.

"Don't even think about hiding from me, Roxy LaFollette. Because I'll find you, and there will be consequences." DK chuckled on the other end of the line. "And you might think about throwing on some make-up and maybe brushing out your hair too."

Chapter 49

He peered around the perimeter again, frowning and deep in thought. Martha had been conspicuously absent today, which was probably just as well. He had a few questions for her, and he didn't think he was going to like her answers, if she was honest with him.

Mac's gaze locked on Barry, who shook his head. Barry was watching for Roxy, assigned the task of making sure she had a front row seat to the final scene's taping. So far, there was no sign of her.

The plan had been hatched over Scotch and more beer at his rented house, Vince and Dane telling him about Roxy's take on what happened in San Francisco. They moved on to how to ensure that she was present to see the message he'd built into the final scene.

His actors had been curious. Justin grumbled about the changes, more put out than truly interested.

"I mean, why can't we shoot what we had in the original script? I already memorized that." As his recovery from his broken leg progressed, so did his level of whining. It hadn't taken him long to return to his former pain-in-the-ass self.

Sheila had been more intrigued. "I see what you're doing, Mac, and I think it works well with the plot. It wraps things up nicely." She tilted her head at him curiously, sympathy winning out in her face. "Is this about the chef?"

Too close to right on target. She'd merely smiled at Mac's denial and said she'd be ready. When they rose to leave the dining room office in his house, she'd given him an uncharacteristic hug.

"Good luck, Mac."

Yeah, he needed a shitload of luck. He needed the jinx to be lifted.

He needed Roxy to be here.

He remembered the men's assurances two nights ago. "Look Mac, Serena and DK will help. We'll swear them to secrecy."

He'd huffed out a groan of disbelief. "They'd keep a secret from a member of the girl tribe, just because you ask?" He was dubious about the chance of this working.

Dane had reassured him. "They love Roxy. It would appear, and I'm just saying this because of how Serena acted when I was prodding about the status of you and Roxy, that the woman has feelings for you too. How deep, who knows. If there's a chance to bring Roxy happiness, Serena would walk across hot coals."

Vince shook his head in agreement. "Yeah, DK too. If Roxy doesn't show up, they'll bring her. They can do it, we promise."

Still, after he visited her with his unsuccessful personal invitation, he had even graver doubts.

"Mac, we need to get going. Can't wait any longer. Can I call the cast and crew back?" His assistant director stood at his shoulder on the boom camera's platform.

It was going to be whatever it would be. Clearly the women couldn't convince her. Disappointment made the sunny day dim.

Sheila and Justin jumped up from their seats, probably as eager to get this finished up as the rest of the crew. It was an emotional scene, one that spread feelings on thickly and was guaranteed to have at least some of the audience in tears.

Of course, there was only one woman he personally wanted to have feeling all of that emotion, one that meant everything to him.

In the stillness of the crowd's sudden anticipation, Barry's waving arms and thumbs-up was a bright spot of commotion.

Mac's gut clenched even as he blew out a dense sigh of relief.

*****

"I don't know why you two insisted I come to this." Roxy was locked between Serena and DK, marching through a crowd that parted like they were royalty.

Serena harrumphed and pinched her side.

"Ow! What was that for?"

"For being so stubborn about coming. It's not like Mac's going to bite, you know."

It had taken both Serena and DK to drag her out of the kitchen office, dumping her chef's coat unceremoniously on a counter on the way out the door. In the truck, they had insisted she take her hair down from its usual bun. Serena shoved a mascara wand in her hand.

"You raided my bathroom? Really? What the hell is so damned important about this? It's just a movie."

Serena and DK both smiled secretively and Serena patted Roxy's shoulder while DK drove fast into the movie set's parking lot.

"Hi Chef! We're – that is, the Boss-man – is so glad to see you here." Barry turned and waved at Mac, who was perched up on a platform suspended from a movable boom next to a large camera. Ten feet or more off the ground, and at a distance, Roxy could still read the open relief in Mac's smile.

She didn't want to, but she couldn't help it. It might be the last time she got a chance to do it.

She smiled back.

Someone was calling for quiet, someone else was calling for positions and lighting triggers and other things that made no sense to her. The crowd became unnaturally immobile, everyone waiting and straining to hear the actors.

*****

He'd written the last scene to reflect the past, and to make a promise for the present and the future. Mac hoped that Madeleine heard it, and that she understood the message he was sending.

Sheila played her part to perfection. "When I needed you to put our love first, you weren't there. You left when I needed you most." Her face reflected the hurt the character was feeling.

Justin moved in closer. "That was a mistake. In fact, the past was all a big mistake. I never left you, at least not willingly." As written in the script, he took Sheila's hands in his, even as she shied away. Then he waited.

Mac stole a look at Roxy. She was watching the act, a neutral expression on her face.

"CUT!" Mac yelled and the actors relaxed and looked to him for direction. He jumped down the three steps from the platform, coming in close enough to whisper hoarsely. When both actors nodded their agreement, he climbed back up and resumed his seat.

Before he signaled for the filming to start again, he stared at Roxy. She was watching him, a slight frown pulling her eyebrows together, leaning back in the camp chair he'd had placed for her at the edge of the set. Confusion raced across her features.

This time, Sheila played the scene with a little more anger and a little more angst. Justin said his lines and took her hands, not hesitating this time in adding the rest of the scripted words.

"I loved you then, and I love you even more now, even if you can't forgive me. You see, I thought you left me. I searched for you for a long time, but you'd disappeared."

The actors pulled closer and Justin finished his lines. "Please, forgive me. Let's start over. I want us to have a chance for a future. I want my future to be with you."

Justin could have been standing on his head as he delivered that statement, because the only thing Mac could watch was Roxy. His heart was pounding so hard he was sure it would be picked up on the tape. No matter. They could edit that out.

What he never wanted to edit out was Roxy in his life.

She was shaking her head with what he hoped was comprehension and understanding heating her face. Blinking rapidly, she turned to stare at him. He couldn't look away.

"Look out!" A cinematographer yelled the warning even as a light mounted on another boom a few feet away swung free from its bracket.

Mac experienced it all in slow motion. He turned towards the cracking sound as the bracket broke. It started to swing in a loose arc, held in that rotation by the cord at its base. It was swinging in the direction of the crowd, which was now starting to exclaim at the problem.

But not everyone was looking at it. Roxy was still looking at him, oblivious to the light and the danger it posed. Mac fought against the sudden paralysis that glued his mouth closed and muted his voice.

Then everything rushed back to full speed.

"Roxy, look out!" His yell and sudden jump to his feet got her attention, and she focused too slowly on the people rushing backwards and the noise around her. She turned towards the object racing towards her.

Even as his feet hit the ground, Mac heard the splitting sound as the edge of the light caught Roxy on the forehead.

Chapter 50

"Get the hell out of my way!" He almost punched a crewmember who didn't move fast enough. Everyone was now crowding around the woman who was hidden somewhere among all of those feet.

"I said move, now!" Mac shoved and elbowed until he was crouched next to Roxy.

"Madeleine? Madeleine! Wake up, sweetheart!"

His knees gave out when he saw her, eyes shut and blood weeping from the spot on her forehead where the light had hit her. He vaguely heard someone calling for everyone to move back.

He eased an arm under her, pulling her up to cradle her head against his chest. The blood was smearing everywhere, on his shirt, on his hands. He didn't care.

Madeleine. After everything they'd been through and when maybe, just maybe, she finally understood that he hadn't walked out on her all those years ago.

He was tempted to destroy every recording of the movie and never let it see the light of day.

"It's the jinx." He whispered the condemnation.

"What'd you say, Boss?" Barry was at his side, a confused question on his face.

He'd been saying it himself, and out loud at that. This was the last straw in this cursed movie.

"Ambulance is three minutes out. Is Chef okay?" Barry's worried face moved to Roxy's other side and he offered Mac a towel to help staunch the bleeding.

"I don't know." The icy compression of his heart barely kept enough oxygen flowing for him to think.

"Mac! What happened! We were standing over there in the back. We couldn't see…" The anxious faces of Serena and DK pushed to the front of the straining crowd. Mac shook his head at them, not even raising his eyes.

All he could see was Madeleine, her eyes closed and her face pale and still. It wasn't like sleep. It was like death.

He couldn't breathe.

"Let me through. Let me pass." The set's nurse bustled up, clucking even as she opened her bag. "My, my. Did anyone see where she got hit?"

"Her forehead," Barry supplied helpfully. He'd moved behind Mac again and was attempting to pull his boss to his feet.

"No, I'm not moving." Mac tightened his hold on Roxy and hovered his body over her protectively.

"Now Mr. Smythe. There, there. I know you feel responsible. But let me help her, alright?" The nurse's quiet singsong voice did little to ease his anxiety.

"Why is still she out cold? Could it have hit her that hard?" He finally looked up into the older woman's kind eyes.

She shook her head in understanding and gently pressed clean gauze to Roxy's forehead, trying to blot enough blood away to see the extent of the injury.

"Coming through. Everyone move out of the way please." An authoritative voice rang over the silent crowd, and everyone took a few more paces backwards.

"What happened?" A paramedic, a muscular man who would have had little trouble lifting both Roxy and Mac as one, was persistently pushing Mac back.

"She got hit in the forehead by a falling light. She hasn't woken up." Mac finally relinquished his hold when the paramedic pushed firmly against his hands.

"We'll take good care of her, sir, I promise." The man gave Mac a brief pat on the shoulder before concentrating on Roxy again.

It was a blur, the taking of vitals, the checking of pupils, the start of an IV. Barry kept trying to pull Mac away. Serena had his other arm, but she was gripping tightly, DK on her other side.

"Why doesn't she wake up?" Mac was asking the question of no one in particular, but Serena squeezed his arm comfortingly even as she continued to watch the activity on the ground in front of them.

He ground his teeth together to hold himself back from crying out her name again. He wanted to yell at her to come back from wherever she was hiding. They had things to discuss.

The paramedic and his female partner rolled Roxy carefully on to a gurney, and along with a team of firefighters, they hefted it across the uneven rocky ground.

Mac surged forward, even as Barry and the assistant director were now trying to pull him back.

"No, not now!" He almost pushed the two of them to the ground in his need to follow the gurney.

"But Mac, we have to finish shooting the scene. We're going to lose the light."

"Mac, we'll go to the hospital. We'll let you know what's happening, okay? And then as soon as you're done you can join us there." DK hesitated, then swung him around so that he looked at her.

"I'm sure Roxy will be fine. She's tough. You know that." Her sympathy was obvious as well.

Hell, everyone on the set probably figured out by now that he loved her. If only she'd open her eyes so he could tell her.

"It's my fault, all my fault. Back then. Now. She wouldn't have been sitting there if..." He bit off the rest of his words.

"Mac. No one blames you for this. It was an accident. And the two of you can discuss back then later. I have a feeling that like you put in the movie, it was all a misunderstanding too." DK gave his arm a last comforting squeeze as she headed for her truck, Serena on her heels.

"Mac? Shall we get things rolling again?" The assistant director was talking at his elbow, using the hushed tones usually reserved for the unhinged.

That was the way he felt right now.

The faster he got things done, the faster he could get to the hospital to see her.

"Okay, one minute." He shook off the man's hand, even as a lighting assistant ran up full of rapid explanations. He waved them both off.

They were getting ready to load the gurney in the back of the ambulance. He was across the distance without knowing how his feet had moved. Standing next to the gurney as it began to lift, he looked down into her still face, the blood leaving dried tracks even while it still oozed.

"Roxy, I know you can hear me. You're too stubborn not to hear me. So listen, and listen hard." He coughed once to hide the hint of tears in his voice, and leaned closer to whisper.

"I love you, Madeleine Roxy LaFollette. Remember that. We are not done with this, not by a long shot."

Chapter 51

Her head ached despite the crap they'd given her, the pounding like the continuing menace of a mallet taken to the hardest steak in the world to tenderize it.

"Ms. LaFollette, we have to keep you for twenty-four hours of observation. It is a precaution, though I do not see any signs of permanent damage. You took a significant blow to your forehead, and you were out for quite a while. A concussion like that means you need to take it easy."

She argued with the doctor, but the small Asian woman had more stamina than she did at that moment. She rubbed at the bandage on her forehead.

"Relax, Ms. LaFollette. You will not have a scar. It ended up being a small deep cut right at the hairline. In a few days, you won't even need a band-aid. And the stitches were done very carefully." The woman smiled understandingly. "I did a rotation in plastic surgery, and I sewed you up myself."

That was the least of her concerns. The vague idea that Mac had said something important to her, something she couldn't remember, was more pressing.

She'd woken up as the ambulance jostled over the bumpy county roads. It hurt like a hell.

"Almost there, ma'am. Can't give you anything until the docs check you out, sorry." The young man had put a comforting hand over hers and squeezed. "Can you tell me who the President of the United States is?"

She'd answered without thinking, craning her eyes around the interior of the small space because her head was immobilized in some sort of brace, searching for the one face she'd hoped to find.

No, it had been a dream, something her addled mind had made up.

She remembered the set, or she thought she did. She remembered the actors' words, or she thought she could. They told her a light hit her on the forehead, but she didn't remember that part.

Probably just as well.

Serena and DK had rushed in as soon as the doctors allowed it.

"Rox, are you okay? Do you know who we are?"

She'd laughed at that, though it hurt.

"Yes, I know who you are. You're my very best worrywart friends who talked me into going to that damn set in the first place." Before they'd had a chance to burst into the apologies she knew were coming, she added, "and I'm glad I went, I think."

This snapped closed both of their mouths around whatever they had planned to say next.

"Was Mac in the ambulance with me?"

Serena shook her head and DK frowned at her question.

"Ah, no. But he was with you after you passed out. People couldn't drag him away. Why?"

She tried to make her pounding head concentrate on the hint of a memory. Hesitating to bring it up, she waited, hoping that a clearer picture would come into her mind. No success.

"I, ah, had the strangest dream. It was Mac, in the ambulance, and he was talking to me."

"What was he saying, honey? Because he was talking to you when you were still on the ground. Could you be confusing the two?"

Despite the lance of pain it cost her, Roxy shook her head. "No, there were lights and beeping, like it was in the ambulance."

Serena covered her clenched fist, and DK held on to her other arm above the IVs. "What do you remember?"

Roxy closed her eyes. It had to be a dream. In fact, her memory of that scene from the movie must be a dream too. Because Mac Smythe couldn't have those kinds of feelings for her.

*****

They'd shot the last goddamned scene, because he knew it was his duty to do it.

"Great job everybody, great work." He'd done the obligatory closing from his perch on the camera platform. "And that's a wrap."

His half-hearted traditional closing brought the expected cheers and claps. Even as he climbed down, his eyes couldn't avoid the patch of ground now brown and dull with Roxy's dried blood. His footing faltered and he would have slipped from the platform if the lighting guy – the same one who was apologizing constantly – hadn't caught him.

"I'm really sorry, Mr. S., really. I hope she's okay."

They had wanted him to change his clothes, Barry and the again-present Martha. He didn't want to. The blood on his shirt and jeans was Roxy's. He wasn't going to give them up without a fight.

Just like he wasn't going to give the woman up without one.

Serena and DK kept him posted. Roxy woke up in the ambulance. They couldn't see her yet because the doctors were doing all sorts of tests. Then they texted that they would be able to see her shortly. Things seemed to be good, or at least as good as they could be until he could be at her bedside.

As the crew was packing, the chatter about the night's wrap party foremost on everyone's mind after the excitement of the accident died down, a sheriff's deputy arrived.

"Sir, I'd like to ask you a few questions about the incident that happened today."

The redheaded woman could have been a movie star playing a cop. He had the random thought while he frowned at her. She was delaying him.

He signaled for his current shadow, Barry. "My assistant can answer whatever questions you have." He moved to brush by her, only to be stopped by her raised arm blocking his way. She was careful not to touch him.

"I understand that you had a unique view of what happened from the top of the camera platform. I'd just like to get your statement. It's routine. We want to rule out negligence. I'm sure you'd like to cooperate on this."

Goddamn, another jinx. It would just be his luck…

"Yes, I'd be happy to answer your questions."

That had taken an hour. She walked him through what happened twice, then had him pace the ground he'd covered to get to Roxy's side.

"You understand, I'm sure, that we all love Roxy around here." The glint in her eye told him that if there was a whiff of any problem, he would personally be visiting the county jail.

And then she'd asked him, politely of course, to come down to the sheriff's office to sign a typed copy of the statement.

At almost six o'clock, the updates from Serena and DK didn't make him feel any more secure.

"She's still awake, so the concussion doesn't seem to have caused any permanent damage. She's talking, and she knows who we are, and she seems to remember today." DK had stopped after that, and the silence on the phone was deafening.

"Is she, ah, asking for me?" The question itself clenched the fist around his heart tighter.

DK remained silent for three beats, and the grip became rigid. "No Mac, she's not asking for you."

He'd stood in his living room, looking down at the blood caking his shirt, and clicked off without responding.

He took off the shirt with care, folding it so that the bloodied sides were facing up. After doing the same with his jeans, he'd laid them over the back of a dining room chair.

Pacing the room and only removing his eyes from the blood when he had to, he searched the programs in his smartphone until he found the phone number for the local hospital. He dialed the general number, waiting impatiently for the operator to pick up.

"Hello. I'd like to talk to a patient, Madeleine LaFollette."

"One moment sir. Let me transfer you."

The pause was so long.

"Med-Surg, Anderson. How can I help you?"

The man's voice threw him.

"I'd like to find out how Roxy LaFollette is doing."

"I'm sorry, sir, are you a family member?"

He swore and heard the male voice at the other end gasp, then softened his tone.

"No, I'm not. I'm a friend." He paused and crossed his fingers. "A very good friend."

He heard clicking keys, and the man said, "And your name? Ms. LaFollette has given us the names of the people we can release information to."

He gave it. More clicking.

The man's voice was more sympathetic this time. "I'm sorry, sir, you're not on her list."

He hung up without a comment. In his briefs alone, he walked quietly to the kitchen, opened a cupboard that held glasses and his favorite Scotch, and moved back to the dining room.

The chair he pulled up was identical to the one that held his clothes. If someone had been sitting in it, they would be knee to knee.

He poured himself a two-finger shot, thought about it after glancing at the clothes again, and added a finger.

Toasting the sight before him, he took a healthy swallow and allowed himself to feel the full brunt of loss.

Chapter 52

A pile driver pounded in his head. How the hell did he drink this stuff for all these years without killing himself?

He was face down on the floor in the dining room, and he had drooled on the carpet. Hammering resonated in his brain. He thought it was his brain pounding to get out of his skull, on to safer and saner heads.

"Mac! Open the hell up!"

He unscrewed his eyes, which complained about the maneuver and threatened to enlist his stomach in the protest.

"Mac, fucking goddamnit, you better the hell open up!"

He centered on the voice. It was Vince. He was upset. Vince was Mr. Snarky Cool, never upset.

That rattled through the alcohol ether in his brain and made him sit up too fast, the world taking a quick spin before he aligned eyes, head and stomach.

Snarky. Roxy. Oh shit.

"Coming, goddamnit. Coming."

Pulling himself upright on a chair, he caught sight of the bloodied clothes. It almost made him lose it, right there on the dining room rug.

Roxy's blood.

"Vince, is Roxy okay?" Talking before he reached for the handle, he yanked the front door open on the last words.

Vince, Dane and Rick were standing on the narrow front stoop, each in different poses that indicated action. Vince pushed by him first.

"What the hell were you thinking, man? You didn't go to the hospital last night."

*****

The sound in her head rivaled a huge cleaver striking a cutting board, but she didn't want any more of the wonder drugs they offered. She'd make do with aspirin.

The sun had risen as they woke her for the umpteenth time. Risk of brain swelling, they said, from the concussion. They wanted to keep making sure she was stable.

As stable as anyone could be with no real sleep and pounding that made putting her head in a bread mixer and turning it on high seem like child's play.

The door opened, and despite the hour, her heart leaped. But when it wasn't the one person she really wanted to see, she faded back into the pillows.

The gray-haired woman in the doorway was vaguely familiar. Roxy struggled to settle the face in her mind.

"Hello Roxy. Or should I say Madeleine? I hope you're feeling better."

"I'm sorry. Do we know each other?" She pushed to sit up straighter in the narrow hospital bed.

"That's not important. What is important is that I have some papers for you to sign. From Mr. Smythe."

Papers from Mac? It didn't make any sense. Maybe she should have taken the nurses up on that last round of wonder drugs.

"You have me at a distinct disadvantage. What kinds of papers?"

The woman smiled, and it looked evil on her.

"Just a simple release of liability, for the accident, you know." The proffered pen and papers were suspended over the bed.

"And why doesn't the esteemed Mr. Smythe bring me the papers himself?"

The woman waved as if the question and the concept didn't matter.

"He's very busy. The wrap party, shutting down the location, going home. You can imagine how it is." The woman moved the papers and pen closer.

"And where is Mr. Smythe now, may I ask?" Two could play at this uppity game.

As the woman smoothed her gray hair and set her face in a grimace of insolence, Roxy got it. It was the same bitch that Mac sent all those years ago, to clean up his 'mess'.

Not anymore.

Offering the pen and papers again, the woman leaned in. "I'm sure that you'll understand that mistakes happen."

Mistakes. Again, she was one of his fucking mistakes. There wasn't a curse word she could think of that would adequately describe her feelings right now.

*****

It was amazing how much high-octane coffee and a cold shower could do to sober someone up. That, and the threat offered by three guys who were your friends and suddenly wanted to beat the crap out of you for your stupidity.

"Why didn't you go to the hospital again?" Rick was quizzing him, even as he pulled fresh briefs and jeans out of a drawer and threw them at Mac. "Shower, cold, fast."

Why hadn't he pushed harder? He'd wanted to go more than his own life.

She didn't have him on her approved list. He probably wouldn't be on her approved list this morning either. The hell with it.

Dane shoved a blisteringly hot cup of coffee in his hands, even as he shaved at his friend's insistent and tried not to cut his own throat.

He was one dumbass guy. Dane didn't say it, but his eyes contained an encyclopedia of words, and none of them were complimentary right now.

"What the hell were you thinking, man?" Vince raved at him during the course of the six-minute drive from his front door to the hospital. Rick made record time and they all piled out of his sedan.

He was pounding up the front walk even as strong hands captured his arms on either side.

"Cool it, okay? You can't go rushing in there like a maniac. Hold on."

Rick and Vince were on either side of him. People were walking by, looking at them strangely until they recognized Mac. Then they whispered behind their hands, and they didn't even try to hide it very well.

Dane punched off his cell phone. "Third floor, three-one-eight. End of the hallway on your right. And Mac?"

He paused, only because the others still held him.

"Serena says good luck."

Chapter 53

"I'm not signing any release."

For a moment, the woman looked confused, one delicately tweezed eyebrow raised. It appeared that few people ever challenged her and the Hollywood legend she represented.

"Of course you're going to sign it. There's no question. It wasn't negligence, simply an accident."

Roxy felt her blood pressure climb, and even though it made her head pound worse, she was grateful for it. It gave her that extra energy she needed to come out with her own fires blazing.

She kept her voice quiet, unwilling to unleash all of the fury she was feeling.

"Please tell Mr. MacGillan Smythe to go fuck himself. And if he wants his papers signed, he'd better find the balls to bring them to me himself." She sat, the exertion costing her as the pounding increased and the monitor beside her bed started beeping in warning.

The woman blinked, twice, before a crafty expression settled in. "Ah yes. You're looking for something else now, aren't you? Not the lovelorn little girl anymore. How much will it take to get you out of Mac's life?"

The question should have shocked her, but instead Roxy felt a hint of triumph. This woman was nothing more than a go-between. Push hard enough, and Mac had to come to her, face to face, and say the words himself.

*****

He should probably have more finesse, but when Mac burst through the door, he was happy for once that he went with his emotions rather than intellect.

Roxy was lying in the bed, pale except for two bright splotches of red high on her cheeks. Anger sparked off her, brighter than the flame on any grill she'd ever run.

Standing at the foot of the bed, Martha was equally angry, the set of her back so straight that rulers could be modeled on it.

Neither woman seemed to notice him at first. Roxy moved her narrowed eyes to him and opened her mouth, even as Martha turned and fixed him with a chagrined stare as well.

"How the hell dare you?"

Thank all the gods. Even if she was swearing at him, she was talking. And it didn't seem like she was the worse for wear either.

"Mac, there you are. I was just trying to explain to Ms. LaFollette that…"

"Explain nothing! You wanted me to sign a release that would leave Mac and the movie off the hook for my injury." Roxy pulled in a deep breath and fixed her gaze back on Mac. "Sending someone else to do your dirty work, just like you did in San Francisco." An accusatory finger was straight as a knife and unwaveringly pointed at Martha.

"Ms. LaFollette, you're overwrought. Perhaps I should go find a doctor and…"

"No, Martha." Mac found his voice, even as this confirmed everything the wolf pack had learned. He had never understood why Madeleine – scratch that, Roxy – had left all those years ago. She seemed to want to stay, and yet…

The older woman suddenly quivered and seemed to shrink under his angry stare. In her hands, she held papers and a pen. Mac moved forward so fast, she didn't even have a chance to blink before he grabbed them from her.

"A release of liability? Who's idea was this?" He couldn't help himself, he towered over her and the older woman shrank even further into herself.

There was no response. Suddenly the room became too airless, and he wondered if he would ever draw a full breath again.

"Martha? Tell me."

Suddenly she looked her age, hair color and face lifts aside. Quivering and shaking her head, she seemed to want to deny it. Then as he continued to stare hard at her, she broke down and cried.

"It was for your own good, Mac. You were an up and coming star, and she would have weighed you down. No rising stars had girlfriends and touted their love all over the place. It just wasn't done."

Her weeping was the only sound in the room. She'd covered her face, though Mac would bet that there was a good acting lesson or two in her display.

"Are you saying that you sent Roxy away in San Francisco?" He waited, and Martha hesitated.

"If you lie to me, Martha, I will know it."

That seemed to shake her out of her indecision.

"Yes." Her voice was tiny behind her hands.

"And this release? It's your idea?"

She nodded.

He didn't have the courage yet to look at Roxy. There was no sound from the bed, and he couldn't even see her out of the corner of his eye. He felt her heat, though, and her presence made him stronger.

"Martha, you're fired. Pack up, go home, and wait for some papers of your own to sign." He stepped away from her, unwilling to be closer than he had to be.

She opened her mouth to argue. Then she saw the set of Mac's face and crumpled again.

"Mac, I…"

"Go, Martha, and be happy that this is the extent of things. I seem to recall a couple of retributive clauses in your contract that might come into play right now."

She gulped and scuttled – there was no better word for it – across the floor and out the door.

When it closed behind her on silent hinges, Mac took a deep breath and turned.

His Madeleine – scratch that, his Roxy – watched him appraisingly with carefully controlled eyes.

He caught her gaze with his and took two steps forward. That brought him to the end of her bed. She didn't scream, and he took that as a sign that he could take the three more paces that would bring him to her side.

Still, she watched him carefully.

He cleared his throat, suddenly at a loss for words. There was no role that had prepared him for this reality. He could only say what was really in his heart.

"Madeleine – Roxy, I don't know how things went so wrong, either back then or now." He waited, and since she still didn't scream, he reached for her hands and examined the small scars dotting them.

"I can only promise you this. It will never ever happen again. I love you." He squeezed her hands and waited. Two lifetimes passed before he felt it.

She squeezed back.

He looked up.

"Goddamnit, Mac. I certainly do love you."

Epilogue

"I still think this was a bad idea."

She swirled the bottle of Prosecco in the ice bucket and checked the antipasto again. Her blue eyes sparked and as she shook her head, the curtain of ash blonde hair waved around her.

"I mean, this is important, Mac."

He would never get tired of watching her in her infinite number of moods. The concussion had barely slowed her down, and the cut had now healed so well that only when he examined it closely – which he did more often than she realized – did he still see it. The day, however, played over in his mind constantly.

He could have lost her, and not because of the accident.

He sat deeper in the long couch and raised a hand to her. Roxy finally shook her head in dismay and moved forward. Once he held her hand, it only took one quick tug to have the rest of her tucked in to his side where she belonged.

"I've told you, this is where I need to be. With you. My Madeleine. My Roxy. Here." He dropped a kiss on her nose.

She wrinkled it at him – he loved that – and turned back to the satellite feed on the TV in front of them. In the wee hours of morning here, it was evening in Los Angeles.

"But what about your reputation? Doesn't this make you, I don't know, unreliable or something?"

God, you had to love the woman. There was no way they were going to be able to beam themselves across the globe and arrive in time for the red carpet, not that she wanted to be there herself mind you, and yet she argued.

He loved that about her.

Dropping another kiss on her nose, he engaged in the argument again. "I doubt it, since the phone is ringing off the hook. Box office on the opening weekend was so big, the money guys are slobbering with glee. And most important?"

He stopped, poised above her as she suddenly smiled at him. Everything he ever wanted was in that smile.

"Yes, Mac? What's most important?" Her voice held the rich buttery flavor that never failed to arouse his tastes.

His voice was husky when he found he could speak again. "You. I have you."

And he kissed her.

'And the Best Picture goes to – 'Jinxed', director and executive producer MacGillan Smythe!'

He was still kissing her when the crowd across the globe went quiet and Sheila began reading his prepared statement.

'Mac would like to thank everyone who was involved in the movie, the movie that at many points we thought must be jinxed. But as he said, it wasn't. Instead...'

Mac hit the off button for the TV. Roxy pushed him back and grabbed for it.

"Mac, what was the end of that?"

He chuckled, throwing the remote over his shoulder and out onto the Italian terrace into the early dawn.

"It will be all over the news tomorrow, because the end was, 'instead, it brought me back to the one woman I adore more that life itself.'"

And he kissed her.

THE END

Excerpt from
BLOOMS ON THE BONES

If you enjoyed *Tastes and Consequences*, stay tuned for the next book in the Flynn's Crossing series, **Blooms on the Bones**.

And here's a taste:

The graceful flute notes triggered by the swing of the front door informed her that another customer had arrived. The holiday season was always hectic, one of the few times of the year when she hired on extra help, both for delivery and to work in her flower shop. Escaping for a brief break, she hoped that a wave of the peace of the season would wash away her pain and sense of foreboding.

"Hello? Is anyone here?" Heavy footsteps tread on creaky old oak as the voice's male owner moved around the downstairs rooms.

Damn, where was Jan? The girl was supposed to be taking care of customers today for the last of the holiday arrangements.

"Hello, I have flowers to pick up…" The man's voice escalated in frustration, and it trailed away as he moved further from the front stairs. His rant grew fainter, this time from her kitchen, off limits to customers. Then, blessed silence.

Her head pounded, and the migraine that had begun as a mild annoyance earlier in the day was now a resounding hammer, complete with flashing lights behind her eyelids. Every noise was magnified a thousand times, and even the scents of her favorite flowers were vile and bitter. She needed a few more minutes for her energy to rebuild to a point where she could function.

The chimes hadn't sounded again, but she might have missed them. She concentrated on fighting off the brutal pain scraping across every nerve ending. Over the years, she'd learned to live with the odd voices that accompanied the pain. Sometimes, like today, she felt compelled to talk back to them, the urgency in her voice intended to send them away, along with the visions they sparked. Her Native American mentors assured her it was normal with her powers, though at times like this, she was more likely to believe Western medicine's diagnosis.

It was only a symptom of her chronic migraines.

At the raw edge of her agony, she sensed him more than heard him, a spirit to take notice of, as compelling as any she'd ever felt. Strong and commanding, an angry current swirled around him. A woodsy aroma came to her next, strangely comforting despite her pounding head. Usually the pain triggered her senses into overdrive, and yet his presence eased her.

The force moved closer. He was here, in her space, invading her privacy. What was the man doing in her bedroom? She needed to correct the situation immediately. These were her personal quarters, and yet he ignored the signs and came up the stairs anyway.

She opened a cautious eye in the darkened room. His big frame filled the doorway, backlit by natural light coming from below. Dark hair was close-cropped and his arms hung at his sides. His build looked fit in a bomber jacket and tailored slacks.

Both eyes wide opened now, she felt a surge that had nothing to do with her pain as a deep spark of recognition lit up her heart. In moments, the cacophony in her head was nowhere nearly as insistent as the magnetic pull she felt from the stranger grew stronger. The emotions surrounding him sucked her in.

"I'm, ah, sorry. I thought maybe someone up here could help me. I'm here to pick up an arrangement?" His husky voice boomed in the small space, and she felt it in her bones. "I heard someone talking up here," he added, by way of explanation. He stared at her, and she wondered what he could see in the dimmed room.

"I'll be with you in a moment, if you could just wait in the display area downstairs..." Her voice was as husky as his, though her tone was low and breathless. Where was this coming from? She hadn't had this kind of reaction in years. And the tumultuous feelings rolling off him were too much to contemplate right now.

The man hesitated, his hands flexing at his sides. She felt the intensity of his stare despite the induced gloom of the space. "I can come back later..." His voice trailed off as he waited for her to comment.

When she didn't immediately respond, he took a slow step into the room. "Are you all right?" His energy changed to worry — she could feel its shift — and he was advancing even further towards her bed until she swore they were breathing the same air. She felt their connection, his eyes seeking out hers in the dark.

She had to get him out of her refuge. He was too much of everything and the odd sensations he was raising had nothing to do with migraines or invasion and everything to do with his spirit.

Who the hell was he?

They both heard it at the same time and eyes jointly turned towards the bedroom door. "I'm sorry, I was out back on the phone. Hello? Is someone here?" The girl's voice sounded uncertain and faint as her light steps squeaked around the downstairs rooms.

His face in faint profile was chiseled and rugged, his expression holding both concern and frustration. Then his eyes flashed back to hers, and while she knew he couldn't see anything in the darkness, she sank deeper into the covers and hoped that her own confusion was hidden from his view.

"I am sorry to have disturbed you." His voice pitched deeper now. He hesitated once more, torn it seemed, between waiting for her reply and making his presence known to the voice below. He glanced between the door and the bed again, and his hand came out towards her. She sat up slightly, pulled by the strange energy that seemed to pour off him.

It felt like destiny.

They froze that way for who knows how long. Then he shook his head and backed out the door as quietly as he had arrived. The release of his potency came as a whoosh sucking everything out of her. It left her breathless and itchy.

And oddly, her migraine was gone.

About the Author

I love to hear from readers, so feel free to contact me through my website, www.yvonnekohano.com, or directly on Facebook as Yvonne Kohano, on Twitter @yvonnekohano, and at yvonne@yvonnekohano.com. Please leave an honest review of this novel at Amazon, Goodreads, or your favorite book discovery site of choice.

Yvonne enjoys channeling her characters' voices and passions as they overcome real world problems and discover love. Her Flynn's Crossing contemporary romantic suspense series is set in a fictional northern California foothills town not unlike the one where she used to live. Of course, the beauty and wonders of the Sierra Nevada Mountains and the surrounding counties play costarring roles in her work.

The first six books in the Flynn's Crossing series follow the developing love interests of the girl tribe, a group of successful women who work through real world conflicts and challenges to find acceptance and love - with some suspenseful happenings thrown in! In the next six books, single guys in the wolf pack find their true loves, but not without their own issues to conquer. Periodically, Yvonne will be adding seasonal novellas to the series, featuring the first person voice of a character from one of her previous books experiencing an event that we can all relate to.

www.ingramcontent.com/pod-product-compliance
Lightning Source LLC
Chambersburg PA
CBHW051333250626
47155CB00007B/2578